HEATWAVE

KENZIE GILMORE
BOOK 3

BIBA PEARCE

LIQUID MIND PUBLISHING

Liquid Mind Publishing

ALSO BY BIBA PEARCE

The Kenzie Gilmore Series

Afterburn

Dead Heat

Heatwave

Burnout

Deep Heat

Fever Pitch (Coming Soon)

Detective Rob Miller Mysteries

The Thames Path Killer

The West London Murders

The Bisley Wood Murders

The Box Hill Killer

Follow the link for your free **copy of *Hard Line: A Kenzie Gilmore Prequel.***

https://liquidmind.media/biba-pearce-sign-up-1/

1

THE HUMIDITY CLUNG to her like a damp cloth. Cloying, suffocating. The palm trees drooped, their fronds limp, even more so than the people who staggered around like zombies, hollow-eyed and wilting. The pavement shimmered like a mirage, and she could feel the heat radiating through her thin sandals with the strength of an underground furnace.

Kenzie darted into the air-conditioned mall and heaved a sigh of relief. Swiping a damp strand of hair off her face, she stood for a moment, absorbing the welcome coolness.

Miami was in the grips of a brutal heatwave, and Fred, the environmental editor at the *Herald*, had warned it wasn't about to end any time soon. *Swampy Summer* they were calling it, and they weren't wrong. The stifling humidity made it feel like you were swimming through the day, drenched in sweat. Kenzie's skin glistened with perspiration and her thick, blonde hair only added to the misery, so she'd scraped it into a ponytail. Glancing at her reflection in a shop window, she grimaced. The smattering of makeup she'd applied that morning had melted off her face hours ago.

The heat was on at work, too. Ever since Clayton had been fired, she'd been the senior investigative reporter on the crime beat. The promotion had come with a frantic schedule, a new assistant she hadn't gelled with yet, and deadlines that made her eyes water. The fact this heat had led to a spate of violent crimes across Miami, didn't help. Tempers flared, literally, in the heat of the moment, and patience wore thin as the relentless temperatures pushed those ready to snap over the edge.

Assaults had doubled, gang violence was on the rise, and there was a spike in homicides. And she was expected to cover it all. Be everywhere. To top it all, the AC in the car had gone on the fritz. It probably wasn't designed to be on full blast for hours on end.

So now she was sheltering in the mall.

An iced coffee made her feel marginally better. She checked her phone. Still no messages from Reid. Understandable though, given the current crime wave. Sweetwater Police Department, where he was based, was situated southwest of the city and included part of the Glades—the accessible part, that is. Those folks were a law unto themselves at the best of times. He had his work cut out for him.

Reid.

A frisson of excitement shot down her spine. She still couldn't believe she'd kissed him like that. It had been impulsive, reckless, and too damn good. Mind-blowingly good, if she was honest. At first, he'd been surprised, then he'd reciprocated, kissing her until they were both gasping for breath.

But it was the look in his eye when they broke away that had startled her the most. Intense, filled with desire and unspoken questions.

And she'd panicked.

At that moment, when she'd felt his breath on her lips, his hand in her hair, it could have gone either way. Her apartment was right there. Just steps from her front door. Yet she'd backed off, stammering an apology.

It was the excitement of the night. The sting operation. The relief it was over and she was safe.

Giving her a long look, he said quietly, "It's okay. I understand."

And he'd gone.

Left her alone with her feelings, her confusion, her desire.

"Excuse me," came a feminine voice beside her. "Are you Kenzie Gilmore?"

Jolted out of her reminiscence, Kenzie glanced up. A teenager stood in front of her, a backpack slung over one shoulder. She wore a pretty summer dress with daisies on it, and a silver chain with an H-shaped pendant around her neck. She looked surprisingly cool given the temperature outside and the general frazzled state of everyone else.

"Yes, I am." Kenzie smiled.

She shifted in her strappy sandals like she wasn't quite comfortable standing there and straightened her dress. "I'm sorry to disturb you. It's just... Well, I need to talk to you."

Kenzie frowned. The girl was nervous. "Sure, have we met?"

"No." She shook her head, then pointed to the vacant chair opposite Kenzie. "Do you mind if I sit down?"

"Of course not."

Kenzie was intrigued. What was this about? The girl was perfectly groomed; manicured nails, styled hair curling softly around her face, a light layer of mascara emphasizing wide deer-like eyes, and just the right amount of lip-gloss.

The backpack was a designer label, she noted, as the girl slid it off her slender shoulder and placed it at her feet, under the table.

"I'm Hannah Radcliffe," she began, voice trembling. "I read your articles in the newspaper. I'm going to do media studies when I go to college. I want to be an investigative journalist, just like you."

Ah, a fan. Sweet. Kenzie broke into a grin. "That's great. Is that what you wanted to talk to me about? Do you need some advice?"

"Actually, no." She wrung her hands under the table. "Not advice, I need your help. My boyfriend was murdered last week and the police aren't doing anything about it. I want you to look into it for me. I want you to find out who killed him."

Kenzie stared at her. Was she serious? But the brown doe eyes fixed on Kenzie were unwavering. Holding her breath, she waited for an answer.

"Um..." Kenzie tried to get her thoughts in order. "Hannah, I'm sorry about your boyfriend, but I'm not sure how I can help. You should take your concerns to the police."

Hannah snorted, a prim, ladylike sound. "The police think he was killed in a drug-related incident. That's what they said." She leaned forward across the table. "Matt didn't do drugs. He hated all that."

Kenzie's heart went out to the young girl. "I'm afraid I don't know the details of the case and there's no way I could get access to the files." She spread her hands out. "You really are better off taking this up with the detective in charge of the investigation."

Hannah's head bowed like a wilting flower, her shoulders caved in on themselves. "I can't." It was a strangled whisper.

"Why not? I'm sure they'd listen to you."

"Because nobody knew we were together. Matt was, well, he was on probation."

At Kenzie's arched eyebrows, she stammered, "F—For stealing a car. It was some time ago, and he was drunk. It was a stupid thing to do, and he regretted it. I swear, he's not a bad person." Her eyes filled with tears. "He was kind and gentle, and I loved him." Blinking, they fell anyway, slipping down her face. "Matt didn't deserve this. He didn't deserve to be stabbed in the street and labelled a criminal and a drug dealer."

"I'm so sorry for your loss." Kenzie reached over and squeezed her hand. The girl was clearly grieving, an emotion she understood well. "Don't you think you should tell your parents? If not them, then someone else? A school counselor, a police officer?"

She needed support. Going through something like this alone was not good for her mental health. That she knew firsthand, too. Endless questions, no answers. Nobody to talk to. It ate away at you, affecting all areas of your life.

"My parents would kill me," she sniffed. "Matt's not the type of boy they wanted me to date. He wasn't wealthy or well-bred. Didn't have a membership in a country club."

Yeah, she knew the type. Matt had been a juvenile offender, probably from the wrong side of the tracks. All types of wrong for their little princess.

Kenzie felt herself wavering.

No. Don't do it. You have enough on your plate.

"Where was he killed?" she heard herself ask.

Hannah wiped the tears away with her French mani nail-polished finger and managed to get herself under control. "South Coconut Grove," she mumbled. "He was on his way home from school."

Kenzie sucked in a breath. How awful. "Stabbed, you say?"

"Yes, in the stomach. I don't know how many times. They didn't tell us much."

"Us?"

"His friends at school. We have—had—some of the same classes."

"Is that how you met?"

She gave a tiny nod. Helpless. Like there was no point to the memories anymore, now he was gone.

"What was Matt's full name?"

Her gaze brightened. "Are you going to help me?"

"There's not much I can do," Kenzie repeated. "But I will ask some questions and see if I can find out what happened." The girl deserved that much. It would save her from wondering.

Endless wondering. No answers.

"Thank you." Hannah broke into a smile. "You don't know how much this means to me. I need to know what happened and find out who was responsible."

"His name?" Kenzie slid a small notepad and a pen across the table. Like all reporters, she kept one in her purse in case she had to jot something down.

The girl wrote Matteo Davis in neat block letters. All capitalized like he was important. Important to her.

"Is there anything else?" Kenzie asked, curiosity getting the better of her. "Was he acting weird in the lead up to his death? Anything like that?"

"Well, now that you mention it, he was worried about something. He told me it was a school thing but didn't say what."

"A school thing? Like a problem with one of the other kids?"

"No," she frowned, her face crinkling. "I don't think so. Maybe something to do with his probation. I suggested he talk to Principal Hogarth about it."

"And did he?"

She stifled a sob. "I don't know."

"Okay, thanks." Kenzie made a note on her pad.

Hannah scribbled her phone number beneath Matteo's name. "That's me. Call me anytime. Day or night." Standing, Hannah said, "Thank you so much, Kenzie. Is it alright if I call you by your first name?"

Kenzie nodded. "Please do."

Hannah shook her hand. "It's been a pleasure meeting you. Thanks again." And she dashed off into the hoard of shoppers, all of whom had the same idea Kenzie'd had, to get out of the stifling heat.

MATTEO DAVIS.

Kenzie stared at the name written on her pad until her eyes went blurry. Then she blinked and glanced away. One phone call, that's all it would take. Reid would be able to help her find out how the boy had died.

Then, hopefully, Hannah could get some closure.

2

REID STOOD on the rocky ledge at Snapper Creek and watched as the emergency services pulled the dead girl from the mangrove fringe. She was tangled up, her hair swept forward over her face, pale arms floppy like a rag doll's, head lolling to one side. She wore a white dress, dulled and stained by the water. It clung to her limp figure making her appear even paler.

Swallowing hard, he brushed the perspiration from his brow with the back of his hand. Another dead teenager. The third this month.

Two police divers stood waist-deep in the murky water and passed her lifeless body to two other men in a motorboat. The side of the canal where she'd been found was pretty much inaccessible, a mass of tropical vegetation, entwined root systems and swampland, which was why they'd launched from the other side.

Turning around, he whistled to the waiting ambulance to get ready. She was coming across.

Behind him was the sprawling residential area of Kendall West, but the two-lane road and maintained lawn that sloped down to the canal meant no one could see the waterway unless they were right at the edge.

"What state is she in?" Reid asked one officer in the boat.

He just shook his head.

Reid took out his phone and snapped a few photographs as they took her out of the boat and laid her on a stretcher. He winced. She was young. A teenager. Couldn't be older than seventeen or eighteen.

The body was intact. No obvious wounds or bite marks. No decomp. The wild animals hadn't had a chance to get to her yet. She hadn't been in the canal very long. Two or three days at the most.

A suited-up CSI professional leaned in. He felt for a pulse. Protocol demanded it, but he was just ticking a box. There was no way she was alive. Then he inspected her face, her eyelids, her mouth, and worked his way down her body. It was a brief overview, a preliminary study. The more thorough medical examination would happen a few days later, in the morgue.

"Cause of death?" Reid asked.

"Hard to say," he mumbled. "No visible injuries to speak of. Slight frothing at the mouth, vomit stains on her dress. No track marks in her arms or other signs of drug use, but looking at her, I'd say she died of a drug overdose." He shrugged. "You'll have to wait for the autopsy for a more concrete diagnosis."

Reid nodded. Out of respect, he watched as she was zipped up and lifted into the waiting ambulance. Only when the emergency vehicle took off down the street, sirens ominously silent, did he walk back to his pickup.

"Looks like another drug-related death," he told his team when he got back to Sweetwater Police Department. Since he'd taken over from the inept Casillas, the general morale and work ethic had improved tenfold.

"The working day starts at nine sharp," he'd told them on his first official day as lieutenant. "I expect you to be here by eight forty-five. There are people depending on us to do our jobs properly and to the best of our ability. No more rolling in at ten o'clock. We need to win back the community's trust."

He'd got several firm nods, a couple of half-assed ones, and a few murmurs. It was a change from his predecessor's lax policies and lazy work attitude. No more freeloading. They were here to solve cases, and this neighborhood had its fair share.

He hadn't fired anyone yet, but it was early days. There were one or two officers loyal to Casillas, who were badmouthing him behind his back. The hushed tones. The conversations that halted when he walked past. It was pretty obvious, but he was waiting to see whether they'd toe the line or be a problem.

Detective Dempsey was in his late fifties, overweight, divorced, and close to retirement. Like Casillas, he wanted to do the bare minimum until he could leave with a full police pension. Whether he deserved it or not was another matter. Reid hadn't seen him pulling his weight much since he'd arrived.

Detective Monroe was similar in age, but unlike Dempsey, he'd been a good cop in his day. Starting out at Miami PD, he'd garnered a reputation as a hard worker and someone who got stuff done. When he hit fifty and packed on a few pounds, he'd been transferred to Sweetwater to handle the paperwork. Demoralizing for such a seasoned detective. Reid could understand why his morale was low. In this game, unless you rose through the ranks, there was nowhere else to go.

It was hoped his years of experience would benefit the younger officers coming out of the academy, but Reid had yet to see that happen. Either Monroe didn't know how to be a supervisor, or he didn't care. The jury was still out on that one.

Detective "Willie" Vargas had turned out to be a smart, motivated young man, and Reid was relying on him more and more as his lead detective. Officer Diaz, the only female police officer in the squad, was also proving to be an asset to the team. It wouldn't be long before she got her detective's badge.

They weren't a big police department, only twelve officers. Five detectives including himself, and seven uniformed police officers in the next room. They all worked the day shift and rotated the nights. The majority were young graduates in their early twenties, with Reid more than a decade older at thirty-five and Monroe and Dempsey at the other end of the scale.

Glancing at them now, he squeezed into the small briefing room, Vargas and Diaz at the front, Dempsey and Monroe at the back. The older two wore tired expressions, like they'd seen it all before, but the rest were leaning forward, eyes glued to the white board behind him. Under Casillas's rule they hadn't done much real investigating, and the novelty of a dead body pulled out of the canal hadn't worn off.

"The victim's name is Sasha Holden." Standing at the front, he faced them. "She was sixteen years old." Diaz cringed.

Sweet sixteen. How different her year should have been.

The photographs he'd taken at the crime scene were pinned on the board. The victim lay on her back in the water, dark hair splayed around her, arms outstretched like she was floating in a swimming pool on a sunny day, gazing at the sky.

Ophelia sprung to mind. He didn't know a lot about art, but his sister had a copy hanging in her house in Philadelphia. She and her husband had taken a trip to Europe back in the days before they'd had kids, and she'd fallen in love with the painting in a gallery in London.

It was the same striking visual, but instead of meadow flowers, Sasha had leaves and bits of mangrove hanging off her.

"Most likely she died after taking an illegal substance," he explained. "But we won't know for sure until we get the coroner's report."

"Pink cocaine?" inquired Vargas.

Reid shrugged. "Could be."

The designer drug, a potent mix of cocaine, acid and God-knows-what else had been turning up on the streets of Miami for weeks now. This concoction was proving to be lethal. Killer coke, they'd nicknamed it. Three deaths, all teens. None of them hardened drug addicts.

"Do we know where she got it?" Diaz asked.

Reid looked at her. "That's what we need to find out. Talk to her friends at school. Find out where they partied. Trace her movements on the night she died, which is probably going to be the weekend. I'm guessing Saturday night judging by the state of her, and when she was reported missing. See what you can dig up."

"Yes, boss." Vargas had started calling him boss when he'd first taken the job as lieutenant, and despite Reid telling him otherwise, it had stuck. Now everyone was doing it. Everyone except Monroe and Dempsey, who were sulking at the back.

Reid looked over at them. "Monroe, Dempsey, will you look into local dealers? Find out who's selling what and where. Reach out to your contacts. Word on the street is that this is a new designer drug. We need to find out who's bringing it in." Grunting, they shuffled back to their desks.

Reid glanced at the other officers waiting for their instructions. "Everybody else, hit the streets. Talk to the residents. Find out where the kids are buying this stuff. Vargas, you and I will talk to her parents." They'd be waiting for news about their daughter. They'd reported her missing on Sunday when they realized she hadn't come home.

Vargas swallowed. He hadn't done a next of kin notification before. Reid wished there was something encouraging he could say to reassure him, but there wasn't. It never got any easier.

Sasha Holden's parents lived in Olympia Heights, several blocks east of where her body was found. They were understandably shocked at the news.

"A–Are you sure it's her?" her father stammered, ashen under his tanned complexion. He was above average height with square shoulders and an upright posture. Except, right now he was stooped over like someone had sucker-punched him in the gut.

There was always doubt. A desperate hope that this was all some terrible mistake.

"She had her student ID card in her back pocket," Reid said.

Sasha's mother collapsed into an armchair. "No," she whispered. "It can't be true."

Reid gave them time to assimilate. It always took a while. The brain had to register what it had been told. That this wasn't a nightmare they were going to wake up from. It was real.

Once the initial shock had worn off, he asked, "Would one of you..." He looked at the father, "be able to come and identify her?"

Mr. Holden nodded. "Of course." He reached for his wife's hand. "It may not be her."

But his wife was sobbing. Grieving tears streamed down her face. She knew.

She knew her daughter was dead.

"I'm really sorry to have to do this," Reid said. "But we need to ask you a couple of questions."

"Surely you should wait until we've officially identified her?" Mr. Holden snapped, then he raked a hand through his hair. "I'm sorry. Sure, go ahead."

Reid nodded. It was hard for anyone to hear. He forgave lapses in manners and angry retorts in these kinds of situations. The shock was enough to render anyone speechless, let alone answer questions. Sasha's father was doing better than most.

"When last did you see your daughter?"

He heaved a sigh, his chest rising, then caving in as he buckled and sat down heavily on the couch. "Saturday night. She went out with friends."

"Was that a usual occurrence?"

"Yeah, fairly usual. They didn't go out every weekend, but they were celebrating completing their SATs. This was Sasha's last year of school." His voice caught, and he squeezed his eyes shut.

It proved too much for Mrs. Holden who stumbled from the room, her sobs echoing down the passage. Vargas looked at Reid who shook his head. Let her go. She needed time to process.

Mr. Holden stared at the carpet under his feet, his arms folded across his chest like he was hugging himself.

"I'm sorry to ask, but did your daughter ever take drugs, Mr. Holden?"

His eyes blazed, momentarily, before the light faded again. "No, of course not. She wasn't wild. Our Sasha was a good girl. She wanted to go to college. Florida State..."

Reid didn't tell him it didn't take a wild teenager to try drugs, especially for the first time. An end of term celebration. Too much alcohol. In the party spirit. It wasn't impossible to imagine she might try the new designer drug everyone was doing.

"Do you know where she went?"

He shook his head. "No, we trusted her. I don't know how she ended up in Kendall West... They usually went out locally."

The body could have floated down, but it was unlikely. The currents weren't that strong. More likely one of her friends panicked and dumped her body.

"Do any of her friends drive a car?" Rob asked.

Mr. Holden thought for a moment, then shook his head. "I don't think any of her friends did, but they were at that age where they were dating older boys. One of them could have had a car."

"Okay, thank you, Mr. Holden. I'm sorry for your loss."

"Shall I come with you now, you know, to look at the...her..." He couldn't say the word. Because if he did, he'd be admitting she was really dead. That it was actually her.

"No, I'll send a dispatch car to pick you up. She's not at the police department, she's downtown." In the morgue, although he didn't say that.

Sasha's father nodded.

Reid said goodbye and strode out. Vargas, a little shaken up, beside him. In the car, Reid turned to his lead detective. His voice trembled with anger, even though he tried hard to keep it even. "I want to find the fuckers who are selling this shit, and I want it taken off the street before I have to tell another set of parents their kid is not coming home."

3

KENZIE KNOCKED on Reid's door, but as usual, nobody answered. He must be out back. She squeezed through the hedge of foliage that ran parallel to the water and squelched around to the deck. Sure enough, Reid was sitting on a wicker chair, beer in hand, staring out over the swamp.

"Hey," she called, hopping onto the wooden structure. Reid's cabin used to be the headquarters of an airboat tour company and had a wide deck and floating platform where his boat was tied up. It was clear he'd just been out for a ride with his T-shirt scrunched in a soggy ball at his feet, and his shorts wet.

Spinning around, he reached for his shirt, but she held up a hand. "Don't worry on my account." She didn't mind looking at his bare chest, and besides, his shirt was soaked. "Did you fall in?" she teased.

He snorted. "Cooled off under the hosepipe."

"Ah." It was so hot the water had all but evaporated off the decking. Leaning back against the railing, she asked, "How have you been?"

They hadn't seen each other since *that kiss*. She hadn't been avoiding him, not really. Just thought it best to put some distance between them while trying to assess what had happened. The problem was, she was no clearer now than she had been then.

He shrugged. "Been better. We pulled a girl out of the canal today. Only seventeen years old."

"I'm sorry," she said. "How did she die?"

"Snorted some bad shit." Reid wasn't one to talk about his emotions, he was more the bottling up type, but the death of a kid had hit him hard.

"That's tough. Are you okay?"

"Yeah, I will be." He gazed out over the Glades. An eagle swooped low and flew over the water, scouting for prey. "What can I do for you?"

A wry grin appeared. "Can't a girl swing by and see how you're doing?"

His eyes narrowed. "Is that why you're here?"

An awkward laugh. "Actually, no. I need a favor."

He nodded as if that's what he'd expected. Kenzie felt bad. Would she have come out here to see him if she hadn't met Hannah in the mall today? Probably not. Not because she didn't want to see him. But she was so confused and didn't know how to explain that to Reid.

"What is it this time?" Sweeping back his errant hair, moist from the water, he raised his eyebrows. Waiting.

About to ask about Matteo but, given his mood and that steely edge to his voice, she thought they'd better clear the air first.

"Listen, Reid, we need to talk."

"Do we?" His shoulders were tense. A muscle worked in his jaw. She couldn't leave things like this. His friendship meant too much to her.

"Yeah, we do."

He fixed his gaze on her. "Okay."

Crap.

She wasn't great at sharing her feelings, either.

"Let's go inside. I'm melting out here."

"Even stuffier inside," he drawled. "If this carries on for much longer, I'm going to have to think about getting AC installed."

He must be the only person in Florida who didn't have air conditioning. But that's not what she was here to talk about.

"I'm sorry about what happened," she burst out, before she lost her nerve. "I shouldn't have kissed you."

He didn't reply, just watched her, his expression unreadable.

"Maybe it was a moment of madness. I can't explain it. Maybe it was the adrenaline, maybe it was my mother's case that made me so emotional. I don't know, but as soon as I'd done it, I knew it would change things between us."

"It was quite a kiss," he said softly.

She shivered, despite the heat. God help her, she wanted to do it all over again.

"Yes, it was." They stared at each other.

She cleared her throat, "But I like our relationship the way it is, and I don't want it to change." Her voice dropped to a whisper. "I don't want to lose you."

Reid stood up. "You won't lose me."

Her skin prickled, and it had nothing to do with the heat. "Won't I?"

"Not if I can help it."

He came closer.

"But what if it doesn't last?" Doubt washed over her. There were so many things that could go wrong, not to mention their respective jobs. He was a police detective, and she was a newspaper reporter. He operated behind the scenes while she broadcast to the world. There would be so many conflicts of interest. "What if—?"

"Shh..."

Her train of thought derailed as his lips came down on hers. The next few minutes were a blur as all the reasons they shouldn't be doing this flashed through her mind. Eventually, she pulled away. To hide how flustered she was, she blurted out, "I really do need your help."

Releasing her, a smile played on his lips. "I'm listening."

When her pulse had slowed to an acceptable level, her brain kicked in. "I need to find out what the police have on a homicide victim, a teenager called Matteo Davis. He was stabbed on his way home from school last week."

Reid frowned. "Are you covering it for the paper?"

"No." She related how she'd met Hannah in the mall, and how the student had asked for her help. "I said I'd see what I could do." Shooting him a pleading look. "I know what it's like to be left wondering..."

Reid leaned against the railing beside her. He knew what she'd gone through as a result of her mother's disappearance. How it had eaten her up inside for twenty years before managing to get to the bottom of it earlier this year, and finally discovering the truth.

"Where did he die?"

"South Coconut Grove."

"That would be Miami PD's jurisdiction. Wait a second."

Walking inside, he came back with his phone. "I'll give Lieutenant Pérez a ring and see if he knows anything. That's the best I can do."

"Thank you." She flashed her best smile.

"Always a pleasure, Miss Gilmore. Congrats on your promotion, by the way. How's that working out?"

"A lot more work without Clayton." Rolling her eyes, "It was easier with two of us, and I never thought I'd say that."

"I can imagine."

"I have an assistant," she said. "Although we haven't really gotten to know each other yet."

Reid held up a finger as he was connected to Pérez.

"Hey, LT. How are things?"

"Yeah, I'm good. I'm calling in connection with one of your homicide victims, Matteo Davis. Young kid found in Coconut Grove?"

He waited while Pérez spoke. Kenzie gnawed on her lower lip. Would the lieutenant be able to give her the information she wanted?

To her surprise, Reid snapped, "What?"

There was a pause. "Have you had it analyzed?"

"What?" Kenzie mouthed.

"Well, I'll be..." He'd forgotten all about her and was staring into space, scowling. "Yeah, it's the same stuff. Do you know where he got it?"

Another pause. "Ortega? He's back?"

Kenzie raised an eyebrow. Ortega had been suspended after an internal affairs investigation. He'd lied to the police and fed her false information that had resulted in the death of Reid's colleague, an undercover operative called Bianca.

Reid had narrowly avoided an assault charge after he'd broken Ortega's nose and sent him flying across the squad room, but luckily the disgraced cop had withdrawn the charges. At least he'd done the right thing there.

"Okay, thanks. I owe you."

Kenzie blew a moist tendril off her face. Perspiration ran down her cleavage. A breeze would help. Anything to break the stifling humidity. "What was that about?"

He exhaled. "That was interesting. Turns out that your boy was found with a couple of grams of pink cocaine on him, the same stuff my canal vic died from."

"You're kidding!" Kenzie stared at him, head swirling. "What does that mean?"

"Means he was probably dealing. He most likely got into a fight with a user and got knifed. It happens."

But Kenzie was already shaking her head. "No, it wasn't like that. Matteo didn't do drugs. His girlfriend was adamant about that."

Reid's expression implied he didn't believe her.

"I'm serious." Thinking back to the earnest young woman. "I don't think she'd lie about something like that."

"Her boyfriend was a young offender. Did you know that?"

"For grand theft auto. It was a once-off. A prank that went wrong. He doesn't have any other convictions."

"Still..." He shrugged. "Who's to say he wasn't dealing on the side?"

Kenzie frowned. "Anything's possible, but Hannah sounded so sure. Maybe I'll see if I can talk to his friends. They'd know what he was into better than anyone."

"Weren't you just saying how busy you were?" He arched an eyebrow.

"Yeah, I know, but something doesn't add up." Her journalistic senses were tingling.

Reid studied her. "Pérez has put Ortega on it. As much as I hate the guy, nobody knows the Miami drug scene like he does."

Kenzie pursed her lips. "Why would a guy with no previous drug offences be involved in a street deal that went bad?" She pictured Hannah's dark brown eyes pleading into hers.

I need to know.

"I don't know, Kenzie. People do strange things for any number of reasons."

She puffed out her cheeks. "If his friends say he was into drugs, then I'll leave it at that."

"And if they don't?"

She hesitated.

"If they don't, there might be a story there."

"You're saying he was framed?" The tone of his voice made her grin. He knew her too well.

"I'm saying he *might* have been." She shrugged. "I'm keeping an open mind."

He glanced up at the sun as if to say, enough already. The smattering of hair on his chest was damp with sweat. "Just so you know, that pink coke is lethal. It's killing kids."

"Pink, did you say?"

"Yeah, it's a synthetic drug that appeared on the party scene a few weeks ago. The girl today was the third victim in a month. These aren't seasoned drug users, Kenz. These are kids, first-time users."

She wrinkled her forehead. "So, if Matteo was dealing, how would he have got hold of it?

"That," he said, his expression serious, "is what we need to find out."

4

REID COULDN'T SLEEP. He had every door and window open in the cabin, and it was still unbearably hot and sticky. Kenzie was right, he should get air conditioning installed. When he'd first moved to the Everglades, it had been to opt out of society, to lick his wounds in a place no one would see him. The lack of amenities played into the self-inflicted guilt that he'd carried with him. He didn't deserve creature comforts. Bianca was dead. What comforts did she or her family have?

Since then, he'd mellowed a bit, thanks to Kenzie and her revelation. Fucking Ortega. That guy deserved more than a broken nose for what he'd done. Still, it wasn't entirely his fault. He hadn't pulled the trigger. It was that cold-hearted bastard, Alberto Torres.

The Morales cartel's man in Miami. The head negotiator. The fixer of deals, amongst other things... *He* was responsible for Bianca's death.

Reid checked the surveillance video on his phone. The battery at the warehouse was running low. He'd have to replace it soon. There hadn't been any untoward activity happening there for a while now.

Not since that convoy of remodeled cars had driven out a month or so ago.

He assumed the interiors had been modified to hide the drugs, so they could transport them across the state and maybe even beyond. Miami was one of the cartel's launch pads for bringing cocaine into the United States. San Diego was the other. From there, the narcotics made their way north along the road network, infecting each city they came to, leaving a trail of death and destruction in their wake.

He blew out noisily. It was a losing battle they were fighting, but they had to try. What else could they do? Even if they took a couple of grams off the street, saved one or two lives, it was worth it.

He clenched his hands. Except he couldn't save the girl he'd pulled out of the canal today. Or the one last week, or the one the week before.

Then this young boy stabbed in a deal gone wrong, with the same pink coke on him. A coincidence? He didn't think so. They had to find out where the boy had got the cocaine from. That was their priority. Kenzie's investigation had given them a lead. First thing tomorrow, he'd put Vargas on it. Who was this boy? What connection did he have, if any, with the higher-level dealers?

He shut down the surveillance app. Nothing to see tonight.

A thought struck him. Could that convoy of vehicles he'd seen leaving Torres's warehouse have been carrying the killer coke? The timing fit. Yet the cartel usually stuck to the classic white stuff. They weren't known for branching out into synthetic drugs. Still, why wouldn't they change things up? A new income stream, a younger, more affluent market, skyrocketing demand. It was summer, schools were out, college students were here for their vacations, it was party central on Ocean Drive.

The ancient ceiling fan whirred around at a mind-numbingly slow pace. No matter what he did to it, he couldn't get it to spin any faster. He hardly felt the breeze.

Sighing, he got up and padded through to the living room, and then out onto the deck. The sky was inky black. No stars. The clouds blocked them out. Unfortunately, they didn't stick around long enough to rain, just to hold in the heat, adding to the humidity. They'd dissipate during the day and build up again in the evening, creating a stifling greenhouse effect.

The water was still and glassy. Not a breath marred its surface. He heard the reeds rustle as a creature edged its way in or out. There was a hollow nocturnal cry, followed by a desperate scampering sound. Usually, he enjoyed the nightly symphony, but right now, he was too preoccupied.

Then there was Kenzie.

Impulsive, headstrong, and emotional. That was Kenzie in a nutshell, even though she tried hard not to be. Her false bravado and the uncanny ability she had to assume another persona when she was undercover could mask her true feelings for a time, but not for long.

He'd known her for almost six months now. Long enough to see through her outwardly composed facade. Her mother's case had shaken her up, left her vulnerable. He'd gotten to know the real Kenzie then, without the mask or the makeup or the false name, and he liked what he'd seen.

He was glad he'd been the one to help her solve it. Now she had closure, even if it wasn't the outcome she'd hoped for. That was the thing with the truth. Once it's been uncovered, there was no turning back.

Just like they couldn't ignore the fact that she'd kissed him.

And he'd kissed her back.

Right here, in this spot.

Staring moodily into the dark water, he watched it swirl around the legs of the deck. Where did that leave them?

Turning his mind back to the current case, he thought about Torres and the cartel. If the killer coke was coming in via their network, it was a new direction for them. Perhaps he ought to speak to Ortega about it.

He scowled into the darkness. Was he ready for that? Would Ortega even talk to him? After the bloody nose, he wasn't so sure.

One thing he did know, however, was that if Torres was bringing in the coke, he was doing it under Lopez's instruction.

Federico Lopez. Head of the Morales cartel.

The man they called The Wolf hadn't been seen in two years. The rumor was that he was dead, except Reid knew that to be untrue. If the cocaine was still coming in, Lopez was still alive. A leadership vacuum would result in a power struggle, and supply chains would be affected. If anything, production had increased. The market was being flooded with product. It took a stable leadership structure to support that, and now it seemed they were expanding into other avenues. Synthetic drugs. The designer high. An off-shoot of their purer product, only more lethal depending on what it was cut with. In this case, a killer substance powerful enough to destroy young lives.

The only way to stop it was to cut off the head of the beast. That meant going after Federico Lopez. And the only way to get to Lopez was through Torres.

Kenzie stood outside the federal building where Matteo's probation officer worked. It was early, but she could already feel the brutal rays from the sun burning her skin. It was going to be another scorcher of a day.

The building was shiny and modern, glass mixed with chrome, with wide windows overlooking the downtown area. Not a bad place to work. She didn't have an appointment, but

she was going to talk her way in.

"I'm writing a feature article on the juvenile offender rates in Miami," she told the woman at the front desk, holding up her press ID card. It was a useful thing to have. It had gotten her into countless clubs, hotels, and VIP events that she otherwise wouldn't have been able to access. "I wondered if I could ask Mr. Hodge a few questions?"

"One moment, please." The woman's eyes lingered on the Miami Herald logo on the card. "I'll see if he's available."

She got up and glided across the reception area to an office. Without knocking, she entered. Clearly, Mr. Hodge wasn't with a client.

A moment later, she was back. "Mr. Hodge will see you now."

Kenzie smiled and went into the office. Immediately, she was hit by the smell of freshly applied deodorant. The chubby probation officer got to his feet. He was sweating profusely despite the AC being on full blast.

"Miss Gilmore, it's a pleasure to meet you. I believe you're from the Miami Herald?"

"That's right." Putting on her best smile, she tried not to inhale too deeply. "I'm writing a piece on juvenile offenders. I know that's your area of expertise, so I'd like to ask you a few questions if you're not too busy."

She surveyed his desk. He didn't appear to be doing anything other than playing solitaire. She could see the green baize reflected in the glass window behind him.

"No, not at all. Please sit down. Can I get you a cool drink?" He fanned himself and looked eagerly at the fridge in the far corner of his office.

"No thank you, I'm good."

The chair squeaked as he lowered his bulk into it.

"I'd like to talk about a specific case." She opened her notepad and pretended to scan it. "Matteo Davis."

The probation officer paused.

"Do you know him?" Kenzie asked. "I believe he was a... client of yours?"

Hodge cleared his throat. Was it her imagination or had the damp patches under his arms spread? "Yeah, he was... before... you know?"

She nodded.

"Awful business. We were devastated when we heard." He shook his head.

Somehow, she doubted that. "Drugs, wasn't it?"

He nodded sagely. "It's the way so many of them go. A real tragedy. They start off with small misdemeanors, then progress to bigger things. Eventually, they either get arrested, imprisoned, or..." He shrugged.

"Murdered?" Kenzie asked.

"There are a lot of violent offenders out there," Hodge retorted, a tad defensively.

"But Matteo wasn't violent, was he? He was in his final year of high school, only seventeen."

"He fell in with a bad crowd," the probation officer insisted. "Other dealers, bad elements, you know how it is."

"No, I'm afraid I don't." Kenzie fixed her gaze on him. "Did you know these people he was hanging out with, these bad elements?"

"No, I didn't."

"Yet you knew they were a bad crowd?"

"I'd seen them around. Hanging out on street corners, causing trouble."

"Was Matteo with them?"

"Yeah, that's what I've been telling you."

"While he was supposed to be at school?" Kenzie asked.

"How the hell should I know?" snapped Hodge. Kenzie was getting to him with her constant badgering.

"Well, I'm sure his teachers will have a record of his attendance," she said breezily, getting to her feet.

Hodge grunted but didn't get up.

"Oh, there's just one more thing." She looked down at him. "I heard from one of his friends that he went to a party last Saturday night. Don't the juveniles in your program have to get permission if they want to attend anything like that?"

"This is a community-based corrections program, Miss Gilmore. Most of these kids are first-time offenders. While they're on probation, they remain active in the community, they go to school, but they must comply with certain conditions established by the court. One of these is regular meetings with their probation officer, another is curfews. Matteo had both. He wasn't meant to be out after eight o'clock at night or before six in the morning, although this is not enforced." He shrugged.

"I see. So, if Matteo wanted to go to a party, there'd be nobody to stop him?"

"Not officially, no."

"Okay, thank you Mr. Hodge. You've been very helpful."

"I have?" He wiped the droplets from his upper lip on the back of his hairy hand.

"Yes." She smiled again. "You have. Don't get up, I can see myself out."

The all-encompassing heat hit her like a furnace when she stepped out of the building. She fumbled in her purse for her sunglasses and was just pulling them on when a lanky teen bumped into her.

"Sorry," he mumbled without looking up. Kenzie noted the skintight jeans, the heavy metal T-shirt, and the eyebrow ring.

"Excuse me." The youth turned around and regarded her suspiciously. Raising her sunglasses, she broke into a smile. "Do you mind if I ask you a question?"

"Er, I guess."

"Did you know a boy named Matteo Davis?"

The boy lowered his gaze, uncomfortable. "Sort of. We weren't friends or anything. I knew him from this place." He nodded toward the building.

"Is Mr. Hodge your probation officer too?" she asked.

He gave an unhappy nod.

"What do you think of him? Do you like him?"

A shrug. "He's my probation officer. I'm not supposed to like him."

"Fair enough." She hesitated, wondering how much to ask. "Do you know if Matteo hung out with a bad crowd?"

The boy stared at her, his dark eyes glittering suspiciously. "Why'd you ask that?"

"Because of the way he died. I knew him, you see." She bit her lip at the white lie. "I didn't think he was into drugs."

"Nah, he wasn't." The hooded eyes were sincere.

"He died with drugs on him, did you know that?" Kenzie pointed out, watching him for a reaction.

The boy's eyes widened. "No way, man. Are you sure?"

She shrugged. "It's what the police report said. Does that seem odd to you?"

"Yeah, it sure does. Matteo didn't do drugs. I didn't know him well, but a couple of us shared a joint after a group session and he declined. Said outright that he didn't smoke."

A small rush of adrenaline shot through her. Hannah had been right. Matteo didn't do drugs. She supposed that didn't mean he wasn't dealing, but it was unlikely.

"Okay, thanks for talking to me." She gestured to the building. "Good luck in there."

He snorted. "This is my last session."

"Wow, congratulations."

"Yeah, thanks. Can't wait to be free of this bullshit." And he shoved his hands into his pockets and stalked inside.

Kenzie walked back to her car, deep in thought. The sun baked down, brutal in its intensity, but already the clouds were gathering. Another couple of hours and it would be overcast. That's when the humidity ratcheted up and Miami turned into a soggy sauna.

Hodge's account of Matteo differed from what this guy had said. Why would Hodge lie? Perhaps he was trying to justify Matteo's death, or maybe he had a jaded opinion of all juvenile offenders?

Whatever the reason, she was sure he hadn't been telling the truth—and that made her want to find out why.

She pulled out the slip of paper with Hannah's phone number on it. Time to inform the high school student she was going to investigate her boyfriend's death. Something wasn't right, she could sense it, and she wasn't one to turn her back on her journalistic instinct. It was time to find out what really happened to Matteo Davis.

5

Pinewood Academy, the school Sasha Holden had attended, was situated in the upmarket area of Coral Gables. Reid had got permission from the principal to talk to Sasha's friends and so he'd brought Officer Diaz with him for backup. Teenage girls were not his forte.

"You do the talking," he'd told her as they walked up the paved path that sliced through rolling green lawns towards the school building.

She'd flashed him an amused grin. "Sure, no problem."

Now, in the overly hot classroom, he sat behind the teacher's desk, surveying the group. Diaz perched on the front of it, so she could address them. Above their heads, the ceiling fan wheezed around, circulating the hot air. It was muggy as hell. Even the walls seemed to sweat.

"I'm sorry for your loss," Diaz began. There were a few sullen nods, while one girl sobbed quietly at the back. "I know you were all close to Sasha."

There were five young women in total who were part of Sasha's friendship group. All showed signs of shock. Pale skin, hollow eyes, haunted expressions. It was clear they'd been very close.

"Were any of you with her on Saturday night?" Diaz asked.

Nobody said anything.

"None of you are in trouble," she emphasized. "We just want to know what happened."

There was another long silence, then the girl who'd been crying sniffed and said, "We went to a bar."

"Stacy," hissed one of the other girls.

"What? I'm not going to lie to the police."

"Thank you, Stacy." Diaz smiled warmly. "We appreciate your help. We know she died after taking cocaine, so you don't have to worry about implicating yourselves. Her death was ruled as by natural causes. None of you are under suspicion."

"Why are you here, then?" asked the teenager who'd hushed Stacy.

"Because we would very much like to find out who Sasha got the drugs from."

"Sasha didn't do coke," said Stacey, wiping her eyes. "None of us do."

There were several nods of agreement. Reid looked for signs they were lying—a downward glance, the flicker of an eyelid, a nervous twitch—but he found none. They appeared to be telling the truth.

"Where did she get it from, then?" asked Diaz.

"It must have been that guy," one of the other girls with curly, auburn hair said.

"What guy?" Diaz was quick to ask.

"The one from the bar. They left together."

That could explain why her body was found in Snapper Creek when she went out in Coral Gables.

The shocked expressions turned sheepish. Guilt at having let their friend go off with this boy etched all over their faces.

"Does this guy have a name?" asked Diaz.

"Nate," the auburn-haired girl said. "He was cute."

"Mich, you can't say that," hissed one of the others.

"It's okay," Diaz interjected. "Anything you can give us in the way of a description is helpful."

Mich shot her friend a triumphant look.

"Do you know his last name?"

She shook her head.

"Anyone?" Diaz looked around. Only blank faces stared back at her.

"What was the name of the bar?" Diaz tried a different angle.

"Monsoon," a couple of them chorused.

Diaz smiled. "And you said she left with Nate?"

"Yeah," said a petite girl with blonde bangs and a high-pitched, squeaky voice. "He picked her up at the bar. We didn't know him, but he seemed nice."

Reid silently took all this in. A random hook-up? Just two kids who met in a bar and did a few lines together, with tragic consequences.

"What time was this?" Diaz asked.

A few shrugs. "About midnight, I guess." It was the auburn-haired girl again.

"Okay, great." Diaz pursed her lips. "Can you describe Nate to me? Was he tall or short?"

"Tall," came the collected response.

"Dark or blond?"

"Dark."

"Any idea if he was at college or if he worked in the area?"

"I think he was a tennis player," Stacy blurted out. "Before she left, Sasha told me he played at one of the local academies."

"Good. That's good." Diaz glanced over her shoulder at Reid. He nodded. Now they were getting somewhere.

"Anything else you can tell me about him?" she asked.

They glanced at each other, eyes vacant and glossy. They'd always remember this. A horrific period in their lives, the loss of a close friend.

"He drove a red car," Stacy said. "I don't know what type. I'm no good with cars."

"It was a Nissan Maxima," the blonde said. "I'm sure of it. My dad has one just like it."

"That's very useful," Diaz told them. "You're doing great. Only a few more questions." She paused, as if gathering her thoughts. Reid knew she was drawing out the tension, making sure she had their full attention. "Would she have taken cocaine to impress this boy?"

"I don't know," murmured Stacey.

"Maybe." remarked the auburn-haired girl. "If she really liked him."

Reid sighed. Sasha had been a novice. The lethal concoction on a sensitive stomach would be absorbed instantly, sending her into convulsions, followed by vomiting, loss of consciousness, and then death. It wasn't pretty.

What a tragic waste of a young life.

Reid got to his feet. "Do any of you know a boy named Matteo Davis?"

Surprised eyes shifted to him.

Walking around the desk, he stood next to Diaz, where he held up a photograph, courtesy of Kenzie's online research. The young boy was laughing, a wide grin on his face. Not a care in the world.

"Who is he?" asked one of the other girls.

"Do you recognize him?"

They all shook their heads.

"Then it's not important." Reid slipped the photo back into his pocket.

"Thanks girls," Diaz told them, smiling. "You've been really helpful."

"It's our fault," Stacy murmured, as they prepared to leave.

Reid spun around. "Why do you say that?"

"Sasha was our friend. We shouldn't have let her go home with a strange guy."

The blonde girl put an arm around her shoulders. "It's true. We should have been looking out for her."

"This isn't your fault," Reid addressed them both. "It was the cocaine that killed her. There are some dangerous products on the street right now. She's not the first one."

Diaz shot him a sideways look. He'd half expected it, it wasn't like him to divulge more details than were necessary. He needed to warn them, though. He had to make sure none of them ended up the same way.

"She isn't?" Stacy blinked back tears.

"No, she's the third this month. Be careful out there, girls. Tell your friends. It's not worth the risk."

They nodded, worry etched on their fresh, unlined faces.

"You did good," he heard Diaz tell them. "We're going to do our best to get these drugs off the street."

"Diaz?" he called from the door. "Let's go. We've got work to do."

6

As REID and Diaz were leaving Pinewood Academy, Kenzie walked into Sunrise Community High School in Coral Gables. A security guard at the entrance pointed her toward the main administrative building. It didn't have rolling lawns or extensive property, but it was impressive, nonetheless. The modern rectangular structure was two stories high and looked more like a stylish tech company in Silicon Valley than a high school. Large white panels covered the exterior, with wide windows looking out over the quad. Kenzie passed a basketball court and two tennis courts surrounded by a running track on her way up to the front entrance.

Kenzie had done her homework and knew the school had an excellent reputation in liberal arts and sciences. Hannah's parents wouldn't have sent their daughter here otherwise.

A boy charged past her with a backpack on, late for class, but other than that, there was no one else around. "Excuse me," she called after him. He half-turned, slowing his pace but not stopping completely. "Where's the principal's office?"

He pointed to the west side of the main block. "Down the hall, last door on the left."

"Thanks," she said, but he'd sped up again and didn't hear her.

The long, wide corridor was flanked by lockers and smelled like sports bags, dust, and sweaty teens. Sighing, she was catapulted back to her own high school years when she was reeling from her mother's disappearance, dodging awkward conversations with people who used to be her friends, and avoiding everyone else. Not a great time in her life.

Her running shoes squeaked on the linoleum floor, made louder by the emptiness. Eventually, after passing a multitude of classrooms, she came to the last door on the left.

PRINCIPAL HOGARTH, read the self-important gold plaque.

She knocked. There was no answer, so she twisted the handle and went in. She was standing in an outer office occupied by a personal secretary who was so busy typing she didn't notice Kenzie standing there.

"Hello?" Kenzie peered over the computer screen at the woman. She was in her mid-fifties with prematurely gray hair, black-rimmed glasses, and an inordinate amount of blue eyeshadow.

Glancing up, she smiled. "Can I help you?"

Kenzie thought she detected a southern accent. She held up her ID card. "Kenzie Gilmore from the Miami Herald. I'd like to speak to Principal Hogarth, please."

"Do you have an appointment, honey? He's really busy."

"No, but I'm writing an article on the best schools in the area," she lied. "I'm sure he'll want to comment. It's a great honor to be selected." A fake smile, designed to flatter.

"Oh, I see." She pushed her glasses up her nose. "Well, sure, in that case... He's with a student right now, but you can go in as soon as he's free."

"Thank you."

Kenzie sat down on a plastic-backed chair. On a small table next to her was a stack of magazines. Tilting her head, she read the titles. Motoring, Engineering, Interior Design. There was also a folded-up edition of the school newspaper, The Sunrise Echo. Picking it up, she scanned the first page.

Student Protest Results in Better School Meals was the leading headline. *Track Team Wins Miami-Dade County Championship*, was the second. There was also a picture of a very tall boy. *Luke Aston Drafted by Miami Heat.*

Clearly, this school was known for its athletic prowess as well as its academic excellence. The door opened and a flushed student came out, books under his arm, eyes downcast. That hadn't been a good meeting.

She got up and glanced at the secretary who gestured for her to go in.

"Mr. Hogarth?" Kenzie enquired, walking into the room. A man in his forties with thinning hair and a bushy mustache glanced up. "Your assistant said you'd be able to see me. I'm Kenzie Gilmore from the Miami Herald."

"Come in. Come in." He got out of his chair and motioned to the one opposite. Kenzie smiled and sat down. It was still warm from the previous occupant.

"What can I do for you?" He smiled, exposing buck teeth.

"Well, it's about one of your students, Matteo Davis. He was stabbed on his way home from school last weekend."

Hogarth hung his head, displaying the bald spot on the top. "Yes, such a tragedy. He was one of our more challenging students, but we were devastated nonetheless."

"Challenging?"

"Yes, he'd had some trouble with the law. He was on probation at the time of his death."

"What kind of student was he?"

Hogarth blinked. "I'm sorry?"

"You said challenging? Did he struggle at school? Was he disruptive?"

Hogarth swatted at his face, missing a bead of sweat that ran down his cheek. "Damn air conditioning's on the blink again. No, nothing like that. He was a smart kid, but it wasn't enough to keep him out of trouble."

"You're referring to the drugs found on him?" Kenzie said.

Nodding, he glanced wistfully at the open window, probably praying for a breeze, a gust of wind, anything to get some relief. The air was so still that it didn't make a bit of difference.

"Was Matteo in a bad crowd, do you know?"

"I have no idea who he was friends with. Patricia might be able to help you. She's more hands on with the kids."

Patricia being the assistant, Kenzie guessed.

"The facilities here at Sunrise are wonderful." She smiled at him, driving home the compliment. "I'm surprised a boy with Matteo's background could afford to go here."

The principal pulled back his lips in what she supposed was a smile. He reminded her of a beaver. "We take in one or two disadvantaged kids every year through our scholarship program. Matteo was one of those boys."

"Had you seen Matteo in the week leading up to his death?" she asked.

His shoulders jerked back. "What do you mean?"

"Was he called to your office? Did you have any reason to reprimand him for anything?"

She was fishing. Hannah had said he'd gone to see the principal, but she didn't know what it was about. He'd just said it was a school issue.

"No, I hadn't seen Matteo for a while."

"He didn't come to your office wanting to talk to you?" She eyed him closely, but his gaze remained steady. "Not that I know of." He clicked through to what she assumed was a calendar on his computer and shook his head. "No, nothing. Sorry."

Scratching her chin, her mind worked overtime. "Did Matteo ever miss lessons? Skip school."

He frowned. "I don't know, I'd have to check his record."

Kenzie flashed her dimples. "Would you mind?"

"What article are you writing again?" he asked, as he tapped at his computer.

"I'm doing a piece on juvenile offenders." She reverted to the same story she'd told Hodge. The best schools in Miami had been a ruse to get past his assistant.

"I don't want the school mentioned," Hogarth insisted. "It would give us a bad name. Our parents are very particular about things like that."

"Oh, don't worry," said Kenzie reassuringly. "The article is on several offenders, not their schools. Sunrise won't be mentioned in the article. I'd just like to know whether he had a bad track record of attendance. It's a pattern, you see, with all these young offenders."

He nodded knowingly. "Yes, it's sad, isn't it? We try to do what's best for them, but they get into trouble regardless."

Kenzie leaned back in her chair while he brought up the attendance records. "Here it is." His eyebrows rose. "Actually, he hadn't missed a day. That is unusual for these types of characters."

"Thank you," Kenzie got up. This fit with the impression she'd been building up of Matteo. A dedicated student, a bright boy from the wrong side of town, in love with a girl from a wealthy family. What had he known that had gotten him killed? Because she was sure as hell it wasn't drugs. "You've been really helpful."

Rising to his feet, he puffed out his chest. "It was a pleasure to meet you, Miss Gilmore. I look forward to reading your article." Kenzie gave him a brief nod and left his office.

"Thank you," she called to the secretary on the way out.

"Sure, honey," came the voice from behind the enormous screen.

Kenzie stalled as a thought occurred to her, then turned around. "Can I ask you a question?"

The blue eyelids rose to meet her.

"Did you know the boy who was killed? His name was Matteo

Davis," Kenzie asked. As the principal's assistant, she'd know everyone who came in and out of this office.

"Why yes, of course I knew Mattie." She shook her head. "Poor lamb. What an awful thing to have happened. He was such a sweet kid, too. Lovely smile."

Kenzie tilted her head in sympathy. "Did he make an appointment to see Principal Hogarth in the week before his death?" She hesitated. "Then maybe he cancelled it or something?"

"Oh, let me see." She pulled up her calendar. "Why yes, he did call in to make an appointment. It was the day before he died." She put a hand on her heart. "Oh, my gosh, that's so sad, isn't it?"

"He saw the principal?" Kenzie inquired, frowning.

"Well, he made the appointment," she said. "But it was the last one of the day and I'd already gone home. I pick my niece up from school on Fridays, so I leave early."

"You didn't see him?"

"No, honey. I didn't." She went back to shaking her head. "Poor lamb."

"Okay, thank you very much."

A quick smile, and the black-rimmed spectacles fell down her nose again. "You're welcome, honey."

Kenzie left the office, deep in thought. Why would Principal Hogarth lie about seeing Matteo? Unless the boy hadn't kept his appointment with the school head. Perhaps he'd changed his mind and decided not to confide in him.

But no, that didn't make sense. Even if he hadn't come to see him, it would still have been on the calendar. Hogarth was deliberately misleading her, and she wanted to know why.

7

"THERE ARE three tennis academies in the greater Miami area," said Diaz. They'd been back for an hour and were following up on what Sasha's friends had said. "I'm cross checking them for a Nate." Her fingers flew over the keyboard.

Reid stopped pacing. He had to get out and do something. "Text the details through to me when you find him. In the meantime, I'm going to check out that Monsoon bar. They should be open by now. Vargas, want to come along?"

"Sure." The young detective jumped to his feet.

The drive to Coral Gables took a little over twenty minutes. He could have put on the siren and blue-lighted it, but there was no real rush, and he was enjoying the AC in the police car. Sweetwater Police Department didn't have the budget for air conditioning and the multiple ceiling fans in the offices didn't create much of a breeze, making the heat even more unbearable. Reid made a mental note to speak to the Chief of Police about that. Now that the department was making a name for itself, it deserved proper facilities. No longer the useless backwater department where the rookies and old-timers were sent anymore, he was tired of being the butt of police jokes.

"How come you were so late this morning?" he asked Vargas, who'd raced in at nine-thirty disheveled and sweaty. He was usually the first one in and the last to leave.

Vargas colored. "I'm sorry about that, boss, but I had an issue at home."

"Nothing serious, I hope?" Reid frowned. He'd thought Vargas lived alone.

"No, I had a... friend stay over last night, and her car wouldn't start this morning, so I gave her a lift home."

Reid grinned. "I understand."

"It won't happen again, boss."

"Not a problem. Just concerned, that's all. Your work ethic is exemplary."

Sitting up a little straighter, he said, "Thanks, boss."

Reid glanced over at him. "You know you don't have to call me boss. Garret will do. Even LT is fine."

"I know." He checked the route on his phone. "We're nearly there."

Monsoon was a trendy pool bar on Sunset Drive, popular with college kids. There was an in-house DJ, and they served cocktails as well as trendy mocktails for those who were underage.

"We try to adhere to the rules," the suave bar manager told them, a worried look on his face. "We ask every kid for ID, and we don't promote underage drinking."

"I'm glad to hear it," Reid said. "But that's not why we're here."

"It's not?" His shoulders slumped in relief.

"This was the last place Sasha Holden was seen before her body was found in Snapper Creek last Saturday night."

His eyes widened. "Hey, man, I don't know anything about that. I'm just the manager."

"Do you have security footage?" Vargas asked.

"Sure."

"Can we see it?"

They didn't have a warrant, but this guy wasn't going to resist. He wanted them gone as soon as possible.

"Follow me." Swiveling on his heel, he made a loud squeak. Reid glanced down. The manager wore shiny shoes and smart chinos with a crisp, white shirt. Overdressed for the weather, but it was pleasantly cool inside the club. Leading them to a back office, he pulled up the security video. "When did you say she was here?"

"Saturday night," supplied Vargas.

The manager clicked on the appropriate file and a video launched, playing at double-time. At first, the bar was relatively empty, but by ten o'clock the place was heaving. People danced inside on the dance floor and outside around the impossibly blue swimming pool with its iridescent underwater lighting. Considering how packed the place was, Reid was amazed nobody fell in.

"There!" He pointed to a dark-haired girl in a white mini-dress standing outside under a palm tree. "I think that's her." It was hard to tell since all he'd seen were the crime scene photographs, but it was the same lithe figure, the same pale skin and dark flowing hair. The same white dress.

The manager slowed the footage so they could watch in real time.

"Yeah, that's Sasha Holden," Vargas confirmed as she threw her head back and laughed. Beside her was a tall, athletic guy with light brown hair and a ready smile. Was that Nate, the tennis player?

Sasha's friends were scattered around her, dancing and laughing. Young and carefree. Their world was still a happy place. They had no idea of the tragedy about to befall one of them.

"Can we speed it up until she leaves?" Reid asked.

The manager did as he was asked, and the images flew by in a whirl of color and movement. The only constant was the azure blue water in the center of the frame.

"Stop!" said Vargas, his eyes glued to the screen. "She's leaving."

The pretty dark-haired girl left with the tall guy, arm in arm. Tossing her hair over her shoulder, she waved to someone behind her.

It was hard to believe this was the same girl he'd pulled from the water yesterday morning.

The couple walked down the road to a red Nissan Altima. Sasha's friend had been right about that. They stopped and kissed, long and passionately, then they got into the car and drove away.

"Freeze it there," barked Reid. The image stilled.

"Can we get a printout of the license plate?"

The manager shrugged. "It's not set up to a printer. The only one we have is in the office."

Shit.

"I've got it." Vargas pulled out his cell phone and took several shots of the screen, zooming in on the back of the vehicle. Reid grunted. Who needed printers these days?

The text from Diaz came through as they were getting back into the car.

"His name is Nate Sanderson," said Reid. "Sandy Bay Tennis Academy."

Vargas raised an eyebrow. "Isn't that the one run by that retired pro, Max Wilson?"

"I have no idea." Reid didn't know much about tennis. "Know how to get there?"

"Yeah."

"Then let's go speak to him and find out what happened to Sasha the night she died."

Nate was on a court when they arrived at the academy. Reid couldn't imagine anyone playing in this heat, yet the two men were battling it out, pounding the ball back and forth, their racquets a blur.

Waiting until the end of the set, they approached the coach.

"Coach, we need a word with Nate Sanderson."

The coach, a broad-shouldered stocky man in great shape for his age, eyed them suspiciously. "What's this about?"

"We'd prefer to speak to Nate about it," Reid replied.

Lifting his head, he called. "Nate! Come over here."

Nate was picking up balls on the other side of the court, but he stopped and came over, picking up his water bottle.

"Yeah?" He took a big gulp from his bottle.

"Could we have a word in private?" Reid asked.

"It's okay," Nate told his coach, who shot them a curious look before going back on the court. Nate turned back to the cops. "This is about Sasha, isn't it?"

Reid gave a curt nod. "What happened, Nate? We know you were with her the night she died."

Sighing, he raked a hand through his hair, damp with sweat. A designer T-shirt stuck to his finely honed body, but despite his athletic appearance, his gaze gave away his immaturity. He was scared, and rightly so.

According to his file, the boy was nineteen and a promising young player. He was cleaning up the ATP circuit. Reid hoped he didn't have to ruin all that for him.

"I don't know what happened," he said. "One minute she was fine, kissing my neck, and the next she said she felt sick and started puking."

"Had she taken anything?" Reid asked.

Nate looked sheepish. "Yeah, one of my friends had given me this bag of coke. Sasha wanted to try it, so she did a line in the car."

"What about you?" asked Reid. "Didn't you have any?"

"No, man. My coach would kill me. I'm on the court at seven in the morning—earlier in this heat. And we get tested for drugs, I wouldn't do anything to jeopardize my career."

"Why did your friend give you the drugs, then?" asked Vargas.

"It was only a gram," he said. "He gave it to me for my birthday last week, but I wasn't gonna use it. I was gonna throw it away, but then Sasha said she'd never done coke before and wanted to know what it was like. So I gave it to her." He swallowed. "I didn't know she was going to have such a bad reaction. I swear, man. If I had, I'd never have given it to her."

"Then what happened? Why was her body in the canal?"

He looked panicked. "When she started throwing up, I pulled over. I helped her out of the car and she ran down the hill to the canal." His voice faltered. "But then she started having some kind of seizure and she lost consciousness...and...and then she died." Voice cracking, he lowered his head.

"Why didn't you call 911?"

"My phone had died earlier in the club." Twisting the water bottle around in his hands, he cracked the plastic. "I didn't know what to do, so I left her there and drove home. When I got back to the dorm, I used a friend's cell to call the police, and said I'd seen a body by Snapper Creek."

"You didn't put her in the water?" asked Reid.

"No way. Why would I do that?"

Reid shook his head. May have been a gator or a wild animal that had pulled her in. They'd have to check with forensics for bite marks or tears in her clothing or on her body.

"Am I in trouble?" he whispered.

Reid could see his knuckles had gone white. "No, not at this stage," he said, watching the boy heave a sigh of relief. "Do you still have that coke?"

"No, I threw it out as soon as I got home."

Fuck.

Vargas glanced at him.

"We need to trace that coke back to the person who supplied it," Reid said. "We won't bring charges against you if you can help us do that."

"How? I was given it as a birthday present."

"Who's your buddy?" asked Reid.

Nate hesitated. "He's not going to get into shit, is he?"

"Not if he cooperates with us," Reid said. "We're not the drug squad. We just want to know where he got it."

"Okay. His name is Tyler Broody. He goes to the University of Art and Design."

"Thanks," said Reid. "And it's best you don't call him before we speak to him. We need to analyze that sample, and I don't want him to panic and get rid of it like you did."

"Yes, sir." Nate chewed on his lower lip. His coach beckoned from the court. "Can I go now?"

"Yeah, you can go."

They watched as he ran back onto the court and picked up his racquet to resume the game.

"You went easy on him," Vargas said, once they were back in the car.

"Didn't want to ruin the kid's career." He angled the air vent so it aimed at his face. "It wasn't his fault she died."

"He gave her the coke," Vargas pointed out.

"True, but he's not a user. Just a dumb kid who was given it as a gift. Everyone deserves a first warning."

Vargas nodded, but Reid didn't miss the secret grin. He wasn't known for his light touch. He cleared his throat. "Let's go find this Tyler Broody."

"This is it," Vargas said as they pulled up in front of an uber-modern building with a slanted roof and reflective glass panels down one side. "The University of Art and Design."

"I can't look at it, it's so bright," Reid complained, pulling on his shades.

They got out of the car and walked inside. Even with sunglasses on, it was dazzling.

"Let's look for the admin offices," Vargas said, shading his eyes.

Walking into the vast lobby, they surveyed a large signpost on the wall. "Down that way," Vargas said, pointing to a glass tunnel.

"Damn, it must be a hundred degrees in here." Reid swiped at the sweat dotting his forehead. At the other side, the air conditioning hit them as they opened the door. Even Vargas, who never complained, sighed in relief.

"Can I help you gentlemen?" asked a woman in a tight skirt, cream blouse, and lethal four-inch heels. Her hair was up in a high bun and she wore oversized glasses that made her look like a character out of a children's movie.

"Yes, we're looking for Tyler Broody." Reid showed her his ID card. "We're with the Sweetwater Police Department."

"Is there a problem?" she asked, adjusting her glasses. "Has Tyler done something wrong?"

"Why would you ask that?" Reid wanted to know.

"Because it's not every day, we get the police coming around."

"Just need to ask him a few questions." Vargas smiled at her, and she relaxed somewhat.

"Okay, I'll see if I can bring up his timetable. Bear with me."

Walking behind a desk, she tapped away at a computer. A few minutes later, she said, "He's in architecture right now. That's on the second floor in lecture theater 207."

"Where's that?" inquired Reid.

She smiled, not without a touch of malice. Reid got the impression she liked making them sweat. "You'll have to go back to the main building and it's up the stairs."

Back through the glass heat tunnel, they went and up the stairs to lecture hall 207. Reid peered through the door. It was a large theater with a small stage and lectern at the front and rows of chairs occupied by students. The class was in full flow.

Vargas hesitated. "Now what? Do we haul him out in front of everyone?"

Reid hesitated. He didn't want to but who knew how long they'd be, and he didn't want to risk losing Broody in the throng.

"I'll go and speak to the lecturer," he said. "You stay here and guard the exit."

Vargas nodded as Reid pushed open the door. The auditorium sloped downwards to the lectern, so Reid walked down, eyeing the class. Several heads turned in his direction as he got to the stage.

"Sorry for the interruption," he said. Then he spoke softly to the lecturer who nodded and turned to his students. "Would Tyler Broody please go outside? Is Tyler Broody here?"

No one moved.

Reid scanned the audience. Instinct told him Tyler was there but keeping a low profile. Several heads turned in one direction. Reid followed them to where a guy shuffled uncomfortably.

"Tyler?" he called. "Would you step outside for a minute? We need to speak with you. It's important."

Tyler got up from his chair. All eyes were on him. He'd have some awkward questions to answer later, but that couldn't be helped. This was important. Unless they found out who was supplying the drugs, more kids would die.

Tyler made his way to the door. Reid walked back up the stairs to where Vargas was waiting, but when he got there, he saw Tyler shove open the door and take off up the corridor.

8

Kenzie didn't leave right away. She waited outside in the school quad under a canopy for Hannah, who was finishing up a lesson.

A bell rang and kids poured out from every doorway like mice, congregating outside. A small shop on the far side served snacks and sodas. No one paid her any attention, and she figured she must look like a teacher, blending into the scenery.

"Have you found out anything?" Hannah asked, coming up to her. She looked bright and breezy in a floral skirt and plain T-shirt, paired with strappy sandals. Her hair was loose and fell around her face in a long bob.

"Both Matteo's probation officer and Principal Hogarth are eager for me to believe he was in with a bad crowd," she said. "I'm not sure why."

"He wasn't," Hannah insisted. "He wasn't into any of that bad stuff. I know his friends, they're good guys."

"Are they here?" Kenzie looked around at the groups of teenagers.

"Yeah." Hannah cast her eyes over the quad. "There! That's Pat.

He's part of their group. That's Chad with him, and Grant's the blond guy by the snack shop."

"Could you get them to come over?" Kenzie asked. "I'd like to talk to them."

"Sure," she said, after a slight pause. Kenzie realized it was because none of them knew about her relationship with Matteo. Still, Hannah went over and rounded them up. They looked puzzled, but came over to talk to her.

"Thank you," Kenzie said, leading them out of the quad and onto the track where it was quieter. "I'm investigating your friend's death, and I wanted to ask you a few questions. You okay with that?"

"Sure," said Pat. "Anything to help Matt."

"Yeah," agreed the blond guy. "No worries."

Kenzie nodded. "Great. Did you know they found drugs on him? A particular brand of pink cocaine."

"Seriously?" asked Pat, staring at her with wide eyes.

"No way." The blond shook his head. "Not possible."

Chad spluttered on his soda.

"Why not?" Kenzie asked.

"Matt didn't deal. He didn't even do drugs," Pat said. Hannah stood a little bit away from the group, and Kenzie could see the boys glancing at her curiously.

"That's not what his probation officer said."

"Well, he's lying," blurted out Pat. "Matt hated drugs. After what happened to his mother..."

Grant elbowed him in the ribs.

"What happened to his mother?" Hannah asked, stepping forward.

"Uh, she OD'ed," Pat said. "That's why he lived with his grand-parents. His father took off after she died."

Hannah gasped.

"I'm sorry to hear that," Kenzie said, but it just reiterated every-thing she'd discovered. There was no way Matteo was dealing drugs.

They were planted on him by whoever killed him. Now she just had to find out why.

"That probation officer was a douchebag," Pat announced, anger written all over his young face.

"What makes you say that?" Kenzie asked, even though she was of the same opinion.

"Because he made Matt go to this party," Pat said. "Fucking weird, man. Excuse me, ma'am."

She waved his apology away. "What party?"

Pat glanced at Grant and Chad, and then back at Kenzie. "He didn't want anyone to know, but it was super strange. The dude said if he went to this party and was nice to the people there, he'd cut six months off his probation."

"Really?" said Hannah. "Can they do that?"

"No," Kenzie replied. "They can't. It's against the rules."

"Well, this guy did," said Pat, and the others nodded in agreement. "Matt thought, what the hell? If he could end his probation early, why not?"

"Did he go?" asked Hannah.

"Yeah, he was told to dress fancy. It was some big mansion in Wynwood. The party itself was weird. When he got there, he said it was only men. No women. Men and teenage boys."

Kenzie stared at him. "No women?"

Pat shook his head. "None. But it gets worse. The men were going upstairs with the boys." His eyes told Kenzie he knew exactly what was happening upstairs.

"Holy crap," she muttered.

Hannah gasped as she caught on to what he meant. "But Matt didn't...?"

Pat scoffed. "No way, man. Some politician dude tried to chat him up, and he pushed him off and legged it. They'd locked the front door, so he jumped out of the window and ran away."

"He didn't want no pedo feeling him up," said Grant.

Kenzie shivered, despite the heat.

Hannah had gone white. "I had no idea."

Pat looked at her. "Why would you? You didn't even know him."

She fell silent.

After a pause Pat said, "Ooh. You're the one."

"What? Her? No way!" Grant said.

Chad gazed at her, intrigued.

"Matt said he'd met someone," Pat told her, "But he didn't say who. He said he couldn't, 'cos it would get you into trouble."

"It would," she whispered.

The boys just stared at her, unsure what to say.

Kenzie took back control of the conversation. "Guys, I'm sure Hannah would appreciate it if you didn't spread this around. She asked for my help in finding out what happened to your friend, and I'm doing that, okay?"

They nodded, their eyes still darting between Kenzie and Hannah.

"What can we do to help?" asked Pat. "We know those drugs were planted on him. There's no way they were his."

"It's true," Kenzie said. "I believe the same thing. According to the autopsy, there were no drugs in his system either."

"I knew it." Pat thumped Grant on the back. "It was a setup."

"By whom?" asked Hannah, her eyes huge. "Do you think it had something to do with that party?"

They all stared at each other.

"That," said Kenzie, "is what we have to find out."

9

VARGAS TOOK off after Tyler Broody, zigzagging around other students in the corridor. Tyler was fast, but Vargas was in good shape thanks to frequent gym workouts and caught up to him at the bottom of the staircase. He tackled Tyler in the lobby, sprawling across the shiny, tiled surface.

Students scattered in surprise, then stood around the perimeter gawking as Vargas hauled Tyler to his feet and handcuffed him.

Reid arrived a few seconds later. "What the hell are you running for?" he demanded, catching his breath. "We only want to ask you some questions."

"I'm not under arrest?" the kid asked.

"No, should you be?" Reid scowled at him. It was hot enough without racing through the damn college.

"No," he said sulkily.

"We know about the drugs," Reid stated. At the kid's look of alarm, he held up a hand. "We're not the Vice squad, okay? Relax. We just want to know where you got them from."

Tyler calmed down. "Hey, can you take the cuffs off? People are going to think you're arresting me."

"Are you going to take off again?" Vargas asked.

"No, I swear." Eyeing the gathering crowd of onlookers. "We can talk in the cafeteria."

"Okay." Vargas took off the cuffs.

Tyler rubbed his wrists. "Follow me."

He led them down a short corridor on the opposite side of the building to an air-conditioned cafeteria. The smell of burgers and fries lingered in the air. Reid's stomach rumbled. It had been a while since he'd eaten.

They got a table at the back. "Okay, spill," he said as soon as they'd sat down. "Where'd you score the coke?"

"There's this guy who hangs out in South Beach. I kinda know him from school, although I think he dropped out after seventh grade."

"What's his name?" asked Rob.

"Sammy Roland," said Tyler, "Although we used to call him Fat Sam."

"That's not very nice," remarked Vargas.

Tyler shrugged.

"And he supplies drugs?"

"Yeah, although he's pretty small-time. Never has more than a few grams of coke on him. Usually it's the white stuff, but this one was something new. More expensive. When I gave him a hard time about the price, he said it wasn't his choice. That's how much it cost."

The new designer drug had a higher street value than the usual cocaine.

"Did you take any?" asked Reid.

"No, man. I gave it to someone for a birthday present. I forgot to get him a gift, so I thought it was a pretty cool idea."

"Your pretty cool idea killed a young woman," Reid snapped.

Tyler gaped at him. "What?"

"Your buddy, Nate, gave it to a girl he met at a bar—and she died."

"Oh, fuck!" He seemed genuinely distraught. "I didn't know."

"Do you have any more?" asked Vargas.

"No man, it was only that one gram. I'm not a regular user. I got it for the college summer party. We break up next week."

Another dead end.

"Do you have a number for this Sammy character?" Reid asked.

"Yeah." He pulled out his phone. "Just don't tell him it was me who passed it on."

"We won't," Vargas assured him. They wouldn't put him in that position. Drug dealers didn't like snitches, even ones they'd been to school with.

Tyler read out the number, and Vargas jotted it down.

"The pink stuff's lethal," Reid told him before they left. "If you know what's good for you, you'll stay away from it, and tell your buddies too."

"I hear you, man. Can I go now? I've got class."

"Yeah, sure."

Vargas tapped the phone number with his pen. "At least we have a lead."

"Yeah, we'll get on that as soon as we get back to the station, but right now, I'm going to grab one of those burgers. I'm starving."

Reid got home to find Kenzie sitting in her car outside his cabin, fanning herself with a notepad, but she waved as he pulled in.

Getting out of the pickup, he remarked, "You look hot," noting her pink cheeks.

"Yeah, my AC packed up. Reid, we need to talk."

Not again.

He gave her a skewed glance. "About us?"

"Er, no. This is something else."

Relaxing, he nodded. "Come inside."

They went into the cabin. "God, it's worse than my car in here." She exhaled noisily. "Seriously, you need to think about getting air-conditioning. No one can live like this. You'll melt."

"It's not normally this bad." Opening the sliding doors, he let what little fresh air there was drift inside. "Want a drink? I'm going to have a beer."

"Bad day?" She arched an eyebrow.

"Long day," he corrected. "We've been trying to hunt down this elusive pink cocaine. It's proving challenging."

Flicking open the top of the beer, he handed it to her, then got another one out of the fridge for himself. "What's your news?"

"Matteo's death." Holding the cool bottle against her flushed face, she said, "It was staged. The coke was planted on him."

Reid frowned. "How'd you know that?"

"Because he hated drugs." She moved closer to him. "His mother OD'ed when he was a little kid. He never touched the stuff."

Reid gave her a long, hard look. "That changes things." It posed a hell of a lot of questions and scenarios they hadn't even considered.

"There's more. I may have stumbled on a pedophile ring."

He stared at her. "Seriously?"

"Yeah, and I think it involves politicians and other people in authority."

Reid collapsed in a wicker armchair. "Explain, please?"

She perched opposite. "I spoke to Matteo's friends at school. Matteo's probation officer, a big sweaty guy called Hodge, told Matt that if he attended this party and was nice to the guests, he'd knock six months off his sentence."

Reid pursed his lips. "What does *nice* mean?"

"Exactly." Kenzie gave him a knowing look. "The kid even saw guests taking young boys upstairs."

"Jesus."

Kenzie leaned forward. "They locked the front door so the boys couldn't leave. Matteo climbed out of a window and ran away."

"When was this?" Reid sat up straight.

Kenzie met his gaze. "The night before he was killed."

10

"IT *MUST* BE RELATED," Kenzie said.

Reid stroked his stubble. "Are you saying Matteo was killed because someone wanted to stop him from talking about the party?"

"Could be." Kenzie's brain had gone into overdrive. "What better way to avert suspicion than to plant this new designer cocaine on him? Make it look like his death was drug-related."

"Hmm... it's an interesting theory and definitely warrants further investigation. I'll talk to Lieutenant Pérez about it tomorrow. His team has more resources than us. They might have better luck tracing where these drugs are coming from."

"Isn't there a DEA field office somewhere in Miami?" she inquired. "Maybe ask them?"

"Yes, I could, although they don't like to share. Let's try Miami PD first."

"Okay." Pausing, she frowned. "Do you think this has anything to do with the cartel?" Reid's nemesis, Alberto Torres, was back in town and operating out of Miami. She knew he'd been looking for him, but so far, the drug kingpin seemed to have kept under the radar.

"Maybe." Reid avoided her gaze. "I'm looking into it, but they don't usually branch out into synthetic drugs. As far as I know, they don't have any lab facilities. Just importers and distributors."

"Maybe they're expanding?" Kenzie suggested.

"Certainly possible." Taking a long pull on his beer, he set it down beside him. "Can I ask you a favor?"

Kenzie raised her eyebrows. This was a first. "Sure, what is it?"

"Will you go clubbing with me?"

She hesitated. Clubbing? Reid?

"Er... sure, if you want to."

Chuckling, his eyes crinkled. "We've got a lead that the pink coke is being sold in a club in South Beach. I want to check it out tomorrow night. Are you up for that?"

Now it made sense. Reid was the last person on earth she'd picture in a club. He was the tough loner, the outdoorsman who loathed cramped, crowded places and overly loud music.

"Sure, I'll be your wingman." And she grinned.

"Thanks. I'll pick you up at eight."

"Make that ten," she amended with a wry grin. "None of the clubs in Miami get going until then."

"Right, of course." He grimaced. "I'm out of practice."

"Ever been to a nightclub?" she inquired, studying him.

"Does work count?"

"No."

"Then nope."

Kenzie rolled her eyes. "Then you definitely need me. Who are we looking for?"

"A dealer called Fat Sam. Tyler Broody, the tennis player's buddy, bought his drugs from him. Said he hangs out at a club called Mojito."

"That's a Latin club off Ocean Drive," she said. "I know it."

"Been there before?"

"Yeah, back in the day. A fun place if you like Latin dance music." But Reid's eyes had glazed over, and she could tell he was already thinking about other things. Clubbing wasn't his thing.

Standing up, she said, "I'd better go."

"Do you want to stay for supper?" he asked, suddenly. "There's nothing in the refrigerator, but we could order take out?"

She gazed at him for a moment. Tempted as she was, she had an early start tomorrow and she wasn't sure where they stood. Something was telling her not to move too fast, because supper could lead to other things, and Kenzie instinctively knew that spending the night with Reid would be dangerous. Exciting, but dangerous.

"Sorry, I can't," she said reluctantly, wincing as his gaze flickered away from hers. "I'm due at the office first thing, and then I want to see if I can track down some of the young offenders who have been at these parties."

His eyebrows shot up. "Kenzie, be careful. If whoever is running this pedophile ring murdered Matteo, there's no telling how far they'll go to prevent their sick secret from coming out. As a reporter, you're particularly vulnerable."

"Don't worry, I'll be careful," she insisted. "I only want to talk to the kids."

He gave a stiff nod. "Keep me posted."

"I promise."

At ten o'clock the following morning, Kenzie was positioned outside the probation office. It seemed like a good place to wait. The juvenile offenders had to report weekly to Hodge. Matteo can't be the only one he'd spoken to about the parties.

It made her feel sick thinking about what occurred at those events. Grown men, respected men, abusing young offenders, offering them a way out of their sentences if they consented to... what? She shivered.

A boy dressed from head to toe in black with a thick chain attached to his jeans and a purple mohawk sauntered up to the entrance. Nah, thought Kenzie. He wasn't the type to be groomed.

Anarchy was written all over him. Their sordid secret wouldn't be safe with him.

Next was a hard-faced, broad-shouldered guy of about seventeen, with closely cropped hair and a crooked nose. He looked like he could handle himself in a fight and frequently did. So she discounted him as well. Too brawny. Not easily coerced.

The next person to walk in was a slim teenage girl with tattoos up both arms. Wrong target market. Kenzie was beginning to think this was a waste of time, when she saw a rake-thin boy of about sixteen walk up. Hands buried deep in his pockets, his eyes were downcast.

Bingo.

Following him in, she watched as he caught the elevator up to the 7th floor. Better and better. That's where Hodge's office was located.

Then she went back outside to wait.

Forty minutes later, the boy re-emerged.

"Excuse me," she said, shoving the newspaper she'd been reading into her canvas bag. "Could I have a moment of your time?"

His eyes narrowed. "What about?"

The sulky expression on his face told her the meeting hadn't gone well. She wondered if they ever did.

"Please, it's important and will only take a minute. It's about your probation officer, Mr. Hodge."

"How'd you know I went to see him?"

"I saw you go in."

Now he looked worried. "You stalking me, lady?"

"No, nothing like that." She showed him her press ID card. "I'm a reporter. I'm investigating the parties Mr. Hodge has been persuading you to go to."

His eyes widened. "I—I don't know anything about no parties."

"Are you sure? Because Matteo told me all about them."

"I don't know no Matteo."

Okay, that had been a long shot.

Time to try a different angle. "Hodge is being watched by the police," she said in a conspiratorial whisper. Not an outright lie.

Hodge was on their radar. "It's in your best interests to tell me about the parties. That way when the police bust him, you won't get taken down with them."

He swallowed. "I didn't have anything to do with the parties, I swear."

"But you have been to one?"

"Yeah, but you can't tell anyone I said so. They'd kill me." He cast a furtive glance back at the building.

"Come on," said Kenzie. "Let me buy you a drink."

They walked up the road to the nearest coffee shop and took a seat inside. Kenzie made sure they sat at the back, out of sight of the door, just in case anyone from the probation office walked in.

"Were you offered a shorter sentence if you attended?" Kenzie inquired, once they had their coffees. The teenager, whose name was Benny, had a grande hot chocolate with whipped cream and sprinkles.

"Hodge offered to release me early. I had six months to go, and he cut it down to two. It was worth it. I'm sick of having these guys dictate my life."

"Isn't he worried you'll tell someone what you know?" Kenzie asked. There was no way they could guarantee the boys' silence.

"Hodge told me that if I ever told anyone what happened at the party, he'd add an extra year to my probationary period. I wanted to get out, man. So I agreed."

"Did you only go to one party?" she asked.

He nodded. "It was sick. They made me..." Kenzie held up her hand. "Okay Benny. You don't have to tell me. I get the picture."

He spooned a dollop of whipped cream into his mouth, a haunted look in his eyes.

"It's over now." She hoped it would give him some comfort. "And there are people you can speak to about your experience."

"No!" shaking his head. "I promised."

"No need to mention anything about the party. Just talk about what happened to you."

"No...I'm good." He kept his eyes glued to his beverage. "I'm not going to risk another probation."

Kenzie gave a small nod. Until this was over and the perpetrators were in custody, she wouldn't be able to convince him otherwise.

"Did you recognize anyone at the party?" she asked.

"They were all loaded," he said. "Wore expensive watches and had fancy cars. And they tipped with hundred-dollar bills."

"They paid you?"

"Yeah, a little something for being a good sport."

She shuddered. A little something to keep you quiet, more like.

Kenzie rifled for a business card. Taking the newspaper she'd been reading out of her bag, she laid it on the table, then delved in again. Where were they?

The boy's gaze was drawn to the picture on the front.

"Here." She finally found them in the inside pocket and laid one on the table. "This is my card. If you remember anything else, or you want the number of someone to talk to, just give me a call."

He didn't take the card, just kept staring at the photograph on the front of the newspaper.

"What's wrong?" Kenzie asked.

"He was there," whispered Benny.

Kenzie frowned. "Who was there?"

Benny tapped the black and white picture. "That man. He was at the party. I saw him."

Kenzie unfolded the newspaper and stared at the image on the front page. Her heart skipped a beat. "Are you sure?"

His eyes hardened. "Yeah, I'm sure."

"Benny, that man is Raymond Talbot, the governor of Florida."

11

Reid picked Kenzie up at ten o'clock that night. He'd never admit it, but he'd agonized over what to wear. Eventually, he'd settled on black jeans, a black shirt and his hair combed back off his face. He'd even had a shave.

"You clean up well," Kenzie said admiringly, when she opened the front door. "I like this new look."

"Don't get too used to it," he grumbled, but he was pleased. If she thought he looked okay, he wasn't going to make a fool of himself. "You look great too."

Amazing, more like. He watched, mesmerized, as she waltzed past him and out of the house, her silver dress shimmering with every step.

"Thanks." She tossed her silky blonde hair over her shoulder, her eyes sparkling.

Oh, boy.

He was going to have a hard time concentrating on the case with her looking like that.

"Are you okay?" she asked when he almost drove into the car in front of them at a stop sign.

"Yeah, sorry. It's just that I'm finding you very distracting tonight. Didn't you have anything less shiny to wear?"

Something that didn't highlight every goddamn curve.

She laughed. "Behave, Reid. We've got a job to do."

He grinned. "Yeah, I know."

This was a new experience for him. Flirting. He'd felt a similar buzz with Bianca, but their relationship had been secret. Stolen moments behind the Miami PD building, nights of passion at her place after a shift ended. With Kenzie, everything was out in the open. He didn't have to hide his feelings.

They parked the car and walked along Ocean Drive to the night-club. Kenzie was right, it was buzzing. A line had formed at the door, snaking down the road, while salsa music blared out from inside.

"Shall we?" She nodded to the back of the line.

"Maybe I could just show my badge," he grumbled. He hated waiting. "But then everyone would know I'm a cop."

"Kind of defeats the purpose, don't you think?" Taking his hand, she pulled him in the direction of the line.

Another novel experience, holding hands in public. God, he hadn't done that since he was in his twenties. She caught him smiling. "What's so funny?"

"Oh, nothing." At her quizzical look, he squeezed her hand. "This. I'm not used to it."

"Me neither, but we should look like a couple. It will allay suspicion."

Suddenly, he didn't feel quite so upbeat anymore. She was playing a role, getting into her character for the night. Kenzie, unlike anyone else he knew, had this uncanny ability to morph into a different person when the situation called for it. A handy skill for a reporter, but it meant he was never sure if she was acting or not. Did she feel anything, or was it all for show?

"What does this Fat Sam look like?" she asked, forcing his mind back to the reason they were there.

"Like his name says," he replied. "He's Cuban, I believe, and wears a backwards baseball cap."

Kenzie nodded. The bouncer let a stream of people into the club. "Here we go."

They paid and got a smudgy black stamp on their hands. Reid followed Kenzie through a short passage and into the club. Immediately, the music became deafening. Sound waves pulsed through his body, making him vibrate.

He glanced around at the bar area, dotted with high tables and recessed lighting. The room was crowded, but not overly full. Women in sequins and high heels drank cocktails, while men in suave shirts and tight jeans drank beer and tapped their feet in time to the music.

On the opposite side of the room was the dance floor. A DJ stood at one end on a type of caged pedestal, glowing green and red, while couples gyrated below.

"How's your salsa?" Kenzie asked.

He shook his head.

She laughed. He bet she was great at it. He'd discovered there wasn't much Kenzie couldn't do.

"Let's get a drink," he said, heading to the bar. He kept his eyes peeled for a fat guy in a baseball cap but couldn't see anyone fitting that description.

"I don't think he's here," Kenzie shouted above the music.

They got a couple of drinks and did a lap of the club.

"That's the VIP area." Kenzie nodded to a raised platform on one side. Reid surveyed the private booths occupied by glittering men and women with expensive smiles and buckets of champagne in front of them. A gold rope and two hefty bouncers separated the exclusive area from the rest of the club.

Reid checked out the VIPs, looking for anyone he recognized. About to turn away, he froze when a man with thick black hair rose and beckoned for a cocktail waitress.

He knew that face. Knew it as well as his own.

"What?" asked Kenzie, noting his change in demeanor. "What's wrong?"

"Torres." His voice was a strangled whisper.

Kenzie followed his gaze. "Oh, shit. What's he doing here?"

"Hell if I know," Reid muttered, his head spinning. "Must be doing business here."

"Maybe he likes Latin music?" she suggested.

"Nah, Torres isn't the type to let his hair down. He's too controlled for that. If he's here, you can bet there's a reason."

Torres wasn't a party animal. He didn't drink or do drugs; Bianca had told him that much. He always kept his wits about him, that's what made him such an asset to the cartel. He didn't make stupid mistakes. He didn't fuck up.

"Will he recognize you?" Kenzie asked.

"Probably not. We've never actually met. He didn't know I was Bianca's handler, and when we raided the bar, he'd already gone." After having shot Bianca and left her lying on the concrete floor. Reid clenched his fists.

"He's coming this way," Kenzie warned.

Reid spun around, not wanting the drug kingpin to see his face, since he kept him under constant surveillance. Kenzie, however had no such qualms. She smiled alluringly as Torres passed, catching his eye.

"What are you doing?" hissed Reid, as the cartel man walked past them towards the bar.

"Diverting attention from you. If he's looking at me, he won't notice you. Besides," she hesitated, her gaze following Torres to the bar. "Since Fat Sam isn't here, I may as well get to know Torres a little better. Maybe I can find out who he's meeting."

"Are you crazy?" snapped Reid. "He's a cold-blooded killer. I don't want you anywhere near him."

Kenzie's voice was deceptively calm. "I think that's my decision, don't you?"

"Kenzie, please," he pleaded. "He is dangerous."

"And this is a crowded club. You've been looking for this guy for years. Now he's here. Are you really going to tell me not to do this?"

Kenzie didn't know he'd already located Torres. That he'd been surveilling him for months. That he had a camera outside his warehouse, for Christ's sake.

"We're here to find out about the pink coke," he said. "Not Torres."

"Two birds, one stone," she said airily, handing him her drink and moving away in the direction of the bar.

He gritted his teeth. Once she'd got an idea into her head, there was no stopping her.

Reid watched Torres turn and smile at Kenzie. She said something and he laughed. Reid felt a tightening in his chest. Torres brought her a drink, and they talked for a while.

Okay, maybe it wasn't so bad. One conversation, then Kenzie would say goodbye and flitter back to him.

To his dismay, he saw Torres lead her onto the dancefloor. He scowled into the flashing lights. What was she doing? The tightening in his chest threatened to choke him. Kenzie had no idea what kind of man Torres was.

Cold, clinical, ruthless.

A murderer.

Except, he had to admit, he looked anything but cold and clinical now. The man could move, his hips undulating as he held Kenzie close, and they sashayed around the dance floor.

Kenzie looked like a writhing goddess, her body moving in time with his, her blonde hair catching the light as she turned. Reid felt his scowl deepening. This wasn't part of the plan. Torres's hand moved down her back, his sardonic face smiling into hers.

She appeared to be having a great time. Reid had to remind himself that she was acting. It's all for show, he muttered, downing his drink in one gulp.

The song seemed never ending. Finally, they walked back to the VIP booth. Reid took up a position in a dark alcove where he wouldn't be seen and watched Kenzie work her magic.

If he didn't know better, he'd think she really liked Torres. The way she leaned towards him, giving him a tempting glimpse of her cleavage. Running a hand through her dance-tousled hair, glancing up at him from under her dark lashes, laughing at what he said.

Torres seemed equally smitten, looping an arm around her shoulders and murmuring something in her ear. When she turned to reply, their faces were very close together.

Jesus. He didn't want to watch this.

Reid downed Kenzie's drink as well, then stalked out of the club. It was warmer outside, but he was just glad to be away from the gut-wrenching sight of Kenzie flirting with Torres, his arch enemy. The man who'd killed his colleague and ex-lover.

Pacing up and down the street, he told himself it was what she did. It wasn't real. None of it was real. That's when he spotted Fat Sam, or at least he thought it was him.

The guy had oversized jeans on and Nike Airs that added at least an inch to his height. He wore a backwards cap and a shirt that flowed over his rotund belly. He was talking to a bouncer, but it didn't look like he had any intention of going inside the club.

Good, because there was no way Reid was going back in there.

Fat Sam moved off down the street. Reid followed, pretending to be glued to his phone. The street was crowded with partygoers, so it was easy to remain hidden. Fat Sam had no idea he was being watched.

A young couple went up to him, and the three talked, their heads very close together. A few hushed words, a fake handshake, and the exchange was complete.

Reid hesitated. He could bust Fat Sam and bring him in for questioning, or he could go after the couple and warn them about the drugs. That way he could get a sample to analyze, to make sure it was the same drug that had killed Sasha Holden and the other teens.

The couple moved away, holding hands. They walked on to the beach. Reid bet they were going to do a few lines, then head back to a club. It was now or never.

"Excuse me," he said, once they'd got to the sand. "I'm with the Sweetwater Police Department and I'd like to have a word."

The man looked as if he was about to run, but Reid put up a hand. "I'm not going to arrest you. I just wanted to warn you that the drugs you just bought are dangerous. There have been several deaths linked to them in the last few weeks."

The girl stared at him, her eyes huge.

"I don't know what you mean," the man stammered.

"I saw you." Reid pulled on the blue forensic glove that he'd put in his pocket for this exact scenario. "I'd appreciate it if you handed over the coke, so I don't have to search you."

The man hesitated.

Reid reached around for his handcuffs. "Have it your way. We can do this down at the station."

"Give it to him, babe," pleaded the girl.

Reluctantly, the guy reached into his pocket and handed over the small envelope of powder. "You're not going to charge us?"

"No. You're free to go."

The couple walked quickly away, oblivious to the fact that Reid had just saved their lives.

He inspected the envelope, then peeled the glove off, encasing the coke in it. The lab would analyze it, and with a bit of luck, it would be the same stuff that had killed Sasha Holden, which would give them a reason to arrest Fat Sam.

As Reid walked back up the beach to the street, he looked around for Fat Sam. But the drug dealer had vanished.

12

KENZIE WAS surprised at how charming Torres was. From everything Reid had said, she was expecting a cold-hearted monster, but he was smart and witty, not to mention a great dancer. It had been a long time since she'd sashayed around a dancefloor like that with anyone.

Still, just because he was good looking and personable, didn't mean he wasn't dangerous. Slowly, she let the conversation drift back to him. He'd already told her he ran a dock loading warehouse. Not very interesting, but she knew it was a front for the illegitimate side of his business, the importation of drugs from Mexico.

"Do you come here often?" she asked.

"Not really. Tonight is a special event."

"Oh?" There were a few other men sitting around with drinks, but since he'd brought her back to the booth, they'd given him space, standing off, laughing and drinking.

"My amigo's getting married," he said. "We're here to show him a good time."

"Which one is he?" Kenzie studied the group of men. Most of them were in their thirties, and like Torres, were well dressed in crisp shirts and shiny shoes. The champagne was flowing, and they'd managed to pick up several women who were hanging around for the free drinks and attention.

There was one man in particular, a burly giant of a man with an earring and slicked back long hair, who'd been giving her the eye. *He* looked dangerous, and she wondered who he was.

"Juan, come here!" called Torres.

One of the younger men came over. He appeared to be a little drunk, which was understandable, given the circumstances. "Meet Kaylee."

She'd reverted to the same fake ID she always used: Kaylee, the freelance writer and waitress. It had served her well before, and she liked keeping things close to the truth.

"Hey, beautiful," he said, taking her hand and kissing it. "Would you like a dance?"

"No, she wouldn't," Torres said, a bit too forcefully, but Juan only laughed.

"Relax, buddy. I'm getting married, remember?"

"Juan and I go way back," Torres said, but the joviality had left his voice. Was there some sort of history there?

"Congratulations." She smiled at him. "I hope you're having a good time."

"I sure am." Slapping Torres on the shoulder, he moved back to the group. Kenzie didn't know what to make of Torres's brief show of possession. It seemed over the top for having just met him.

"He seems nice," she remarked.

But Torres was on to other things. "How about another dance?" Lowering his voice, "It's the rumba." The rumba was a very sexy dance, and Kenzie wasn't sure she liked the gleam in Torres's eye. Then it flickered as he gazed across at Juan, and he was momentarily distracted.

Kenzie glanced between the two and wondered at their relationship.

She shook her head. "No, thank you, Alex. I have to go."

"Are you sure?" He seemed disappointed.

"I'm sure." She flashed him a seductive smile. "Thank you for a wonderful evening."

Letting Torres walk her to the exit, she wondered where Reid had gone. She hoped he wasn't too upset with her. Surely, he'd be able to see that it was a smart move. Now that she'd made contact, she could tell him why Torres was at the bar tonight, and it was nothing sinister.

Kenzie walked out onto Ocean Drive. Still sickeningly humid despite the late hour, there was no breeze off the sea.

Where was Reid?

She glanced up and down the street but couldn't see him. Maybe he'd given up and gone home? No, he'd never leave her alone with Torres.

Walking back to the car, she found him leaning against the trunk, staring moodily out over the ocean. When he heard her heels on the pavement, he turned. "Good night?"

His icy tone was enough to make her shiver. "Come on, Reid. I was working, probing him for information. It's what I do. I'm an investigative reporter, remember?"

"Did you find out anything?"

"Yes, actually. I discovered why Torres was at the club. His friend Juan is getting married. That was his bachelor party."

"Is that what he told you?"

"Yeah. I met his friend and congratulated him. He was suitably drunk."

Reid grunted.

"You don't believe him?"

"No, I don't. I know Torres. He doesn't believe in pleasure without business."

Kenzie studied him. Hard eyes, tension in his jaw, neck, and shoulders. She hesitated, then said, "Do you know what I think? I think your opinion of Torres is clouding your judgement."

"My opinion?" He gave a harsh laugh. "The man's a killer,

Kenzie. I've seen the evidence. I've seen the mess he leaves behind, how little people mean to him."

"I know." This wasn't constructive. "Look, I'm sorry if my actions tonight made you worry, but I know what I'm doing."

"Just like you knew what you were doing getting on Ingleman's yacht?"

Kenzie frowned. She couldn't believe he'd brought that up. Earlier in the year she'd been abducted after going after a corrupt businessman. "That's not fair. He was on to me. I didn't know it at the time. If I had, I'd never have gone to the party on his yacht."

Reid gritted his teeth. "What's to say Torres won't figure out who you are?"

"Not tonight, he won't." She attempted a smile, but he didn't smile back. "I gave a false name, and he probably won't remember it, anyway."

"Don't be so sure. He barely drinks, he's smart and controlled. If he likes you at all, he'll have you checked out."

"And all he'll find is Kaylee's social media profiles engineered to support my cover story." She'd set them up after last time, including pictures of herself working at the restaurant and hanging out in coffee shops. She didn't have many followers, but enough for it to look legit.

"Torres is a charmer," Reid warned. "I've seen it happen before."

Kenzie rolled her eyes. Not this again.

"I'm not Bianca," she said. "I know he's a gangster, and I'm not about to fall for him, if that's what you're worried about." How could he even think that? Didn't he know her by now?

"I don't know." He raked an agitated hand through his hair. "You're so good at playing roles, Kenzie, that I don't know if what you're doing is real or not."

She touched his arm. "It's not. I promise you."

Giving her a hard look, he nodded. "If you say so. Let's go."

The drive back to her place was in silence. Reid dropped her off, wished her good night, and took off down the road. Kenzie watched him go. That was another thing she'd found out tonight.

Reid had a jealous streak. That was new. He'd never shown it before.

Sighing, she opened her front door. This was because they'd kissed. Kissing meant giving in to feelings that were sometimes better left under the surface. Feelings made things awkward. Maybe they needed to have another talk.

It was a good thing she hadn't told him she'd given Torres her phone number.

Reid floored the airboat until it sped over the surface of the water with eye-watering speed. It was dark, and the swamp was deserted, the only light coming from the full moon and smattering of stars far above. The sporadic cloud cover was still there, locking in the heat.

Tilting his head back, he let the breeze run through his hair and cool his heated face.

Kenzie.

Damn it.

He felt bad about the conversation they'd had, and was slightly confused by his own behavior. He'd never thought of himself as a jealous man before. Even with Bianca, when she'd seduced Torres as part of her undercover role, he'd gone with it. He hadn't liked it, but it hadn't bothered him the way seeing Kenzie flirting with Torres had.

He scowled at the night.

Kenzie was getting under his skin. When he'd seen her laughing with Torres, he'd wanted to punch the guy in the face.

This was not good.

He couldn't afford to let Kenzie become a liability. *She* was clouding his judgement, not Torres. The only problem was he liked being with her. She made him feel hopeful in a way he never had before. The future seemed brighter with her in it.

One question played on his mind. Would he have reacted the same way if they were still friends, if he hadn't kissed her?

He grimaced as the wind whisked away the moisture at the corners of his eyes and billowed his shirt out behind him. Maybe he was overreacting. Torres was a dangerous man. He wouldn't think twice before taking Kenzie out if he suspected she was investigating him. That's why he was concerned. It had nothing to do with jealousy.

He gave a loud snort.

Who was he kidding?

Perhaps Kenzie had been right all along, and this wasn't a good idea. He didn't want to lose her either, but if things continued like this, he couldn't see it ending well.

He sighed, the wind snatching at his breath.

Taking a bend, he felt the boat slide across the inky black water. Sawgrass brushed the hull but offered no traction. The airboat was designed to fly above the surface. It was a weightless feeling and one he relished. He only wished he could apply the same principle to his emotions. Don't get involved, keep a clear head. That was his usual motto.

Except Kenzie had gotten to him, and he hadn't seen it coming. Not until she'd kissed him.

As he approached the mangrove forest, he slowed down so he could navigate through the submerged roots and branches successfully. Even though he knew this part of the Glades like the back of his hand, it was a dark night, and he didn't want to be stranded out here. He was grateful for the brilliant headlights illuminating the water in front of him.

The powerful jet engines drowned out any night sounds, and usually drowned out his thoughts too, but not tonight. The realization that he had to back off, that he had to let her go, was eating at him, leaving a foul taste in his mouth.

He'd seen it in her eyes, too. The doubt.

Why are you acting like this, she seemed to be saying?

How could he explain it was because he had feelings for her? That he cared? More than he'd initially thought. He'd already lost one woman to Torres. He thought back to her words that day on the deck.

I don't want to lose you.

How ironic that for them to stay together, they had to move apart.

He shook his head, the wind tugging at his hair. Talk about screwed up.

When he got to the other side of the mangrove forest, he opened the throttle again. The airboat surged forward, roaring across the surface. It was isolated out here, no one to hear him, no one to care. He'd left civilization far behind.

It was near here he'd discovered Sarah Randall's body last year. The visual of her yellow dress floating in the twisted roots would never leave him. He'd come out to the Glades to forget, but it was becoming a place of memories, and not necessarily good ones.

Sighing, he turned the boat in a large arc and headed back the way he'd come. When he was close to home, he cut the engine and drifted for a while, letting the silence ring in his ears. Soon the nightlife sounds filtered back, the rustling in the bushes, the cries from luckless prey and the swish of a predator's tail. Familiar nocturnal sounds. The hunter and the hunted. The circle of life.

He'd been hunting Torres for years now. Studying him, following him. He'd even broken into his house to look around, although he wouldn't admit that to anyone, not even Kenzie. It would mean the end of his career, but back then he hadn't given a shit. The need to know was far greater.

That's when he found the photograph.

Torres and Bianca.

Their arms around each other. The water lapping in the background. They were smiling into the camera, the deep smiles of two people in love.

He shivered, despite the balmy night.

Damn it, Kenzie.

He'd wanted to scream at her to stay away. That this man kills women. Yet all he'd managed to do was sound possessive and condescending. What a mess.

He started the engine again and cruised the rest of the way home. At least he'd cooled down, even if he hadn't solved anything.

Tying up the boat, he made his way up the walkway toward his cabin. Thank goodness tonight was behind them. Kenzie had left the club, her cover story intact. Torres was none the wiser. Hopefully, she wouldn't have to have anything more to do with him.

Kenzie couldn't sleep, and it wasn't the heat. She'd had a cold shower, and the AC was on low, which made the ambient temperature just about bearable. No, it was the uncomfortable feeling that had gripped her since she'd left the club.

Usually, Reid went along with her investigating, knowing she was good at it. He'd seen her in action before and it had never bothered him then.

Maybe she was being too hard on him. To be fair, Torres had killed his ex-colleague, but she still thought he'd overreacted. He'd been after Torres for years and she'd been safe in the club.

Thinking about Reid was giving her a headache. Flipping over, she tried to get comfortable on her other side, shifting her thoughts to Governor Talbot instead. Had he really been at the pedophile party? It seemed ludicrous that a man in his position would take such a mammoth risk. Except the kid had seemed adamant.

Giving up on sleep, Kenzie sat up and turned on the bedside lamp. Reaching for her laptop, she googled Governor Talbot and pulled up his Wikipedia page.

The Honorable Raymond Talbot. Head of State.

She stared at his photograph. He had distinguished features, a hawk-like nose and hair that was more salt than pepper. His preferred residence was an elegant Miami mansion, in addition to the official residence in Tallahassee. Rolling manicured lawns, perfectly pruned flower beds bursting with color, pillars around the gated entrance and a gravel pathway leading up to the front of the house. It was stunning.

He was married to Helen Talbot, a plain-looking woman with a hapless expression and a vacant smile. Her most rewarding feature was her hair. Full and glossy, it hung around her face in a stylish bob. They'd been married for twenty-two years and had two grown children.

Kenzie thought for a moment. What she needed was an appointment with the governor. Perhaps he'd be interested in an interview with the *Herald*?

Of course, she couldn't ask him outright if he was involved with a pedophile ring, but she could get a feeling for the man. She was a pretty good judge of people, thanks to her unusual upbringing. Being hyperaware of what people thought of you was not a habit she'd willingly taken on, but it was one she'd adopted all the same. And there was no doubt it was useful in her job.

Slowly, a plan began to form in her mind, and by the time she dozed off, she knew what she was going to do.

13

"Excuse me?" Trevor Nolan, the Political Editor at the Miami Herald, reluctantly turned away from his screen and blinked at her.

"What do you know about Governor Talbot?"

"A lot. Can you be more specific?"

"His personal life." She perched on the end of his desk. Trevor was the one with his finger on the political pulse of the city, so if there were any rumors, he'd know.

He squinted behind his thick glasses. "Why? What have you heard?"

"Is he happily married?" she inquired airily.

"Yeah. I haven't heard anything to the contrary. There's no scandal associated with him, if that's what you mean. He's got a boring wife, kids at college, and a dog called Pooch." He shrugged.

"Any same-sex tendencies?"

Trevor nearly fell off his chair. "Holy crap! What have you heard?"

"Nothing." She hastily held up her hand. "Only hearsay. Totally unfounded rumors. I'm still looking into it."

"Oh, okay." He readjusted in his seat, deflated.

She didn't move.

He peered at her from above his glasses. "I know that look. What do you want from me, Kenzie?"

Kenzie grinned. "I want to interview him. Can you help?"

"About being gay?"

"No, of course not. Politics, of course."

Trevor chewed on his lower lip as he cogitated. Eventually he said, "I could do a forerunner to the elections later this year. Any legislative changes? Policy initiatives? You know the drill."

She did, although politics wasn't her forte. Still, it was a foot in the door. No way he'd turn down an interview with the *Herald* in the months leading up to an election.

"Great, thanks Trev. I owe you."

"Yes, you do." And went back to blinking at his screen.

Governor Talbot was only too happy to be interviewed by the Miami Herald. "How does nine-thirty tomorrow morning sound?" his personal secretary asked. "He's got a breakfast meeting at eight, but we can squeeze in a quick one after that."

"Perfect." Kenzie smiled into the phone.

"Will you have a camera crew with you?" asked the secretary.

"No, it'll just be me."

The governor might be used to performing for the cameras, but this was a newspaper article and she wanted him as relaxed as possible, not thinking about his target audience or what his best angle was.

After that, she tried to call Reid, but it diverted to voicemail. He was probably busy. Given what had happened last night, it may be for the best. A little breathing space might be a good idea.

At that moment, Reid was talking to a sweaty Vargas who'd been following Fat Sam all afternoon. "He's making a killing selling to college kids on summer break," he said, wiping perspiration off his forehead.

"Jesus," muttered Reid, thinking of all that lethal coke on the streets.

"I brought him in." Vargas handed over a plastic evidence bag in which was the signature small envelope. "He's being processed."

"Good work." Reid thumped him on the back. "Let's get this analyzed. I'm hoping not all of it is as deadly as the stuff Sasha and the others took." Vargas handed it to Officer Diaz, who'd already completed the paperwork for the lab.

"Did you find out where he was getting it?" Reid asked.

Vargas gave a small grin. "Yeah. Before I arrested him, I followed him into a tacos place down on Washington Avenue. I thought he was grabbing lunch, but while he was there, you'll never guess who walked in."

Reid wasn't in the mood for guessing. "Who?"

"Jago Martinez."

Reid's eyebrows shot up. "The same Jago Martinez who runs the Warriors?"

The Warriors were a street gang, Cubans mostly, who operated out of the Miami area. They covered the same turf as the Kings, hence the drug war that had erupted last year. Since the Kings had mostly disbanded, the Warriors had filled the gap.

"The one and only."

Reid exhaled. "You know what that means? The Warriors get their drugs from the Morales cartel." He'd confirm that when he interrogated Fat Sam.

"You were right," Vargas summed up. "The pink coke *is* being brought in by Federico Lopez."

Torres was Lopez's man in Miami.

Reid gave a terse nod. "Yeah, that's what I was afraid of."

They were expanding. The cartel was breaking with decades of tradition and expanding into new markets. A bold move, with way more risk, but potentially higher returns.

"Let's get that stuff to the lab," he reiterated. "And great work this morning. Now we know who we're dealing with."

"What are we going to do, boss?" Vargas asked, twisting the lid off a bottle of water.

It was a damn good question. Drug gangs weren't his specialty. Ortega, at the Miami PD, was best suited for that. He had CIs he could tap for information, and he knew all the players. Yet this was *his* department's case. Three dead teenagers in as many weeks, and they were dying on his turf. The last thing he wanted to do was hand it over to Miami PD.

To Ortega.

That would suck, both for professional and personal reasons. Still, he needed to know if his old adversary had heard anything.

"I'm heading out." Reid grabbed his car keys off the desk. He'd interview Fat Sam when he got back. "Knock off early, Vargas. You deserve it. Take that girl out you're seeing."

He didn't miss Vargas's grin as he pranced out.

Reid called Ortega from the Miami PD parking lot. He wasn't keen on going inside, where Ortega had the advantage. His turf, his office, his team. At first, he thought the detective wouldn't pick up, then he heard his voice down the line.

"Ortega."

Hesitant. Curious.

He'd know it was Reid calling. They still had each other's cell numbers on their phones from when they were part of the same unit.

"Hey," Reid said. "I heard you were back."

"Yeah."

There was no love lost between them, although Ortega had quashed the assault charge he'd been going to hit Reid with, thanks to Kenzie's intervention.

"I just wanted to say thanks for dropping that charge," he ground out.

Damn, that hurt.

The weasel should never have laid it to begin with. He'd deserved the bloody nose, and the suspension.

Ortega grunted.

Reid pushed on. "Listen, I need to talk to you. Not about that," he added quickly. "About a case I'm working on."

"Why me?" Ortega was as suspicious as ever.

"There's a drug angle."

A pause. Then Ortega sighed and said, "Where are you?"

"Downstairs, in the parking lot."

"I'll meet you there in five."

When Reid got out of the car, the humidity hit him like a furnace. Christ, it was hotter today than yesterday, if that was even possible. Heat radiated off the asphalt, causing a mirage, and through it, Ortega appeared. Ten minutes later, not five, but Reid let it slide. Let the guy make his point. As usual, he looked suave and annoyingly fresh. Reid, on the other hand, needed a shave, and his hair was just long enough to be scruffy.

"What can I do for you?" Ortega asked, hands in his pockets. He was trying to remain casual, but Reid could tell by the tension in his shoulders that he wasn't as calm as he pretended.

"I take it you've heard about this pink cocaine that's hit the streets?"

"Yeah, nasty stuff. A few fatalities."

"Us too," Reid said grimly. "Do you know where it's coming from?"

Ortega shuffled from one foot to another. "I've heard rumors," he said. "Word on the street is it's the Warriors distributing it."

"That ties in with what we've found," Reid confirmed. "We traced a local dealer back to Jago Martinez."

Ortega didn't react. He already knew. Reid bet his snitches had confirmed it.

"Isn't it a little out of character for the Morales cartel?" Reid asked.

Ortega shrugged. "I guess, but the landscape's changing. Cartels are using established pipelines for all sorts of things these days. Drugs, guns, human trafficking, you name it."

It made sense. They were multitasking, creating different revenue streams using the same networks.

"Any news on Lopez?" Reid asked.

Ortega shook his head. "Nah, not a peep. My guess is he's gone back to Mexico and is controlling operations from there. It's safer with the warrant out for his arrest. He doesn't need to be on American soil. Alberto Torres has everything under control."

"You watching him?" Reid wanted to know. He hadn't seen any police presence at the warehouse.

"He's popped up under a different name," Ortega said. "He's married, runs a legitimate business. Doesn't put a foot wrong. We've got nothing on him."

Alex Guerra.

Reid had discovered that while searching his premises.

"Could be he's gone straight," Reid suggested, even though he knew it wasn't true. He wanted to gauge the detective's reaction.

Ortega snorted. "These guys never get out. The bastards just get smarter."

He was right about that.

"You're not treating those drug deaths as suspicious?" Reid asked.

"Nah, those kids took some bad shit, but it's not homicide. We've got our hands full with real murder cases. You know how it is."

And there it was. The thinly veiled insinuation that he didn't get real cases over at Sweetwater, that they were just some backwater excuse for a police department.

"What about Matteo Davis?" he asked, ignoring the jibe.

Ortega frowned. "Who's he again?"

"The kid. The stab victim. He was found with drugs on him."

"Oh, yeah. We're looking into it, but it looks like a drug-related stabbing."

"Even though the kid didn't deal?" Reid met his gaze, his own unfaltering.

Ortega shifted uncomfortably. "Listen, man, I wish I could stand here and shoot the breeze, but I've got work to do."

Reid wasn't going to get anywhere with that one. They'd made up their mind. The drugs found on Matteo's body meant it had to be drug-related, right? Just like the killer intended.

"Sure thing."

Reid watched as Ortega turned and strode back into the building. Unless he could find out who planted the drugs, Matteo's killer would never be brought to justice. One of many lost in the system.

Reid got back into his car and turned the AC on full blast. As soon as he got back to the station, he was going to call Pérez and get the case transferred. Miami PD would be happy to get rid of it. Reid could waste his time hunting down a junkie. They had better things to do.

14

Kenzie pulled up outside the governor's Miami residence and handed her press ID card to a uniformed guard at the gate. The security officer scrutinized it, nodded, then waved her through. Pulling away, she heard his walkie talkie crackle, notifying the officers at the mansion she was on the way up.

As expected, another guard showed her where to park and then directed her into the house. A woman in a smart dress suit was waiting to greet her. "Good afternoon, you must be Kenzie Gilmore. I'm Carol, the governor's personal assistant."

Kenzie shook her proffered hand. "Hi, yes I am."

"This way, please."

The woman took off at a fast pace, leaving Kenzie to catch up. The mansion was enormous, but tastefully decorated as she'd expect of a governor's mansion. Large chandeliers hung from the ceilings, the floors were polished Italian marble, and in every room, ornamental tables were crowned with vases of flowers.

"He's in his office," she said, over her shoulder. "We're almost there."

The governor's office was positioned at the end of a long corridor.

It was pleasantly cool inside, allowing Kenzie a few moments' reprieve after her frantic rush to get there. Keith's last-minute correction to her copy had delayed her.

Carol rapped twice on the office door and then, without waiting for a reply, opened it. Kenzie followed her in. "Governor Talbot, Kenzie Gilmore from the Miami Herald is here to see you."

"Thank you, Carol," Talbot said, his gaze on Kenzie.

"Good afternoon, Governor." Giving him her best smile.

"Come and sit down," he told her. "It's a pleasure to meet you."

Carol left the office, and Kenzie took a seat opposite him. He had a vast oak desk with an intricate design carved into it. It reminded Kenzie of the Resolute desk in the Oval Office. Perhaps Talbot had lofty ambitions. "Thank you for agreeing to see me on such short notice."

"That's alright. I had an opening in my schedule, so it was good timing. I believe you want to ask me some questions?"

"Yes, about your political goals for the upcoming year," she said, regurgitating what Trevor had told her in the rushed five minutes before she left.

"I have an ambitious schedule," he said, and launched into his plans for the new term. Kenzie nodded and smiled in all the right places, but her mind was elsewhere. The artwork of beautiful young men on the walls, the male bust on the windowsill behind him, the framed photograph of his two daughters, but none of his wife. All very suggestive, but it didn't necessarily mean he was gay.

She studied him while he talked, content to let him rattle on. His hands were smooth and manicured, his suit tailored, and she was sure the hair at his temples had been touched up. But then, he was constantly in the limelight, so why wouldn't he want to be the best version of himself? None of this proved he was part of a pedophile ring. She needed to dig deeper.

Once he'd finished talking, and she'd asked all Trevor's questions, she said, "A friend of mine saw you at a party last Saturday night. Richard Weatherly, maybe you know him?"

"Weatherly, no, I don't think so." He scrunched up his forehead. "Which party was that?"

"Lakefield Road."

Talbot went white. The color literally drained from his face.

Well, well, well.

If that wasn't a sign he'd been there, she didn't know what was.

He took a moment to recover, then cleared his throat. "Your friend must be mistaken, I spent Saturday night at home with my wife. One of those rare occasions when we had nothing going on."

Kenzie smiled benignly. "Oh, I'm sorry. He must have been mistaken. Thank you so much for talking with me. I know how busy you are."

"Anytime," he rasped, walking her to the door. As if by magic, his PA was there waiting. "Carol will see you out."

He closed the door behind her before she had a chance to say goodbye.

Now, *that* was interesting.

Kenzie walked back to her car in somewhat of a daze. Had she uncovered a pedophile ring that stretched up into the highest echelons of power? Young offenders, persuaded by their probation officer to perform lurid acts on wealthy, powerful men for tips and early releases?

It seemed unconscionable that anyone in Talbot's position would do something like that. Risky too. What if he was spotted? Or someone took a photograph of him? How would he explain that?

As it stood, she had nothing concrete. The word of a juvenile wouldn't hold water, particularly not against a man like the governor. Perhaps that's what he was counting on. The boys were threatened with longer sentences if they revealed anything, so none of them would take the risk. The other members had as much to lose as the governor. Reputations, marriages, careers—all destroyed if their terrible secret got out.

One thing she did know was they would strive to protect themselves, no matter what the cost. Even kill to keep someone quiet. Matteo was proof of that.

Kenzie glanced up at the elegant mansion before getting into her car, scanning the external facade until locating the governor's study. A dark shape stood in the window, looking down at her.

She shivered as an eerie feeling crept over her. She'd just put herself in the firing line. Still, she'd got what she came for. At least now she knew, even if she couldn't prove it.

Unnerved, she got into the car and called Reid. It rang for ages, then diverted to voicemail.

Damn.

She really felt like talking to him about what had happened, even though she knew he'd be upset with her for mentioning the party.

He was always so rational and matter of fact about things. Talking to him made her feel better. These last few months he'd seen her anxious, down, distraught, fearful and happy. She'd cried in front of him, raged, and stomped up and down. She'd even collapsed in his arms.

Stopping at a red light, she realized he'd never done any of those things in front of her. Except raged. He'd done that a couple of times.

Reid kept his own emotions locked away. Even now, she was only touching the tip of the iceberg. Even when she'd kissed him, he hadn't looked happy. Surprised, more like, and something else. Something that had set her heart racing, but it wasn't happiness.

That little display of jealousy at the club the other night was the most upset she'd ever seen him. A warm feeling ran through her, replacing the uneasy one. It was amazing how just thinking about Reid made her feel better.

She drove to the garage she'd booked to get the car air-conditioning fixed. It would take twenty-four hours, she was told as she handed over the car keys. Then she walked down the road to the bus stop.

It was just pulling up when her phone rang, and she answered without looking at the screen. "Reid, I'm so glad you called me back. I really need to talk to you."

"Reid?" asked a voice she recognized.

Her heart skipped a beat. Shit, it was Torres.

"Oh, gosh. I'm so sorry," she said. "I thought you were someone else."

"Clearly."

She cringed.

Damn. Damn. Damn.

And she'd said Reid's name.

"It's so good to hear your voice," she lied, although she had been wondering if he was going to call.

"Likewise, but I seem to have caught you at a bad time."

"No, not at all. How are you?"

"Good. I know it's late notice, but I was wondering if you were free tonight. I thought we could go for a quiet drink and get to know each other."

A red flag, if ever there was one.

The drugs, the dead teenagers, Matteo...Reid thought it was Torres's organization that was bringing in the lethal cocaine. And she already knew Torres had killed Bianca.

Climbing on the bus, she threw caution to the wind. Screw it, it would be a chance to find out what he was up to. Perhaps she'd discover something Reid could use in the investigation.

"It just so happens I am free tonight."

"Excellent. Shall I pick you up?"

"Um, why don't I meet you there?" She'd get a cab. It was safer than him knowing her address.

"Sure."

He gave her the address and said goodbye. She was almost home when Reid returned her call. Glancing at the screen, she hesitated. Only minutes ago, she'd been desperate to talk to him, but now she wasn't so sure. How would he react knowing she was going out with Torres?

He'd be angry, even angrier than when she told him what she'd said to the governor. She bit her lip, something she always did when she was undecided.

Maybe she'd wait until tomorrow to tell Reid. It was always easier to apologize after the fact than to explain beforehand. That way, if she did find out anything, she could use it to soften the blow.

She let the call go to voicemail.

15

REID ENDED THE CALL. Maybe she was working late, or on her way home. He'd try her again later. The palm-fringed avenue he was driving down, opened, exposing the rolling greens of the golf course on the right and elegant, well-maintained homes on the left.

He'd intended to get takeout and go home, but after a long, hot day at the precinct, he was enjoying the cool air-conditioned interior of the car and was not in any hurry to get back to his sauna of a cabin.

The interrogation with Fat Sam had brought nothing new to the investigation. The low-level dealer wasn't important enough to know anything. Sure, he got his drugs from Jago Martinez, but who didn't? The Warriors were the new suppliers on the street. And no, he didn't know Matteo Davis, didn't recognize him from the photographs either. It had been a long shot, anyway.

Reid drove on until he saw a set of wrought iron gates come into view, and behind it, a colonial-style villa with its columns and ornate crest. Torres's silver Audi was parked in the driveway. Reid pulled over and watched, but had no idea what he was looking for, if anything.

The blinds were drawn, so he couldn't see inside the house. After ten minutes of resting his head back against the headrest, he muttered, "The hell with it." No sense wasting time, so might as well go home.

He was about to pull away when the front door opened and Torres walked out. Reid cut the engine and hunkered down. Crap, he hoped the gangster hadn't seen his lights.

But Torres didn't look in his direction. Walking down the stairs, he beeped his Audi, making the headlights come on, and opened the car door.

Reid noted the smart suit and crisp white shirt, the slicked back hair, the swagger. He was meeting someone, and it wasn't his wife.

Could it be the other cartel members? Lopez, even?

Torres got into his car and reversed out of the driveway. Reid kept very still, not even risking a peek until he heard the soft screech of the Audi turning up ahead. Sitting up, he glimpsed a silver flash before it disappeared around the corner.

Reid followed.

Taking the corner carefully, he breathed a thankful sigh when he spotted Torres. The traffic was thicker here, forcing the gangster to slow down. Reid crept closer, all the while maintaining a safe following distance, letting a couple more cars tuck in front of him. The silver Audi was easy to keep an eye on.

"Where are you going?" muttered Reid.

Toward Miami Beach, it turned out. Reid followed until Torres pulled over outside a cocktail bar off Collins Avenue called Swizzle. Hidden between two hotels and flanked by palm trees, it was easy to miss.

Perfect for a clandestine meeting.

He watched as Torres got out of the car and checked his watch. Definitely meeting someone. Then, to his horror, Kenzie walked up the road.

What the hell was she doing here?

She smiled as Torres spotted her.

No. It couldn't be.

They embraced, and then he put a hand on the small of her back and led her inside the bar.

Reid stared at the entrance, feeling sick.

Had that really happened? Kenzie had met his arch enemy, the man responsible for so many deaths, not only Bianca's, and walked into a cocktail bar with him.

Was she out of her fucking mind?

He took out his phone to call her, then stopped, too mad to speak to her right now. They'd only get into a fight, and he didn't want that. She wouldn't change her mind, anyway. He knew her too well.

The best thing to do was keep an eye on her, make sure she was okay. But damn it, of all the headstrong, foolish things to do...

Then he frowned as a thought occurred to him. How had Torres got hold of her? A shiver shot down his spine. Kenzie must have given him her number.

He hissed out a slow breath.

Why hadn't she told him?

Seething, he wondered what to do. He could follow them in, but Kenzie might see him. Would it matter? Torres didn't know who he was. How ironic that Reid had been hunting the gangster for two years, investigating every aspect of his life, and the man didn't even know he existed.

But he would, soon.

Reid was going to destroy the entire organization. Once he had proof new synthetic drugs were being brought in by the Morales cartel, he was going to go to the DEA and get it shut down. Kids were dying. It was time these scumbags were taken down.

Kenzie sipped her cocktail and smiled at Torres.

"Please, call me Alex," he said in his silky accent. He really was a very good-looking man. He didn't have the same gruff, physical appeal as Reid did, but was handsome in a suave, devil-may-care kind of way. Except she knew he was anything but. Reid had said he was cold and calculating, that nothing he did was without a reason.

She gazed into his eyes. What was his reason for bringing her here tonight? "I was surprised you called," she said. "I didn't expect to hear from you again."

"I wanted to see you. I enjoyed our chat the other night. You're an intriguing woman."

She stirred her cocktail. "Thank you. Do you come here often?"

"Sometimes. I like the ambiance. And it's quiet enough to talk. You don't have to shout to be heard."

That it was. The high tables dotted around the interior were occupied by groups of professionals. Bankers, lawyers, and accountants in standard-styled suits and loosened neck ties. All enjoying a cocktail after work. The couples stuck to the booths, more intimate that way, and there was a scattering of singles at the bar.

The background music was jazzy and light, the decor classy. She liked it too.

"Tell me more about yourself." His hand brushed against hers. They were sitting at a low table at the back in two round-back chairs. There were only a few of these types of tables, and they were all positioned along the back wall.

"I'm a freelance writer." She rolled her eyes. "But I'm still building up a client list. That's why I waitress three nights a week."

She didn't, but he didn't know that.

"At a restaurant?"

"Yeah, you wouldn't know it. Just a small Thai place in Wynwood."

His dark eyes danced in the dim lighting, always watching.

"What sort of things do you write?"

"Oh, nothing important. I provide content for bloggers, websites, social media posts—that sort of thing. There's a big demand for it, as you can imagine."

"I'm not really into all that, I'm afraid," he said. "My business is very hands-on." He grinned. "We don't require much of a social media presence."

"No, I don't imagine you do." An off-dock warehouse, he'd said. "Where are you based?" she asked.

"Near the port where all the other off-dock warehouse companies are located. It's more convenient that way. When they offload from the ships, we then transport the containers to our warehouse or wherever they need to go, but no need to talk about that."

She laughed. It was deadly boring, but she got the feeling that was the point. Keep the conversation away from business.

"Did your friend enjoy his party?"

Torres smiled. "He had a great time. We partied long into the night."

She doubted that. He'd only sipped his drink the night they'd met, and it was no different tonight. The scotch on ice sat on the table between them, untouched.

Alex, or rather Alberto Torres, was not a big drinker. Like Reid had said, he was too much of a control freak for that.

"Do you have a family?" she asked. "Kids?"

He shook his head. "I haven't been so fortunate as to find the right woman."

Liar.

She knew he was married.

"What about you? Is there anyone special in your life?"

At that moment, she glanced up and saw Reid walk in.

What the—?

She spluttered on her gin cocktail.

"Um, no, not really. There was someone, but...but it didn't work out."

What on earth was he doing here? How did he know?

Was he following her? Had he pinged her phone?

Walking to the bar, he sat down. She watched as he ordered a drink and paid, without once looking in her direction. This was not a coincidence.

Then she got it. He must be tracking Torres somehow. How had she not thought of that before? That's why he was so furious at the club. He didn't need her to do his work for him, because he already knew what Torres was up to, and probably where he'd been this whole time.

She felt like kicking herself. So much for her little subterfuge. Reid would be furious with her for not telling him about this.

Taking a gulp of her cocktail, she stiffened her back. Still, she was an investigative journalist, and she was going to defend her position. Torres was the biggest drug dealer in Miami, if Reid and Ortega were to be believed, the Morales cartel's main man. It was his drugs that were flooding the market. If she could bust his organization wide open in the press, it would be the scoop of the decade. Not to mention it would get that harmful stuff off the streets.

Why shouldn't she go after Torres herself?

Turning to her date, she asked, "Has there ever been anyone special in your life?"

For a moment, his eyelids flickered. "There was," he said, then his voice hardened. "She died."

"Oh, I'm so sorry. What happened?"

Shrugging, he pretended it was no big deal, but she sensed a bitterness there. A regret. "Car wreck, but it was a long time ago. I always think one has to live in the moment, don't you?" Swiftly changing the subject.

"Absolutely. Life can be very fleeting. I lost my mother at a young age, so I'm always aware of how fragile it is."

Now why had she gone and said that?

His eyes bore into hers. Suddenly, she felt like he'd seen right through her. "I'm sorry to hear that. I didn't know my parents."

"You didn't?"

"No, they passed away when I was very young."

Now she felt bad. At least she'd had her father to look after her, even if he had wallowed in his own grief for a decade.

"It doesn't seem like it's held you back," she remarked. The conversation was getting a little too personal for her, encroaching on real life. Her mother, his parents.

A ruthless drug dealer.

A killer of innocents.

What was she doing?

"No, it hasn't." He straightened his back. "If anything, it's made me stronger. I have built the business up single-handedly in a very short time, and now we're one of the most successful firms in the port area."

"That's admirable," she acknowledged. Especially since it was only his sideline. "I'm still building my career after a few false starts." No lie there, either. Many times she'd wondered how different her life would have been if she hadn't had her accident, if she'd been allowed to graduate from the police academy. She'd be a detective by now, like Reid. May even have met him, worked together.

"You'll get there," he said.

The music changed to a bluesy number, and Kenzie leaned back in her chair. Reid still hadn't turned around, but she knew he was watching them in the mirror above the bar. His back was taut, his broad shoulders stiff. She could just imagine the look on his face.

They chatted about mundane topics for a while longer, Torres ordered another round of drinks. Kenzie excused herself and went to the restroom. She wasn't surprised to find Reid waiting for her when she came out.

"What do you think you're doing?" he hissed.

"Investigating. What are you doing? Following me?" She'd never admit she was glad to see him. It helped knowing he was close by. Torres didn't seem to be a threat, but all that would change in an instant if he figured out who she was.

"No, I was following *him*," he growled. "Imagine my surprise when you showed up."

"I was going to tell you." She bit her lip. "But I knew you'd be mad at me."

"Damn right I'm mad," he growled. "Torres is a cold-blooded killer, but you already know that."

"I know," she whispered. "Don't worry, I'm fine. Look, I have to get back, but I'll call you when I get home. We'll talk then."

He gave a curt nod and stood back to let her pass.

Kenzie got back to find Torres on his feet. "I decided against staying for another drink," he said abruptly. "Let's go dancing. I know this great Latin club around the corner. It's the real deal, not like the place we went to the other day."

Kenzie hesitated. Reid was still in the restroom. But she didn't have time to think up an excuse as Torres led her out of the bar. They walked along Collins Avenue to 11th Street and into a club called Havana. There was a line outside, but the bouncer waved Torres through with a respectful nod. It seemed he was well known in the local community.

A couple of dances, she promised herself. That's all. Then I'm out of here.

She'd make an excuse, leave, and call Reid, who could meet her on the corner and give her a lift home. She'd caught a cab to the cocktail bar since her car was in the garage.

The thought made her feel better, and she smiled and gave a flirtatious nod.

Taking her hand, he led her onto the dance floor.

16

REID GOT BACK from the restroom and stared at the empty table.

Fuck.

Where had they gone? He glanced around the bar but there was no sign of them. They must have left. Running outside, he peered up and down the street. Nothing.

Goddamn.

Spotting Torres's car, he relaxed. At least they were still in the area. They couldn't have gone far. He tried a few bars nearby, but they weren't there. No way to get into any of the clubs without waiting in line, and no sense doing that when he didn't know for sure they were in any of them. The only thing to do was go back to the car and wait.

The hours ticked by. What the hell were they doing? Then it struck him, Torres could have left his car here and gone home with Kenzie. He drove up and down the street looking for her car, but it wasn't there. Trying the next road, and the next, working around the whole area in a grid. There were no parking lots close enough for her to have used, and she wouldn't have parked miles away.

So what had happened? Had she given him a lift home, gone back to his place?

Heart thumping painfully in his chest, he didn't want to think about the implications. No, she wouldn't have done anything as foolish as that. This was Kenzie, for God's sake. Besides, Torres was married. His wife was home.

Then a cold chill sliced through him. There hadn't been a second car in the driveway.

Surely Kenzie wouldn't be that impulsive?

He gritted his teeth. If she was onto something, she may well have gone back to his place to have a poke around. A crazy, foolish thing to do, but knowing Kenzie, a possibility. She'd gotten into sticky situations before.

He punched the dashboard. Damn it, Kenzie.

He couldn't take the chance.

Reid put his foot down and took off in the direction of Torres' house. The roads were quiet, since it was after two o'clock in the morning, and he made record time. Stopping outside the colonial villa, he stared through the gates.

The driveway was deserted.

He heaved a sigh of relief. She wasn't there. Then he saw a flicker as the blind moved. There was a light on inside the house. Someone was home. If it wasn't Torres's wife, it must be the man himself. But then why had he left his car outside the bar? Had he drunk too much to drive?

Torres? Nah.

Reid got out of the car and looked up at the wall. Although he'd scaled it once before, he didn't want to risk it again, not without a damn good reason. And there was no indication Kenzie was there.

He took a long look at the house again. She said she'd call when she got home, but hadn't. He needed to know she was okay. He fired off a text message, not caring that he might wake her up.

No reply.

And he could tell she hadn't read the message either.

A light went on in one of the upstairs rooms. Reid watched, sucking in his breath. A female figure walked past, silhouetted against the light. Slender, big breasts, curly hair.

He exhaled. Thank God it wasn't her.

Must be the wife. Maybe she'd got rid of the Merc, or it was parked somewhere else. The light in the room went out.

Reid got back into his car. Logic dictated Kenzie wasn't there. But neither was Torres.

Would she have been crazy enough to take him back to her place?

He gulped. If she had, it had nothing to do with work. She'd never risk him knowing where she lived, not unless she was under duress, or had fallen for him.

Neither were very good options.

The first made him sick with worry. The second, sick for an entirely different reason.

Reid started his car and raced off in the direction he'd come. When he got to the highway, he headed for Bay Harbor Island, where Kenzie lived. The drive seemed to take forever, when in fact it was a little over twenty minutes at this time of night.

There was no traffic. The city had gone to sleep long ago.

He flew over the speed bumps in the road leading to her condo complex, his front bumper scraping the ground as he landed. Almost there.

Shutting off the engine, he gazed up at the house set back from the road. The blinds were drawn, the lights off, and her car wasn't there either.

Where on earth was she?

He stood outside staring at the house. Should he knock? Should he break in and check to see if she was okay? Where the hell was her car?

Peeking through the darkened windows, he strained to see inside.

The shutters were open, and he knew she always shut them before she went to bed. She hadn't been home.

A sick feeling tore at his gut.

Something was wrong, he could sense it.

Sitting down on the doorstep, he exhaled, forcing himself to think. What to do? Call Vargas to ping her cell phone? He knew it was on because his text message had gone through, even though she still hadn't read it.

Go back to where Torres had parked his Audi and wait until he collected it, then demand to know what he'd done with Kenzie? A sick feeling hit him in the gut. What if they were still out, dancing the night away, watching the sunrise?

Those were possibilities he hadn't considered. It would explain why Torres's car was still there. He groaned, fighting a wave of exhaustion.

Settling for the middle ground, he rang Sweetwater PD and spoke to the officer on duty. He told him to send a patrol vehicle to sit on Torres's car until he came back, then notify Reid.

Getting back into his car, he rolled back the seat. Nothing to do but wait, and if he hadn't heard anything when dawn broke, then he'd panic. Right now, he was too goddamn exhausted to think straight.

A tap on the window woke him up. Blinking, he saw Kenzie glaring at him through the glass.

His heart leaped. She was alive.

He opened the door. "Thank God, I was worried."

"Jesus, Reid. Did you sleep out here?"

He gave an annoyed nod. "I was waiting for you. You said you'd call."

"Well, I'm sorry, I forgot. When I got home, I was so tired, I decided it could wait until this morning."

"What time did you get back?"

She gave him a strange look. "Around midnight, why?"

His heart sank. Was she lying to him? There was only one reason to do that, because she'd been with Torres all night. Where, he had no idea.

"I came to see you," he said. "You weren't home. That was at three this morning."

She fixed her direct blue gaze on his unshaven face. "Well, you should have knocked. I was fast asleep at three this morning."

He frowned. "I don't understand. The shutters weren't closed."

"I told you, I was exhausted. I went straight to bed."

He scratched his head. "But where's your car?"

"It's in the freaking garage. The AC broke and I couldn't drive around in this heat without it. I caught a cab to the bar last night."

Reid felt like a complete idiot.

"You mean... you weren't with Torres?"

"I was, but only until eleven-thirty, then I got a cab home." She stared at him. "I can't believe you thought I—"

"I didn't," he interjected, cringing inside. "Dammit, I was worried about you, that's all. Torres is a dangerous man."

She studied him, her clear gaze roaming over his face. "I was about to go into the office, but since you're here, why don't you come in and we can talk. Maybe you should freshen up first, and I'll put some coffee on."

That sounded good. "Thanks."

He followed her into the house. How had he got it so wrong? The thought never occurred to him she might not have her car. Kenzie didn't go anywhere without the little Honda. Miami wasn't that sort of city.

In her bathroom, he splashed some water on his face. He needed a shave, but it would have to wait. Two days' worth of stubble made him look grislier than ever. Reemerging, there was a mug of coffee waiting on the countertop.

He picked it up. "Did you learn anything last night?"

"Alex, I mean Torres, is nothing like I expected. The more I get to know him, the harder I find it to believe he's a member of one of the biggest cartels in the state."

"Not just a member," Reid said. "The Operations Manager, the cartel's main man in Miami."

Kenzie gave a thoughtful nod. "He told me about his off-dock warehouse. How he'd built it from scratch. How he'd lost his parents at a young age. If he hadn't shot his girlfriend through the head, I'd actually like him."

Reid gave her a warning look. "Bianca was taken in, too. He has a way of getting under your skin."

She pulled a face. "I'm not in danger of being seduced by him. He's just a dichotomy, that's all."

Reid exhaled. He couldn't believe he'd overreacted like that. This was Kenzie, for goodness' sake. The level-headed reporter. The prize-winning journalist. She used people to get a story, of course she wasn't going to fall for a known drug kingpin.

"Where did you go after the cocktail bar? When I got back from the restroom, you'd disappeared."

"To a salsa club," she said. "I tried to stall him until you got back, but he was insistent. I don't know why, unless he saw you."

"Wouldn't have made a difference. He doesn't know me."

"Maybe he recognized you from the club."

Reid frowned. That was a possibility. Was Torres on to him? "Do you know why he left his car outside the bar?"

She shrugged. "No, maybe he had a few too many and didn't want to drive. Who knows?"

Reid gulped down his coffee. After the night he'd had, he needed it.

"I'm sorry I overreacted." He put the mug back down on the counter. "I didn't know about your car."

She leaned over the counter. "You know, Reid, ever since we... kissed, things have been a little weird between us. You haven't been acting yourself."

He didn't reply.

She was right, he was acting like a fool. His judgement was completely screwed up. He couldn't think straight.

"I know you're worried about me, and you have every right to be. Torres killed your colleague and your ex-girlfriend. I get that. But I investigate, that's my job and I'm good at it. Sometimes it means I have to take calculated risks to get a story. You can't camp outside my house to make sure I'm okay."

"This isn't a story," he said. "This is about getting drugs off the street, about saving lives."

"I know that but getting the lowdown on the cartel is a story too. A big one."

His gut twisted. "Don't go there, Kenz. It's too dangerous. Besides, you might get in the way of our investigation."

"I was trying to help," she retorted. "You're the one who wanted to find him."

He didn't meet her gaze.

"I knew it!" She snapped her fingers.

"What?"

"You've known where he's been the whole time. That night at the club, that wasn't the first time you'd seen him since we bumped into him six months ago, was it?"

He sighed. "Look, can we not talk about this?"

"Why? Because it's true?"

"I knew where he was living, yes. But I don't have anything on him. Neither does Ortega."

"He knew too?" She threw up her hands.

"That's not the point," Reid said. "What you've done is put yourself on his radar. He's got people who can find out who you really are. What then? Do you think he's going to just forget about you? He'll know you're using him to get information on the cartel. It's only a matter of time."

A flicker of fear flashed across her face, but she tried to cover it up. "You're overreacting. I'll probably never hear from him again."

Reid wasn't so sure.

"Oh, there was one thing I forgot to mention. I overheard him talking on the phone about an upcoming conference."

Reid froze. "What conference?"

"I don't know. He didn't say."

"What did he say?"

She closed her eyes, remembering. "The conference is next week. I'll see you there." Opening her eyes, she shrugged. "That's it. Do you think it's important?"

Damn right it was important, and it could only mean one thing.

Lopez was coming to town.

17

KENZIE STILL HADN'T TOLD Reid about what she'd said to Governor Talbot. This morning didn't seem like the right time. He'd been too preoccupied with Torres.

She still couldn't believe he'd slept outside her house in his car. Torres had shot his colleague and lover, she got that. He would understandably be concerned, perhaps even irrationally so, but it was his motivation that worried her. Was it concern, or was it jealousy?

If it was the latter, then that was a problem. It wasn't like Reid to fly off the handle, and even though he hadn't come out and said it, she knew he'd been worried she'd fallen for Torres's charms. Sure, he was charming, and rakishly handsome, and clearly very smart—but he was also just a source.

And she wasn't Bianca.

Governor Talbot's wife got out of the chauffeur-driven car and went into the grocery store. Kenzie had been waiting outside the mansion this morning and had followed her here. Unlike her husband, Mrs. Talbot didn't have armed security. An oversight on the army's part, Kenzie thought. She was an easy target for kidnapping and coercion—if anyone cared that much about the governor's policy.

Kenzie put her plan into action. She'd decided yesterday she wanted to speak to Mrs. Talbot. Her husband had been lying about the party, she was sure of it, and there was no one better than his wife to disprove his alibi.

A group of kids were hanging out in the corner of the parking lot, skateboards under their arms. Kenzie walked over to them.

"Hey guys, I need a favor. Who wants to earn twenty bucks?"

A few minutes later, one of the skateboarders walked into the grocery store. Kenzie followed a discreet distance behind, keeping out of sight. He stomped down the aisle and bumped into the governor's wife, knocking her off her feet. She fell to the ground with a yelp, dropping her shopping basket. Fruit and vegetables scattered over the floor.

"Oh!" she cried. "My shopping!"

"Sorry," yelled the boy, and took off out of the store.

Kenzie bent down to help her. "Oh, my gosh. Are you okay? I saw what happened."

"Y—Yes, I think so."

Kenzie took her arm and helped her up. "Let me get those for you." She gathered the fallen groceries.

Mrs. Talbot was smoothing out her skirt and dusting off her knees. "Thank you so much. I don't know what happened. One moment I was standing there, the next I was on the floor!"

Kenzie handed her the basket. "You seem a little shaken up. Let me buy you a coffee. There's a place next door that does a wonderful Americano."

The woman nodded gratefully. "Yes, that would be good. I think I need to sit down for a second."

Kenzie grinned. It was as easy as that.

Mrs. Talbot, or Helen, as she asked to be called, was a well-spoken, articulate woman with a quiet sense of purpose. Kenzie liked her.

"I must admit, I know who you are," Kenzie said. "I recognize you from the papers."

The woman sighed. "It's the price you pay for being married to a man with political aspirations," she said. "You're always in the public eye."

"It must be hard," Kenzie sympathized. "Particularly this time of year, in the lead up to elections."

Helen nodded. "The campaign trail starts in a few weeks. That's the hardest part. On the road for hours on end, staying in hotels, smiling for the cameras. Sometimes I think my face is going to crack."

Kenzie felt genuinely sorry for her. "Do you think your husband will win a second term?"

Helen nodded. "The early polling is positive, although just between you and me, I wouldn't be too upset if he didn't. Is that terribly disloyal of me?"

"No, I get it," Kenzie said, and she really did. "I couldn't do what you do."

"I'm sorry, here I am rambling on, and I haven't asked you anything about yourself. Do you work in the area?"

"Yes, just around the corner. I'm on my lunch break. I have to say, I do admire your husband. He's made some positive changes during his current term in office."

She didn't want to steer the conversation away from Talbot.

"He means well," Helen said. "And he works hard. He really does try to make a difference, not like some of these politicians who are only in it for the power and the glory."

"Do you get some time together at least?" Kenzie asked. "It's not all work, is it?"

"Not very often." Her shoulders slumped. Kenzie could sense her weariness.

"Perhaps you should make some time for a romantic dinner," Kenzie suggested. "Or a quiet night at home, just the two of you. Unless you already do that, in which case, just tell me to shut up."

Helen looked at her for a long moment, then shook her head. "No, we haven't done that for months. Perhaps I should suggest it."

There goes his alibi, Kenzie thought.

A rare night in. Yeah, right.

"Well, I must dash," Kenzie said, once she'd finished her coffee. "It was lovely meeting you, Helen. I've got to get back to work."

"Of course. Thank you for the coffee." Helen gave her a tentative smile. "And for helping me in the store."

"You're very welcome. Good luck with everything." Kenzie slung her purse over her shoulder. Once the governor's dirty little secret came out, she'd need it.

Reid called Pérez and got the Matteo Davis case transferred to Sweetwater Police Department. He encountered no resistance. As he'd thought, Miami PD was happy to offload it and bring down its caseload.

"Several grams of coke were found on his body," Reid told his team. They were in the biggest room in the precinct, previously a storeroom, which Reid had converted into an incident room, complete with a whiteboard. Vargas had stuck up a photograph of Matteo taken at the crime scene, and a "before" photograph supplied by his girlfriend Hannah. "The kid didn't do drugs, and he didn't deal. He had no drug connections whatsoever."

"Are we saying the drugs were planted on him?" Diaz asked. Reid hadn't discussed the stabbing with anyone at Sweetwater PD yet. This was the first they were hearing about it.

"It looks like it," he acknowledged. "And we have to find out why. He may have witnessed something that got him killed."

They all gazed at him expectantly, all except Detective Dempsey, who was rolling his eyes.

"Something wrong, Dempsey?" Reid asked, singling him out. He was getting sick of his constant sniping and bad attitude.

"No, I just think it looks like a drug-related homicide, that's all."

So did everyone else.

"Except we know different." Reid turned back to the team. "The night before he died, Matteo went to a party where sexual abuse was happening." He didn't know how else to phrase it.

"Seriously?" asked Diaz.

"Yeah, according to his friends and the other young offender Kenzie Gilmore spoke to, juveniles were being coerced into sex in exchange for an early release from their probation."

"Holy shit," she muttered, shocked.

There was a dull murmur amongst the rest of the team.

"His girlfriend intercepted Kenzie at the mall and asked for her help. She wanted justice for Matteo."

"Has she given a statement?" Vargas asked.

"No, and she won't. Her parents don't know about the relationship. No one does, and we want to keep it that way. Considering what happened to Matteo, if the men behind this know she's involved, we could be putting her at risk."

"We'll need the victim's friends' testimonies and that of the juvenile offender to prosecute," said Monroe, who was standing next to Dempsey. "Provided we catch these guys."

"Yeah, and we'll bring them in at the right time. After what happened to Matteo, I'm not going to put any more young lives at risk. That goes for the girlfriend, too."

The detective gave a reluctant nod. Dempsey muttered something in his ear, derogatory, no doubt.

"What do you want us to do, boss?" Vargas asked.

Despite the two older detectives' 'seen it all before' attitude, there was an excited buzz in the air. This was a new case, a homicide. Not a robbery or a drug overdose. There was an actual perp out there, someone who'd stabbed Matteo and someone they needed to catch.

"First, I want us to dig up all we can find on Matteo's probation officer, William or 'Bill' Hodge. He's the one who reportedly told Matteo about the party. Let's check his bank account." Reid glanced up. "Monroe and Dempsey, can you get on that? He must be benefiting from this somehow." He frowned. "The rest of you, look into his connections, particularly political. I want to know who his friends are."

Diaz raised an eyebrow. "Is there something you're not telling us?"

He didn't meet her gaze. "These parties are pretty exclusive events. The guest list will be..." he hesitated, searching for the right word. "Noteworthy."

Her eyes widened. "Got it."

He didn't mention the governor, not yet. It would be better to see if his name popped up anywhere during the investigation.

"What about the drugs found on him?" Monroe asked. "Weren't they the same as the ones the girl we pulled out of the canal took?"

So the old guy did read the police reports.

"Correct," he said. "Thanks for pointing that out. If they were planted on him, it would be by someone who wanted to make it look like a drug-related death." His eyes met Dempsey's over everyone's head. The disgruntled detective scowled back at him. "We've got a local dealer called Fat Sam in custody, thanks to Detective Vargas here, but he's just one of many supplying this synthetic drug. It's more likely we'll catch whoever is doing this by working the party angle, but if you have contacts on the street who could find out, use them."

Monroe nodded, more purposefully this time, while Dempsey grumbled in the corner.

"Diaz, why don't you give Monroe a hand?" Reid said, as an afterthought.

She glanced up, surprised. "Oh, yeah, sure." He'd never paired anyone up with the old-timers—as they were known in the department—before, but Monroe showed promise. Reid got the feeling he wasn't ready to hang up his badge just yet.

Dempsey, on the other hand, was a problem.

After the briefing, Reid had a quiet word with a uniformed cop fresh out of the academy. He'd started last month and was still finding his feet.

"Officer Hamilton, can I talk to you for a moment?"

The officer turned white, then nodded. "Ah, sure. Is something wrong?"

"No, you're good. I need a favor, but you can't tell anyone else about it."

His eyebrows shot up. "Yes, boss."

"And don't call me boss." Vargas's phrase had caught on.

"Yes, bo—" he broke off, and cleared his throat. "What do you need me to do?"

"Keep an eye on Detective Dempsey for me. If he leaves the office, tail him, but don't let on that you're there. You don't need to take any action. Just follow him and report back to me, and only me. Do you understand?"

If he was surprised by the request, he didn't show it. "Yes, boss. Sorry, Lieutenant."

Reid nodded. "Remember, tell no one."

He had a bad feeling about Dempsey. He couldn't put his finger on it, but he didn't trust him.

If the tail revealed nothing, he'd call it off after a few days. The guy had six months to go. It wasn't worth making a fuss over.

18

IT WAS LATE when Reid finished the report he was writing. It was Vargas's turn on night duty, and the sergeant was settling in with a pizza and a couple of case reports he was going to go through.

The rest of the team had gone home hours ago. Reid glanced out the window at the moody sky. Dark clouds had been gathering all afternoon, but it was still humid as hell. Maybe tonight it would rain.

He said goodnight to Vargas and was walking out the door when a slim redhead came in holding a canvas bag. "Can I help you?" he asked.

She broke into a wide smile. "You must be Detective Reid Garret." Looking him up and down the way one would a prize stallion. "I've heard so much about you."

He frowned. "Sorry, you are?"

"Shannon Maisie, pleased to meet you. I'm here to see William."

He blinked, momentarily confused. "Oh, you mean Vargas?"

Her eyes glittered. "Yeah, Detective Vargas. I've brought him a snack." She held up the bag.

"Shannon, what are you doing here?" came Vargas's voice from inside.

"I bought you something to eat." Sidling past Reid, she cast a flirtatious glance over her shoulder as she went.

"Sorry, boss," he said, turning pink as she put an arm around his waist. "I didn't know she was coming."

"That's okay," he nodded at Vargas. "But make it quick."

"Yes, boss."

So that was Vargas's new woman. Interesting. He'd never have put the two of them together. Not that Vargas wasn't deserving, more that she was not what he'd expected the young, steadfast detective to go for. A naughty grin, flaming red hair, a cheeky demeanor. Reid got the feeling that woman was no stranger to bending the rules when it suited her. Vargas couldn't be more different. Still, they said opposites attract.

Stretching his neck, he got into his car and started the engine. It purred to life. He was feeling good. They'd had a productive afternoon. The team was working well together.

All except Dempsey.

He'd left at three to "talk to a contact," but Officer Hamilton had reported that he'd gone home. Reid wasn't going to confront him about it. If he was at home, he wasn't causing trouble, and that was the main thing.

Diaz and Monroe had looked into Hodge's bank statements. At first, they hadn't found anything suspicious, but then Monroe had suggested looking into his wife's accounts and bingo! They discovered regular cash deposits in the amount of ten thousand dollars each.

A quick search revealed his wife was a hairdresser, and her salary was clearly marked on her bank statements, so unless she was up to something on the side, these payments were for her husband.

To supply boys for the parties?

They'd discussed bringing Hodge in for questioning, but Reid didn't want him to tip off the network, which was what he would do —and then they'd never catch any of them. There was no proof that any of this was going on. The money could be for anything. The word of a juvenile offender would mean nothing, and that's if they could even get him on record.

Still, they were making progress. Slowly, they were slotting the pieces of the puzzle together, and if all else failed, they'd bring in Hodge and use him to set up a sting operation. It was risky, but it might be their only play.

Reid yawned, looking forward to a cool shower and collapsing into bed.

He was headed west along SW 8th Street, the main thoroughfare that led into the Glades, when he first spotted the lights in his rearview mirror. They glowed with a bluish tinge making them more noticeable than usual. Two miles later, they were still with him.

Frowning, he took an early turn with the idea of going around the block to see if the headlights would follow.

They didn't.

Relaxing, he got back onto the highway and drove home. He had just turned onto the gravel road that led to his cabin when he noticed the blue lights were back.

What the hell?

He kept going. No choice, there was nowhere else to go. This was one straight road into the Glades. No side streets, no turn offs.

The lights were gaining on him, so he decided to drive past his house and pull over at the Gator Inn. There were people there, and it was less isolated. After that, there was nothing but swampland.

He didn't get the chance.

Headlights loomed up ahead. Someone was coming toward him on the road. They got brighter, and he veered to the side, his pickup bouncing over the uneven ground, so they could pass, except they didn't.

The oncoming vehicle skidded to a stop diagonally in front of him, causing him to slam on the brakes.

Fuck.

This was not good. Four masked men leaped from the stationary vehicle, all carrying semi-automatic assault rifles.

"Get out of the car!" came the hollow yell.

Reid took his cell phone from his pocket and slid it down between the car seats. Then he opened the door. Slowly. No sudden movements. Not with that amount of firepower aimed at him.

"Get down on your knees!"

Toppling forward, he lifted his hands above his head. No point in arguing with these guys. Four against one were unwinnable odds.

The car with the blue headlights pulled up behind, effectively blocking him in. Nowhere to go.

A beast of a man with a tattoo snaking up his neck approached and patted him down, looking for his service pistol. It was in the glove compartment. "Where's your phone?" he growled.

"Left it at the station."

"Get up," he ordered. Mexican accent. Reid did as he was told, he knew when he was outnumbered. All he could do was wait and see where they were taking him, and who was in charge. Judging by the hardware and the accent, he had a pretty good idea.

They bundled him into the trunk of the car that had been tailing him, and a few seconds later he felt it turn and race off, gravel stones pinging into the undercarriage. They drove for a good twenty to twenty-five minutes before the car finally slowed down. It made a sharp ninety-degree turn and went over a bump. A driveway. They'd reached their destination.

Reid braced himself, wondering if it was worth exploding from the trunk, but then decided against it. Those men were well trained, judging by the hard stop they'd performed on the road in the Glades. They'd be anticipating his move, expecting it even. He was likely to get himself killed pulling a stunt like that.

The trunk popped open, and he blinked as a flashlight was shone in his face.

"Get up," the same voice ordered. This guy was in charge of the attack team.

Reid climbed out of the trunk and knew exactly where he was.

Torres's warehouse.

The heavy air carried the scent of salt and fish, along with the faint odor of diesel fuel. The wide, squat building in front of him was in darkness, the roller doors shut.

The barrel of a gun pressed against his back. "Move."

They were taking him to the side entrance.

"Why have you kidnapped me?" he asked, slowing his step. "You know I'm a police officer, right?" The penalties for kidnapping or killing a police officer were infinitely worse than a civilian. The force never took kindly to one of their own being gunned down. Even someone like him.

He got no reply.

The tattooed Mexican opened the door and prodded him inside. "That way."

They led him down a short passage to the office at the end. He'd been here before. Once, months ago, when he'd first discovered this place. He'd broken in to have a look around, to see if he could find anything relating to Bianca's murder, but there was nothing. Torres had reinvented himself as the off-dock warehouse owner, Alex Guerra. Businessman. Entrepreneur. Stand up citizen.

Drug dealing scum.

The door was open. Reid went inside. A metal chair had been placed in the center, but apart from that, the room was empty. The filing cabinets, the desk, all gone.

Even the grimy windows had been boarded up from the outside. There was no way he was getting out that way.

He studied the single chair. Sturdy. Solid. Even if it toppled over, it wouldn't break. They'd thought of everything.

"Sit down." The gun barrel ushered him forward. Reid glared at the Mexican. He didn't like being ordered around, and he didn't enjoy having a gun trained on him.

His patience was wearing thin.

"What the fuck am I doing here?" he growled. "I want to speak to whoever's in charge."

The hombre curled his hand into a fist and punched Reid in the gut, ramming the air out of him. Doubling over, he gasped. That's what he got for making demands.

The gun barrel gestured to the chair. Reid sat, but he wasn't happy about it.

"Where's Torres?" he demanded. "I want to speak to Torres."

The men exchanged a look.

Gotcha.

They hadn't been expecting that.

They secured him to the chair with plastic ties and left another badass Mexican in charge. This one had a gold tooth and stubble you could light a match on. The others, including the tattooed giant, cleared out. Gone to speak to the boss, no doubt.

Reid took a good look around. Now that he had some time, he realized the floors were smooth concrete, the walls made of aluminum or steel. The whole place smelled of bleach, which was never a good sign. They'd removed any trace of Torres ever being here.

He sighed. Things were not looking good.

Vargas was on duty, but he had no way of contacting him. Even if he'd kept his phone, it would have been taken off him during the search. At least this way, when he didn't make it into work tomorrow and they searched his car, they'd find it and know something had happened.

Torres's men would park his pickup outside his house, make it look like he'd gone home and then mysteriously disappeared. Mugged on his way back from Smiley's Bar. Confirmed when his body was discovered half-eaten by gators days from now.

Or a drunken accident. The detective who couldn't cope with the responsibilities of being a lieutenant. Who'd cracked once before.

They weren't going to let him go, of that he was sure. Not now he knew who they were. Didn't seem to be very many options left. Just as he was lamenting his fate, the door was flung open and in walked the man himself. The man he'd been watching for two years, the man who he didn't think knew who he was.

Torres.

"Good evening, Detective Garret," the drug kingpin drawled.

So much for that theory.

"Alberto Torres." He eyed him darkly. "Guessed it was you."

Torres pulled up a chair and sat down opposite him. Not close enough so that he was within reach, but near enough so they could look each other in the eye.

Reid found he was shaking. Not with fear, but with rage.

If he hadn't been tied up, he'd be ripping Torres's head off right about now. Here was the man who'd shot Bianca, blown her brains out from less than a foot away in a bar in Little Havana. What he wouldn't give for one chance to wipe that arrogant smirk off his face.

Now, perhaps, he could finally ask him why. Or maybe a better question was how? How could you shoot the woman you professed to love? Or had their relationship meant nothing to him? Had Bianca been deceived? Had she fallen for the enigmatic gangster, and he'd let her believe it?

"It's about time we had a little talk." Torres's haughty gaze roamed over Reid's face, but it was tinged with curiosity. "Why are you following me?"

"You know why," Reid responded.

A half nod, a lifting of the chin, the eyes never leaving his face. "You're still upset about your agent."

And there it was, out in the open.

"Bianca," he gritted. "Her name was Bianca."

"I know her name." A curt reply. His gaze shifted ever so slightly. Was it regret? Reid couldn't be sure.

"Did you even think twice before you pulled the trigger?"

"She betrayed me." His voice was cold. "She played me for a fool. It was the article that did it. The article written by your friend, Kenzie Gilmore." He gave a rough laugh. "I must say, I was surprised to discover you were working together after what happened."

Icicles gripped his heart. "Kenzie has nothing to do with this."

The bastard had known. He'd known about Kenzie right from the start.

Damn!

Once again, they'd underestimated Torres. He should have known, should have seen it coming.

Torres smirked. "So, she's more than a friend, eh? That *is* interesting."

Reid glared at him. "She was acting on my orders. Leave her out of this."

"Don't worry," he murmured with all the sincerity of a snake. "Your girlfriend is safe for now. I must say, though, she's a lot of fun. You should take her dancing sometime. She can really move."

Reid stiffened, straining at the ties.

Torres shook his head. "Conserve your energy. You'll need it later."

That meant they were going to torture him, pump him for information. They wanted to know if he knew about their boss coming to town. The upcoming conference.

At least he wasn't after Kenzie, although he imagined that would change if he didn't cooperate. He had no illusions that once they were done with him, they'd kill him. He was law enforcement, they couldn't let him go.

Not after this.

The only hope left was that Vargas would find the surveillance app on his phone. If he opened it and saw the warehouse, he might be able to locate it. It was a long shot, but it was the only shot he had.

"What do you want from me?" Reid hissed.

"Why are you following me? Why set up your honey trap? Why now?"

Now that Lopez is coming to town?

"We want to know who's supplying the pink cocaine. It's killing people, innocent kids."

Torres shot him a hard look, but Reid held his ground. It was the truth.

Not the whole truth, but the truth, nonetheless. "I pulled a teenager out of the canal last weekend, the third in as many weeks. They're snorting your shit and dying. Did you know that? Or don't you care?"

"I care." His tone suggested otherwise. "It was a bad batch, that's all. This is a new revenue stream for us. We're still ironing out the kinks."

The kinks? That's what they were calling it?

"You mean it's not all like that?"

"No, most of it is pretty harmless. A party drug. By the time we realized there was a bad batch on the market, it was too late. It was already on the street."

Reid narrowed his eyes.

"You don't believe me?" Torres shrugged. "Do you think I want to send kids to the hospital? It's bad for business."

That was all he cared about. At least it wasn't the entire shipment that was lethal. Thank God for small mercies. "We can't have that," Reid snorted, derisively.

"Who else knows about me?" Torres asked, fishing now, trying to find out if they knew about the impending conference. No matter what happened, Reid couldn't let on that they knew. Even if he didn't make it out of this alive, he knew Kenzie would tell Ortega, and he and the DEA would be all over it. There was an arrest warrant out for Federico Lopez. Torres had somehow dodged that, having escaped the scene of the massacre two years ago, leaving no trace of himself. The gangsters they'd caught had told them Lopez had escaped but said nothing about Torres.

Except it was *his* bullet that had killed Bianca.

His gun left at the scene, even if it didn't have his fingerprints on it. They'd traced it back to another shooting the year before. The victim had survived, and he'd identified Torres as the shooter.

Bianca's last words to Reid had been in the form of a text message:

He knows.

"My department," Reid said. The more people who knew, the less point there was in killing him.

"You're lying," snarled Torres. "If your department knew, you wouldn't be using your girlfriend to suck up to me."

Reid shrugged. "Honestly, they know. We've been trying to trace the coke for weeks."

"Except you didn't know it was our product until five minutes ago."

"We suspected."

Torres laughed, a mirthless sound. "Suspected means you have no evidence."

"We have Fat Sam."

"Who?"

Crap, he didn't even know the low-level dealer.

"No one, it doesn't matter."

"No," scoffed Torres. "It really doesn't."

He got up.

"Make sure he's telling the truth," he said to the tattooed Mexican who had come in while they were talking. The giant nodded, flexing his fingers.

Here it comes, thought Reid.

Torres muttered something that Reid didn't catch, then, without a backwards glance, left the room.

Reid braced himself. This was going to hurt.

The thug puffed out his chest as if psyching himself up for a workout, then he stood in front of Reid, legs apart, hands clenched.

Reid squeezed his eyes shut and turned away as the first blow landed.

19

Kenzie could no longer delay. She had to speak to Reid. He'd know what to do. Governor Talbot had no alibi for the night of the party and given his reaction, she'd bet good money that he had been there.

She called twice and left messages both times, but so far, he hadn't returned her calls. She was afraid he was ghosting her.

Come on, Reid. Pick up.

This wasn't the time to worry about their relationship status. There were more important issues at stake. The young offenders who were being abused for one. She had to get those parties shut down. The corrupt probation officer, Hodge, needed to be apprehended and arrested for what he was doing.

They needed a plan.

Kenzie paced up and down her kitchen, debating what to do. Why didn't he pick up?

To hell with it. If he wasn't going to call her back, she would go to him.

Decision made, she grabbed her keys and ran out of the door. She'd picked her Honda up from the garage that afternoon, complete with a new air-conditioning unit, although now it was fixed, the temperature seemed to have dropped.

Ominous clouds obscured the moon, making it very dark. She drove carefully across town and out to the Glades where he lived. The dirt road seemed endless tonight, and she heaved a sigh of relief when she finally turned into the gravel parking lot outside his cabin.

It was in darkness. That was unusual.

Turning off the car, she got out. Reid's pickup was there, where he always parked it. She felt the hood; it was marginally warm, so he must have been back about half an hour.

Kenzie knocked on the door, wishing he had a bell, but there was no answer. That wasn't surprising. He hardly ever heard her knocking, particularly when he was out on the deck.

Sighing, she scooted through the hedge and around to the back, her feet squelching in the swampy grass. Now her socks and shoes were all wet. Pulling herself up, she crouched under the railing and stepped onto the deck.

How strange this side of the house was dark too.

"Reid?" she called, her voice echoing off the murky surface of the water all around her. No reply. She rapped on the sliding glass door, but there was no response. No indication anyone was home.

Turning around, she stared down the floating walkway to where his airboat was moored. Still there, its white hull bobbed on the inky black water.

Could he have walked to Smiley's? The local bar was only a couple of miles away.

She squished back to her car. It wouldn't hurt to have a quick look. They could talk there over a beer.

But he wasn't at Smiley's Bar.

The place was pretty lively, and she got two wolf-whistles and her ass pinched as she walked around looking for him.

Where the hell was he?

At a loss, she pulled out her phone. The parking lot was busy, with swampers, truck drivers and locals arriving for a night of revelry.

She dialed Sweetwater PD. Vargas answered.

"Hi, Willie," she said. "It's Kenzie. Is Reid there?"

"No, ma'am," he replied, polite as ever. "He left a couple of hours ago."

"Do you know where he went?"

"Home. Told me he was bushed."

She frowned, an uneasy feeling gripping at her chest. "He's not at home, Willie. I was just there. He's not at the swamp bar either."

A pause.

"Have you tried to call him?"

"Yeah, repeatedly. Do you want to try? He might not be answering me."

Willie didn't ask why. "Hold on," he said.

She waited while he dialed Reid's cell.

"He's not picking up." She heard the concern in his voice. It made her even more worried.

"What if something's happened?" Panic gnawed at her throat, threatening to choke her. She didn't want to think that, but they had to consider the possibility. "His truck's at home," she added. "Why would his truck be there and not him?"

Willie pondered this for a moment. "I don't know," he said. "It doesn't sound good. I'm coming over."

"Okay."

Kenzie got into her car and drove back to Reid's place. It was still eerily quiet, so she waited in her car until Vargas arrived.

"I've got his spare keys," the detective said. "He always leaves a set at the station."

She nodded, not sure what good that was going to do. The pickup was empty

Vargas opened the driver's door and climbed in. Leaning over, he opened the glove compartment, then gave a snort. "His firearm is here."

Kenzie shook her head. "What does that mean?"

"No way he'd leave it in his vehicle overnight," Vargas said. "It's against policy."

"Oh."

The bad feeling deepened. Above them, the sky grumbled. A forked laser lit up the Glades like a flash on a camera. Suddenly everything was bathed in white light, then the darkness returned. They were in for one heck of a storm.

Vargas sat in the driver's seat, looking around him.

"Anything else?" Kenzie called.

"Not that I can see. Why don't you try to call him again?"

She hit redial.

A buzzing sound came from inside the pickup.

"Did I dial you by mistake?" Kenzie glanced at her screen. No, she'd called Reid.

"It's his phone," exclaimed Vargas, reaching down between the seats. "Now what the hell is that doing here?"

Another crack of thunder made Kenzie jump. Louder this time. The storm was moving in, and before long, it would start to rain.

"It's not good, is it?" she whispered. "He wouldn't leave his phone behind."

"It was wedged down between the seats." Vargas scratched his head. "A strange place to put it."

"Maybe it fell down there," Kenzie suggested, although Reid usually kept it in his back pocket.

Vargas got out of the truck. "I think I'm going to put out an APB," he said grimly. "I don't like this."

The first drops of rain landed on their heads. They had to get under cover, and quick.

Vargas got back into the police vehicle and leaned over, throwing open the passenger door. "Jump in."

Kenzie hopped in, and just in time. Big splotches landed on the windshield, smearing their view. It was only going to get worse.

"What if he's inside the house?" she asked, the thought suddenly occurring to her. "Maybe he's injured." Or worse.

Vargas nodded. "I'm going to call for backup. We'll go in and take a look."

"Can't we go in now? You can break the door down."

Vargas hesitated. "It's against protocol."

"To hell with protocol. He might be bleeding out in there." She got out of the car, ignoring the rain, and ran to the front door of the cabin. "Come on, help me."

Vargas hesitated, but only for a second, hopping out of the police car to join her. The rain looked like tiny spears in his headlights. Shoving his shoulder against the door, it shook on its hinges but held fast.

"Harder!" she yelled. "1-2-3!"

Together, they threw themselves against the timber frame. Splintering, it fell backwards, taking them both with it. Kenzie was first to her feet. It was pitch black inside. She felt around for the light switch. There!

The hallway was empty.

"There's nobody in here either," called Vargas, walking into the living room. "I don't think he's been home."

"Check the bedroom."

"Okay." Reid's house was three cabins stuck together. He'd knocked through walls after he'd bought the place from the airboat company. The door from the living room into the bedroom was open. "No, nothing."

Kenzie checked the adjoining kitchen and bathroom. Vargas was right: Reid hadn't been home. A small sense of relief flowed through her. At least he wasn't lying here injured. Then a darker fear took its place.

"If he's not here..." She looked at Vargas. "Then where on earth is he?"

20

Kenzie waited in the police vehicle while Diaz and a bunch of uniformed officers traipsed through Reid's cabin and re-searched his vehicle.

"I don't think they'll find anything," said a dripping Vargas, getting back in. She'd never seen him look so forlorn.

"Where's his phone?" Kenzie said. "Let's see if he made any calls this evening."

"Yeah, that was my next move." Vargas opened the glove compartment where he'd put the phone and took it out. He pressed the start button, and the screen lit up. The battery was at fifty percent.

"I don't know the passcode." Vargas slumped in his chair.

"It's 287250," Kenzie said.

He gawked at her. "How'd you know that?"

"It's his sister's birthday. Backwards."

Vargas shook his head and entered the code. The phone unlocked.

"I'm in."

Kenzie watched as he pulled up the recent call list and scrolled through the numbers. "Apart from the five calls from you and the two from me, he hasn't made or received any calls since earlier this afternoon."

Damn.

She ran a hand through her wet hair. What now?

Diaz's drenched figure dashed from the house and jumped in the back seat. "We found nothing else in the vehicle," she said, wiping her face on her sleeve. Kenzie wasn't surprised.

"Try Lieutenant Pérez at the Miami PD. Maybe he heard something. Perhaps Reid called him because he didn't have his phone on him."

"Good thinking," said Diaz, and got out her phone. Five minutes later, she shook her head. "No one's heard a thing."

"Crap," Kenzie muttered. "Now what?"

Vargas was still studying Reid's phone. "This is odd," he murmured.

"What?" The rain pelting down on the roof made it hard to hear.

He raised his voice. "I said, this is odd. There's a surveillance app on here. As far as I know, we don't have anyone under surveillance."

Kenzie frowned, then it clicked. "It could be Alberto Torres. Reid may have been watching him." She leaned over to look.

Vargas glanced at Diaz. "News to us."

Kenzie didn't want to get into it. Reid had his own reasons for not telling anyone about that. "Can you open it?"

"Yeah, I'm in." He tilted his head to the side. "It looks like a warehouse of some sort, but the picture's bad, and it keeps dropping out."

"Let me see." Kenzie took the phone from him. "Crap, I can't make out anything from this."

The image fizzled and cut out, then came back filled with static, then cut out again.

When it flashed back on, she took a screen grab, but it was still grainy.

"Good idea," Diaz said, impressed by her quick thinking.

"Sorry." She handed the phone back to Vargas. "That's the best I can do."

The image on the app was completely blank now.

"Does Torres own a warehouse?" Diaz asked.

Kenzie shook her head. "I don't know. Reid didn't mention it. I only found out because...well, it doesn't matter." She wasn't going to go there. They didn't need to know how he'd tracked Torres to the club where she'd met him.

"It's possible," Vargas said. "Maybe he found out Reid was onto him."

Kenzie nodded. That was the most likely scenario.

"What should we do with this?" Diaz asked, glancing at them. "We'd better tell someone."

"I'll call Ortega," she said, sitting up. "Reid told me he'd been tracking Torres, too. Perhaps he knows where this warehouse is."

She dialed his number. They hadn't spoken since she'd persuaded him to drop the charges against Reid. Would he even want to speak to her?

Please pick up, she prayed.

It took several rings, but he did. "Kenzie? Are you okay?"

It was late. He must think there was something wrong.

"Actually, no. Xav, I need your help." She hadn't called him that since before he'd been suspended.

"What's wrong? Are you hurt?"

"It's not me. Reid's gone missing."

"Oh." Flat. Uninterested. "Why is that my problem?"

"Because we think Torres has kidnapped him."

"Jesus, Kenz. Are you serious?"

"Deadly. He's disappeared. His pickup is outside his house with his firearm and phone inside, but no Reid. The house is empty."

"What makes you think Torres has got him?" Alert now, authoritative.

"We found an app on his phone. A camera app. He's been watching a warehouse, and we think it belongs to Torres."

A pause as this sunk in.

"Where is the warehouse?" Ortega asked.

"I don't know." Kenzie heard the desperation in her own voice. "But Reid was tracking him, and we suspect he was made. Reid mentioned that you... might know where Torres is?"

A pause.

"Don't know of any warehouse, but I do have his address."

"We need to go and talk to him, Xav. He may know where Reid is."

"Do you have any proof that Torres and his gang have taken Reid? Anything at all?"

"I feel it. Besides, who else would it be? Reid's been working the pink cocaine case. It has to be him."

A grunt. "Yeah, okay. Let's go talk to him, but I'm taking point."

"Fine." Relief flooded her body. "Thank you."

"Who are you with?"

"Detective Vargas and Officer Diaz from Sweetwater PD."

"Let me talk to Vargas." A detective outranked an officer. Kenzie handed over the phone.

"I've got the address." Vargas said, hanging up. "He's going to meet us there."

"Okay, so what are we waiting for?" Kenzie asked. "Let's go."

"You can't come on a police op," Vargas said. "I'm sorry, Kenzie, it's against..."

"I know." She opened the car door. "But there's nothing to say I can't follow you in my car. I'll stay back, I promise. If Reid's in trouble, I want to be there."

Vargas hesitated, but Diaz nodded. Eventually, he gave in. "Okay, we're heading to South Beach. Stay back and don't get out of your vehicle. Got that?"

"Yes, I've got it."

She shut the door and ran to the car. No way were they keeping her away. Not if Reid needed her.

There was another crash of thunder, and the swamp lit up. The storm was right overhead. She shivered and started the car. The police vehicles reversed out of the driveway and onto the dirt road. She heard a growl as the gravel kicked up as they took off, and a short while later, flashing blue lights filled the night sky, along with the howl of sirens.

She followed them, the windshield wipers whipping back and forth. It was raining so hard she could barely make out the road ahead. If it wasn't for the blue lights, she'd lose sight of them altogether.

The drive took the better part of thirty-five minutes. Kenzie didn't dare go as fast as Vargas and the others, and after a while, they pulled away. Damn it. Now she'd have to text Willie for the address.

She slowed down on the causeway to South Beach. Her wipers couldn't keep up with the deluge.

A blinding set of headlights appeared right behind her.

"What the—?"

She squinted into her rear-view mirror. The car was so close she could make out two figures in the front. Men, she thought, judging by their size and breadth. Other than that, they were a blur.

She gently put her foot on the brake, hoping to force them to slow down, except they didn't. Instead, they rammed into her and jolted her forward.

"Hey!" she yelled.

Speeding up again, she tried to put some distance between them, but they stayed with her. Fear gnawed at her gut, but she tried to keep calm. Maybe if she pulled over, they'd drive past. There wasn't much space on the causeway, but she slowed down and veered across the yellow line.

A terrible scraping sound made her jump. They were right beside her, pushing her off the road!

"What are you doing?" she yelled at them. "Are you crazy?"

Slamming her foot on the brake, she tried to stop, but another sideways push sent her dangerously close to the barrier. There was a dull screech as the tires fought for traction, but the road was wet and they slid sideways.

A large telephone pole loomed out of the greyness in front.

She screamed, shoving the brake pedal to the floor, but she knew the car wouldn't stop in time. With a sickening crunch of metal, she hit the pole—and everything went dark.

21

REID WOKE up in a world of pain.

His head pounded and every muscle ached, but at least he was alive. He tried to open his eyes, his vision was blurry. Actually, it was only blurry in one eye, the other he couldn't open at all.

Groaning, he tried to sit up, gasping as pain radiated through his side. He probably had a fractured rib. He had a vague recollection of the chair falling over and that big Mexican son-of-a-bitch kicking him in the side. That's when he realized he was lying on the ground. His wrists and ankles were still bound, but the chair was gone.

He opened and closed his mouth, making sure his jaw wasn't broken. It was tender, but the pain was bearable, and he still had all his teeth. That was something.

Wincing against the pain in his side, he managed to maneuver himself into a sitting position. A wave of dizziness swept over him and he closed his eye again. Damn, his head hurt. He probably had a concussion. That bastard had really done a number on him.

Once the vertigo had passed, he tried to take stock of his situation. How long had he been out? It was impossible to tell what time it was since there were no windows. The door was firmly shut, and the only air vent was close to the ceiling and not big enough to see through.

The only thing he knew for sure was that he'd been here overnight. That brute had questioned him for hours, punching him in the gut or the face when he didn't like Reid's answer. When it had stopped, he had no idea. He'd blacked out.

Reid hadn't said a word about the conference. He was hoping Torres didn't know Kenzie had overheard his telephone call.

Had he been missed yet? Had Kenzie or Vargas found his pickup? His phone?

Time lost all meaning as he sat there, semiconscious, waiting for the pain in his head to subside. He'd managed to shuffle to the wall, so he could prop himself up and his rib didn't hurt so much. He must have dozed off again, because he woke up with a start a while later and his vision was clear. In his good eye.

He used the wall to get to his feet, but they were bound so tightly that walking was impossible. The most he could do was a double-footed hop that had him toppling forward onto his knees.

Shit. He didn't have much time. Now they'd questioned him, they had no more use for him. It was only a matter of time before he ended up as fish food.

Laying on his side, he listened, but the only sound he heard was the rain falling on the corrugated iron roof of the warehouse. It was strangely comforting.

How long did he have? Even now, were they planning his demise?

He kept working his ankles and wrists back and forth to break the ties, but they held fast. What he needed was something sharp or jagged to cut them with. The office was empty. There was nothing he could use.

Or was there?

A rusty pipe in the opposite corner caught his eye. It was close to ground level, which was why he hadn't noticed it before, sticking up about half an inch through the concrete.

His pulse ticked up a notch.

He shuffled toward it on his butt and took a closer look. Yeah, the end was jagged and covered in rust. It had been sawed through but wasn't flush with the ground.

Reid rolled onto his back and jerked the wrist-ties over the rusted metal, feeling it catch his skin. Back and forth he zigzagged until he felt a stickiness running down his fingers.

Snap.

It broke apart.

Yes!

He shook out his hands to get some blood flowing back into them. His shoulders ached from his arms having been pulled back for so long. Still, there wasn't time to enjoy his victory. He had to get these ties off his feet so he could walk.

Spinning around on his behind, he tried to catch the ankle-ties on the side of the pipe. Damn it. The edge was too low.

Gritting his teeth in frustration, he twisted on his side and tried from that angle. Same problem. The jagged edge was just out of reach.

"Come on, please," he murmured, pressing his heels into the ground. The only chance he had was to attack the next person to come through that door, and he couldn't do that if he couldn't stand up.

Then he heard the handle turn.

Shit. Too late.

He spun round, expecting to see the Mexican standing there, ready for round two, but instead, it was Torres.

The gangster held a finger to his lips as he came inside, shutting the door behind him. "Shh...We don't have long."

Reid stared at him. Had he gone mad?

"Come on," Torres whispered. "We've only got a few minutes to get you out of here before Nacho comes back. After that, you're a goner."

He helped Reid to his feet.

"W—What..." Reid stuttered, "are you doing?"

"Getting you out of here."

Torres bent down and, using a switchblade, cut through Reid's ankle ties.

"I don't understand..." Reid began, but Torres interrupted. "Agent David Palmer, DEA. We can talk later. Right now, we've got to move."

Reid stared at him, at a loss for words.

"You're law enforcement?" he managed to get out.

"Yeah, that's why I'm helping you. Come on, if we get caught, we're both finished."

Torres, or rather Palmer, helped him through the door. It felt like the floor was tilting to the side and he swayed dangerously.

"Lean on me," Palmer urged, and together they struggled down the passage.

A soft rumble made them freeze. Reid's heart filled with dread. It was the roller door of the garage entrance to the warehouse.

"Shit, they're here."

A bout of nausea hit him, and he felt like throwing up, but he gripped Torres's shoulder. "Keep going," he whispered.

"No, it's too late." The agent looked at Reid. "Can you run?"

Reid nodded. He'd have to.

"Okay, then hit me."

"What?"

"Hit me and make it look good. Then take off. Got it?"

Footsteps echoed through the warehouse. They had seconds until they were discovered.

"Now," hissed Palmer.

Reid swung and sent a right hook straight to his jaw. Palmer flew backwards, careening into the wall and knocking his head.

Reid didn't wait for the men to come into the corridor, he took off.

He burst out of the side door and into the street. It was pouring rain, and he could only see out of one eye, but he kept going.

There was a shout behind him and the sound of heavy footsteps.

No way, not again.

Reid gritted his teeth and put on a burst of speed, ignoring the agony in his side and the pounding in his head. The only thought was to get away.

22

Kenzie opened her eyes and groaned. What had happened?

Then it came rushing back. The men in the car behind...the screeching metal...the fear...the crash.

Why was she wet? She touched her face, expecting to see blood, but it was just water. It was still raining. Tilting her face upwards, she felt the drops pound against her eyelids.

A voice asked, "Can you hear me?"

Her eyes fluttered open. Everywhere was grey, the sky, the rain, the road. Then she saw the car and gasped. It was wrapped around the pole, looking very sorry for itself.

"Are you okay?" the voice asked.

Mentally she inspected every part of her body, starting at the head and working down to her toes.

Twisting her neck to see who was behind her, she murmured, "I think so."

"Easy," he said, helping her into a sitting position. "You were incredibly lucky." The voice was male, mid-twenties, maybe thirties, with a genuine note of concern in it.

A face came into focus. Dark hair, brown eyes, a smattering of freckles. He was taking her pulse, his hand on her wrist, his eyes on his watch. "I can't believe you're not badly hurt."

"Neither can I." Grimacing, she held her head. Perhaps she wasn't completely unscathed.

"That's a nasty bump where you hit the steering wheel, but other than that, you appear to be fine. No broken bones. I checked you over."

She studied him. "Who are you? A doctor?"

"Vet, actually, but same thing at the end of the day. Humans are just big animals." He smiled at his little joke.

She couldn't quite manage it.

The rain was ricocheting off the asphalt, and in the background, a steady flow of traffic continued over the causeway.

"Did you see the car that ran me off the road?" she asked.

"No, sorry. When I came along, you were already bent up like a tin can. I'm afraid your car's totaled."

"Great." She tried to get to her feet, but the world spun.

"I'm not sure you should get up just yet. Just wait for the paramedics to get here?"

"I'm okay," she insisted swaying unsteadily.

"You may have a concussion." He looked concerned. "I'd recommend going to the hospital and getting checked out."

Reid. He was still out there, somewhere.

"I can't. I've got somewhere to be."

"Oh, where's that?"

She hesitated. What was there to say? A Mexican drug lord's house. How crazy would that sound?

A burst of dizziness hit her, and she gripped his arm. Sirens could be heard coming along the causeway. "On second thought, maybe I will get checked out."

"Good idea." He lowered her back onto the wet ground. It felt like sitting in a puddle. If only this rain would let up. That struck her as funny. She'd prayed for rain to break the heat for the last three weeks, and now that it had, she wanted it to stop.

A giggle escaped her, then she started shivering. Why was it so cold? This was Miami.

The man beside her took off his jacket and put it around her shoulders. She realized he was older, mid-thirties.

"What's your name?" she asked, as the ambulance pulled up and a paramedic got out, but he didn't get a chance to respond.

"Are you the driver of this vehicle?" The paramedic knelt beside her, and the man moved back, out of the way.

"I think she's in shock," he said.

"I'm fine," she mumbled, but the world was spinning again.

"Look at me, ma'am." The paramedic studied her pupils, then gave a curt nod. "Definitely a concussion." Surveying the mashed-up car, he raised his eyebrows. "You're lucky you're alive."

"I know."

This wasn't her first road accident. The first time had been just before she was due to graduate from the Police Academy, although she didn't remember much. A screech of tires, scraping metal, and glass breaking. Sounds she'd never wanted to hear again.

Except now they were running on a loop through her head like a nightmarish soundtrack.

This time, thank goodness, she'd been lucky. Last time, not so much. The accident had ended her career on the police force and laid her up for months.

She looked around for her rescuer, but he was talking to a police officer who'd arrived and was cordoning off the area. Her crime scene. His jacket was still draped around her shoulders.

"Come on," said the paramedic, taking her arm. "Let's get you to the hospital for a scan."

She let him help her to her feet. Together, they hobbled to the waiting ambulance. It was a relief to get out of the rain, and she sat on the chair and closed her eyes, while they belted her in and shut the door.

Only when she heard the siren come on, did she remember she hadn't thanked the man who'd helped her.

. . .

"Your CT scan was clear." The doctor's smile hovered in the air.

Why was he so happy, when she felt so awful?

She was in a ward at Jackson Memorial Hospital with a headache that was worse than any hangover in memory. A nurse had given her a couple of painkillers, but they hadn't done anything to stop the thumping elephants in her brain.

"We'll keep you overnight for observation, but it's just a precaution. Tomorrow you can go home."

She managed to nod.

"There are some people here to see you. I'll let them in now."

Her heart jumped.

Reid. They'd found him.

Then it plummeted again as a deflated Diaz and Vargas traipsed in. Defeated expressions announced bad news.

"Are you okay?" Vargas looked terrible, even worse than her. Tie askew, shirt rumpled, and his hair stuck up every which way.

"We couldn't believe it when we heard." Diaz, who only looked marginally better, sank down on the end of the bed. "What happened?"

"Somebody drove me off the road," she said. "Literally. Pushed me into the outer barrier on the causeway, and I crashed into a pole. There was nothing I could do."

"Torres's men?" Vargas looked worried.

She'd been thinking about that. "I don't know. I don't think so. This didn't feel like him." Torres would be more subtle. This was brazen, aggressive. An act of desperation. Not his style. "Any news on Reid?"

Vargas shook his head. "Torres's house was empty. We knocked and waited, but there was no response. Without a warrant, we couldn't search it."

"I doubt you would have found anything anyway," she muttered.

Torres, under his guise as Alex Guerra was a stand-up citizen. No way he'd leave evidence of a kidnapping lying around his house.

Looking up at them, she asked, "What are we going to do?"

"I don't know," Vargas admitted. "I feel so helpless. The boss is in trouble and there's nothing we can do about it."

Then she remembered the phone conversation with Xavier. "Was Ortega there?"

"Yeah, he was there, not that it did any good. I called him when I heard about your accident, and he's on his way here."

Ortega had visited her often in the hospital after her first accident. He was the one person who'd kept her sane when her world was falling apart around her. He'd been a good friend back then.

A few moments later, the door burst open and Ortega strode in. "Kenzie, Jesus Christ. Are you okay?" His gaze flew to the bump on her forehead, the size of a plum, and almost the same color. "Ouch!"

"Yeah." She winced. "I'm fine, though. Thanks for coming. You didn't have to." But she was glad he had. Not only for herself, but because they could talk about Reid, and what was being done to find him.

"Of course I did. What the hell happened?"

She told him the story, and he winced when she described how her Honda had been totaled. "You had a lucky escape."

Didn't she know it. Thanks to the vet who'd pulled her from the wreckage and called the ambulance. Her gaze flickered to his jacket on the chair beside the bed. There was nothing in the pockets, she'd already checked. No way of finding out who he was.

"Do you know who did this?" Ortega asked.

"Actually, I might have an idea."

"Who?" asked Vargas and Diaz, simultaneously.

She bit her lip. "Yesterday, I went to see Governor Talbot."

"Governor Talbot?" Ortega frowned. "What's he got to do with this?"

"I've been investigating a possible pedophile ring," she explained.

"Young juvenile offenders are being exploited for sex by wealthy older men. I think the governor's involved."

All three stared at her, aghast.

"You're serious?" Ortega asked.

"Unfortunately." She told them about her meeting and what she'd said. "He looked like he'd seen a ghost. I'm convinced he was there. He also had no alibi for the night of the party. I checked with his wife."

Diaz was shaking her head. "How'd you get to his wife?"

She shrugged. "That's not important, but we can trust her."

"Holy shit," muttered Ortega. "You tell Talbot you suspect he's involved in a pedophile ring and the next day you're run off the road."

"Yeah."

"Did you get a license plate?" Vargas asked.

She shook her head. "It was raining too hard. I couldn't make out anything other than it was a dark color and there were two men in the front."

"That doesn't help much."

It didn't, but it was all she had. Anyway, they could investigate that later.

"What about Reid?" she asked. "Have you managed to trace Torres yet?"

"No, we're looking for him," Ortega said. "But he seems to have gone off grid."

Her eyes widened remembering. "I have his phone number. Would that help? It's probably a burner, but you might pinpoint his location."

Everyone stared at her.

"Y—You have his number?" Ortega stuttered. "How?"

She crinkled her forehead, knowing she was going to get flak for this. "I ran into him at a club and engineered a meeting. We hit it off, and I gave him my number."

"For fuck's sake!" Ortega erupted. "You know what happened to the last detective that tried that." Regret marred his features. Bianca's death was on him, and he had to live with that for the rest of his life.

"Not you too," she huffed. Reid never let her forget it.

Reid.

Where was he now? Was he hurt? Injured?

Gulping hard, she tried to focus on what she had to say. Finding him was the only way they could help, and to do that, they needed to know about the conference.

"The boss knew?" Vargas gasped.

"He was with me when we ran into him. I knew he'd been looking for the guy, and we suspected it was the Morales cartel who was bringing in the lethal pink cocaine, so I decided to see what I could find out."

Diaz was staring at her with newfound respect. Ortega was still fuming silently, shaking his head. "That's what my sources say, too. The pink coke's a new revenue stream for them, but a lucrative one."

"Did you find out anything?" Diaz asked.

"Only that there's a conference coming up. Reid thought Lopez might be coming to town."

There was a shocked silence as her words sank in. Eventually, Ortega said, "And you're only telling us this now?"

"Things have been a little crazy," she grumbled. "Anyway, Reid knew, and now he's missing. It's got to be related. Torres must have known he was following him. Maybe he even knew who I was." She shuddered. That wasn't a welcome thought.

Ortega looked grim. "I wouldn't underestimate Alberto Torres. If you're right, and he was onto Reid, then this is worse than we thought."

Kenzie felt weak. "What do you think he'll do to him?"

"You know they can't let him go." Ortega said gently. "It doesn't look good for him, Kenz. I'm sorry."

She paled as the world seemed to tilt again, and she gripped the sides of the bed. Diaz looked down while Vargas ran a hand through his hair.

"Can't we do something?" she whispered.

"Give me Torres's number." Ortega pulled out his phone. "Let's see if we can trace him. Vargas, you and Diaz come with me back to Miami PD. We'll get our experts to look at that screenshot Kenzie took. There's a chance we can find out where the warehouse is."

They nodded eagerly.

Kenzie threw back the covers. "I'm coming too."

"No, you're not," Ortega said. "You're not well enough."

"I'm fine. The doctor gave me the all-clear." Not strictly true, but close enough. He'd said she was out of danger.

Getting out of bed, she reached for her clothes. "I'll be five minutes. Don't you dare leave without me, Xav."

Ortega shook his head and stalked from the room, muttering about how impossible she was. Vargas followed, while Diaz stayed to help her get dressed.

"We'll find him," the female officer said, more to herself than Kenzie.

"I know we will."

She refused to believe he wasn't coming back. Reid was a survivor, he was tough. He'd hang in there till the bitter end. Somehow, they'd find him. They would.

23

REID ZIGZAGGED through the warehouse district in the blinding rain, trying to find a place to hide. It was daytime, but the low clouds and driving rain reduced visibility to almost nothing. Sprinting across a busy road, he darted between two fish factories. A truck was offloading the catch of the day, and he ducked behind a giant container that stank to high heaven. The footsteps behind him petered off, and then faded to nothing.

Thank God.

He leaned against the container, catching his breath.

His head was spinning. What the fuck? Torres, a DEA agent. How?

Questions flew through his brain, but he couldn't make head nor tail of them. It was too surreal. And yet here he was, alive and enjoying the sensation of the rain on his battered face.

When his breathing returned to normal, he still didn't move. He couldn't. The pain in his side was excruciating. Every time he tried to straighten up, it felt like a knife jabbing between his ribs. The wild sprint through the streets had made it worse.

He slid down to the wet ground and waited until the pain had subsided. They must have found his truck by now, his phone. They were probably trying to trace Torres and work out where the warehouse on his app was.

He grimaced. He'd have some explaining to do over that.

When he could stand without gasping, he walked out from behind the container and approached the men in high visibility jackets, offloading the fish. They glanced up, startled. He must be a sight. Still couldn't see out of his one eye, and there was a big gash on the side of his cheek. He was probably covered in blood. The men began backing away.

He held up a hand. "I'm with Sweetwater PD," he began, realizing how ridiculous that sounded. He didn't even have his badge on him. "My name is Lieutenant Garret, and I need to use a phone."

The men stared at him, and he wondered if they spoke English.

"Phone?" he said, raising his right hand to his ear.

One of the men pointed to an office on the side of the factory. It was a walk, but what choice was there?

Cringing, he limped over to the office. The woman inside screamed when she saw him and backed into a corner. He sighed. This wasn't going well.

"Lieutenant Garret, Sweetwater PD," he said, trying to keep his voice calm. "There's been an...incident, and I need to use the phone."

"You're a cop?" She arched an eyebrow. He couldn't blame her; he didn't look like one at the moment.

"Yes, ma'am. I need to use your phone. It's an emerg..."

"My husband's a cop." She broke into a relieved grin. "What the hell happened to you?"

"Ma'am, I just need to use your phone." He didn't have the energy to explain. "I have to call the Miami PD."

"Honey, you're in luck. That's where my hubby works. Let me grab my keys, and I'll take you there."

Even better.

He followed her out to the car. It was still pouring down, but he was so wet it hardly mattered.

"Sure you don't want me to take you to the hospital, honey? No offense, but you don't look too good."

No kidding. "I'm sure, thanks."

She chuckled. "I should see the other guy, right?"

If only... that Mexican bastard had it coming.

Beatrice, as she introduced herself, talked all the way there. Her husband, Dwayne, was a beat cop. Had been for the twenty-five years they'd been married. Still had ten years to go until retirement, and she worried about him every day. His head was pounding when she dropped him off.

"Say hi to my Dwayne if you see him, honey," she called, and took off out of the parking lot.

"Jesus, is that you, Garrett?" asked an officer in the parking lot.

"Yeah, I need to see Pérez."

"Shit, sure. Come on. Let's get you inside and get that eye looked at. What the hell happened?"

"It's a long story," he groaned. "Can you get me past security?" They'd never let him up looking like this.

"Yeah, follow me."

The officer, whose name Reid had forgotten, had a word with security, and they let him through without a second glance. There wasn't much that shocked them anymore.

The officer took him up to the homicide division. "Want me to come in with you?" he asked at the door.

"No, I've got it from here."

Pushing open the door, he walked across the squad room towards the lieutenant's office but didn't get far before seeing Vargas and Diaz standing beside Ortega's desk.

There was a screech, and Kenzie flew across the room and into his arms, engulfing him in blonde hair, a warm embrace, and the faint smell of perfume.

He closed his eyes briefly, enjoy the moment before his legs gave way.

Vargas grabbed his arm. "Shit, boss. Are you okay?"

Ortega jumped up. "Sit down, Garret, before you fall down."

Reid collapsed gratefully into his chair. "Thanks."

"You're alive." Kenzie gawked at him as if she couldn't believe he was actually there. He was having a hard time believing it himself. Then he noticed the bump on her head.

"What happened to you?"

"Oh this," she shrugged, not meeting his eye. "I'll tell you later."

Pérez marched out of his office. "Christ, Garret, you gave us a scare. We've got half the force looking for you."

"Well, you can call them off. As you can see, I'm fine."

That was debatable.

"What the hell happened?" Pérez demanded, standing in front of him. A small crowd had gathered around Ortega's desk. Everyone wanted to know what had happened to him.

"I'm going to call for a paramedic," a young female officer said. Detective Ryan. Reid remembered her from the Swamp Strangler case.

"Good idea," agreed Diaz, giving her a nod.

"Was it Torres?" asked Ortega.

Reid nodded. "Yeah, his men snatched me outside my cabin. They wanted to know if we knew about..." he glanced at Kenzie.

"I told them," she said.

"About the conference. Lopez is coming to town. I'm sure of it."

"Do you know when?" Pérez asked.

"Next week." He glanced at Kenzie again.

She nodded. "I think it's at the Ritz-Carlton."

That was news. He shot her a questioning look.

"I remembered something else Torres said. After the phone call I overheard, he rang the Ritz-Carlton Hotel and booked a suite. I didn't connect it at the time, but if Lopez is coming to Miami, it would make sense, right? They could be meeting there."

Reid felt like hugging her.

"Which one?" asked Diaz. "There are several in Miami."

She shook her head. "I don't know, sorry."

"I take it you didn't let on that you knew about the meeting?" Pérez asked.

Reid rolled his eyes. "Of course not. Would I look like this if I had?"

Pérez smirked. Diaz just shook her head.

"Torres knew I was following him,", his gaze meeting Kenzie's. "He knew who you were too, right from the beginning."

"Damn. All this time I thought I was playing him, but he was the one playing us."

"He's smart," Reid acknowledged. He hesitated. Should he tell them about how Torres had helped him escape? That he was working for the DEA?

Nothing made sense. There were things that didn't add up.

First, he must have been undercover for years. Since before Bianca. Way before. And secondly, how could he condone shooting an innocent woman? A fellow law enforcement officer, no less. It was unconscionable.

A chill ran down his spine. Had Bianca known? Was that why she'd fallen for him? There were so many questions, but no answers. He had to talk to Torres. Somehow, he had to track him down.

"How did you get away?" Ortega asked.

"There was this rusty pipe in the corner of the room," he explained. "It had a jagged edge and I used it to snap the ties, then when the door opened and Torres came in, I hit him and ran for it. I managed to get out through a side door before the other goons noticed I was gone. A lucky escape."

There were several silent nods. Everybody knew there was no way the cartel would have let him go.

"Thank goodness." Kenzie clutched his hand. "I knew you wouldn't give up without a fight."

He smiled at her, then grimaced. Crap, his face hurt. That reminded him. "Torres has a big Mexican guy doing the dirty work for him. Name's Nacho. He's covered in tattoos, shouldn't be too hard to ID. I'm willing to bet he's got quite a rap sheet."

The paramedic hurried in carrying a medical bag, but stopped short when he saw Reid. "You need an ambulance," he told him.

"Patch him up as best you can," Pérez ordered. Reid shot him a grateful nod. He wouldn't be going to a hospital any time soon. His ex-lieutenant knew him too well.

"What now?" asked Vargas as the paramedic dabbed Reid's face with antiseptic. It stung like hell and he sucked in a breath.

"I'll put out an arrest warrant for Torres, or Alex Guerra as he's called now," said Ortega, who he was convinced was enjoying his discomfort—just a little. Payback for the broken nose. "And this enforcer guy, Nacho."

Reid knew he ought to tell them what he knew, but could Ortega be trusted? He'd blabbed once before. Granted, that had been because he'd had feelings for Bianca too, but Reid didn't want to put the DEA agent's life at risk. One word from anyone here, and he was history. The cartel didn't take kindly to that kind of thing.

"Won't they come after you again?" Kenzie inquired, frowning.

"Nah, they know I'm coming after them. Even if we go back to the warehouse, it'll be empty. They'll have moved on, gone underground until the conference." They'd already gotten rid of any fingerprints or DNA in the office. That bleach smell had been strong, recent.

"Shit," said Vargas.

"Still, we should make a show of raiding it," Pérez said. "Let them think we're following protocol. It'll throw them off the scent of what we're really doing."

Reid nodded. It wasn't a bad idea.

"Which is what?" asked Kenzie.

"We're going to crash their little party." Reid met Ortega's eye.

The Miami PD detective nodded. "That can definitely be arranged. I'll have to speak to Wilson at the DEA field office. This is their jurisdiction."

Reid froze. Would Wilson let on about Torres? Probably not. He wouldn't risk his own agent.

"Let's hold off contacting the DEA until we have more intel," he suggested. "At the moment, it's just an overheard phone call. Let's check out the Ritz-Carltons and find out which one they're meeting at, and what suite he booked."

"I'll get on it," Vargas said.

Ortega pursed his lips. "I'll reach out to my CIs. Maybe they heard something."

"Good," said Pérez. "I'll set up the raid on the warehouse for this afternoon. Let's not waste any time."

Reid jerked his head away as the paramedic inspected the gash on his cheek. "That needs stitches," he warned. "You're going to have to go to the emergency room whether you like it or not."

Reid muttered something unintelligible beneath his breath.

"I'll get a squad car to drop you," Pérez said.

Kenzie jumped up. "I'll come with you."

Reid hoped he hadn't made a mistake not outing Torres. Guilt gnawed at him as they drove to the hospital but, at the same time, he felt like he owed the DEA agent. He'd risked everything to save him. The least he could do was return the favor.

24

"TORRES *KNEW* THE WHOLE TIME," Kenzie grumbled, as they pulled into the hospital parking lot. "I feel like such a fool."

"How would you have known?" he said.

"Because you warned me, but as usual, I didn't listen." She shook her head. The manipulator had been out manipulated. She'd underestimated him, a mistake she wouldn't be making again.

Reid shrugged. "No harm done."

She glanced at his split cheek and swollen eye. "I wouldn't say that."

The uniformed officer dropped them at the front entrance. "Want me to wait?"

"No thanks, I'm going to get a rental," Kenzie said. "There's a place around the corner." It would only be for a day or two, until she could get a loaner from the insurance company.

"Back already?" asked the ER nurse when she saw Kenzie. "Having problems?"

"No, it's not me," She gestured to Reid. "It's him."

The nurse noticed the slice down his cheek and her eyes widened. "Oh. Take a seat, I'll get a doctor."

"Was that about the lump?" he nodded to her forehead. She touched it and winced; it was still tender. "Are you going to tell me what happened?"

"It's not connected," she blurted. "At least, I don't think it is."

"What's not connected?"

"Promise you won't be mad?"

"Kenzie? What's going on?"

She told him about her conversation with Governor Talbot.

"What the hell were you thinking?" he exploded, causing the other patients to look over. "You practically accused him of being a pedophile."

"True, but how else was I supposed to find out if he was there?" Knowing he wasn't going to like this next bit either, she filled him in on the accident.

He listened, horrified. "You could have been killed."

"I think it was more of a warning. To get me to back off."

"Don't be so sure. Look what happened to Matteo."

That was true.

Reid dropped his head into his hands.

"This way, sir," said a nurse, appearing in front of them. Reid shot Kenzie an exasperated look, then followed the nurse down a passage and into a treatment room.

Kenzie took the opportunity to walk around the corner to the car hire place and rent a vehicle. Not ideal, but it would do for the interim. The headache was building up again, so back at the hospital, she got a cup of coffee and took another painkiller. Not too strong, just strong enough to take the edge off.

Reid came back, sporting a row of neat stitches in his cheek. The damaged eye was clean, even though it was purple, and the shirt was partially open, displaying a tight bandage around his torso. Still pale, but the smeared blood was gone, and he looked much better than before.

"Let me take you home," Kenzie said. "You need to rest."

"So do you," he told her. She acknowledged that with a nod of her head. What a fine pair they made. Anyone seeing them walk out of the hospital would think they'd been in a car accident together.

"I'm not going to give up," she told him, as they drove across town to the cabin. The rain had finally stopped, but many of the roads had localized flooding. Water sprayed up like a wave as they drove through a large puddle. "We have to take them down. Stop them from abusing young boys like this."

"We will." He put his hand on her thigh, and she froze. He'd never done that before. "All I'm saying is, be careful. No more brazen insinuations. Let him think you've learned your lesson and you're backing off."

It felt warm, and she liked it there. "Yeah, okay. Maybe stealth is the way to go."

Giving her leg a quick squeeze, he let go. Irrationally, she wanted him to put it back.

It's just the emotions of the last few days, she told herself, was feeling fragile and overwrought. Sleep, that's what was needed. A good night's sleep would make everything right again.

Well, almost.

She pulled up outside Reid's.

"What the–?" The door had been taped together, a result of being broken open earlier.

"Oh, yeah. They had to bust in to look for you."

"Fair enough. I'll get someone round to fix it. Would do it myself but..." he nodded downwards towards his ribs.

Kenzie could only imagine how painful it was, although this was the first time he'd mentioned it.

She hesitated in the hallway. "Do you need anything before I go?"

"No, I'm good."

He didn't bother going into the lounge, just headed straight for the bedroom and laid down on the bed. That was a sure sign he wasn't alright.

"Can I make you something to eat? How about a painkiller?" She had a stack of those in her purse.

"Kenzie, I'm fine. Don't fuss." He didn't look fine. In fact, he was pale and exhausted.

"Okay, if you're sure."

Turning, she headed for the door.

"Kenzie?"

"Yeah?"

He paused, as if wrestling with his conscience. His conscience won. "There's something I need to tell you."

She turned back to face him. "What's that?"

"Better sit down,"

Frowning, she backtracked and sat down on the end of his bed. It felt weird being in his room, on his bed with him in it.

"Okay."

He hesitated, as if unsure how to continue, then he said, "I didn't tell you guys the whole truth back at the station. There's more."

She stared at him.

"I did cut through my ties, the ones on my hands anyway." He paused, as if unsure how to proceed.

She waited.

His voice dropped. "Then Torres came in and helped cut through the ones on my feet."

"Excuse me?" She shook her head. "I thought you said Torres..."

"Yes, I did."

She stared at him. Were the painkillers making him groggy? Was he talking nonsense? "I—I don't understand. Torres...the bad guy, right?"

"He helped me escape, Kenz. There wasn't time to explain, but he told me he was an undercover DEA agent and to get out before they killed me."

She almost fell off the bed. Perhaps she was hallucinating. "What?"

"It's true. I couldn't believe it myself. Then we heard footsteps, and he told me to hit him. There wasn't time for both of us to get away clean, so I punched him in the face and ran for it. He went down. That's the last I saw of him."

Kenzie said nothing for a full minute, trying to process what she'd heard.

Torres a DEA agent.

Torres helping Reid escape.

Could it be true?

She thought back to the two evenings she'd spent with him. On both occasions, he'd drunk very little, preferring to keep a clear head. He'd flirted, but she'd always felt he was holding back. Now she knew why. He'd been playing a part, acting a role, just like she had.

The two of them had been dancing circles around each other, except he'd been aware of her little charade the entire time.

"This is hard to believe," she murmured, still in shock. "How is it possible?"

"I don't know, but he did help me escape. I hope he didn't get into too much shit for it."

"But he's the cartel's man in Miami. How does an undercover agent rise that high up in the cartel hierarchy without getting caught?"

Reid just shrugged.

Then Kenzie gasped. "What about Bianca? Did he shoot Bianca?"

Reid just shook his head. "I don't have any of the answers. I'm just telling you what happened."

"Holy crap," she whispered, running a hand through her hair. "You don't think this will have blown his cover, do you?"

"I hope not. I hit him pretty hard."

She nodded, hoping he was right.

One thing was for sure, she had not seen that one coming.

"Don't you think you should have told Pérez?"

"Couldn't risk it," he said. "Torres put his life on the line for me, risking the entire undercover op. If he is DEA, he'll have a handler. I want to see if I can track him down. Also, you know what happened with Ortega last time. The fewer people who know about Torres the better."

He was right. They couldn't risk Torres's life. He was in the thick of it. If the cartel even suspected he was an agent, he was worse than dead.

"He'll lie low until the conference," Reid guessed. "They won't want anything to derail the talks. That's probably when Torres is planning on bringing Lopez down, when he's on American soil."

"If it is," Kenzie said, "it's the culmination of God knows how many years of undercover work."

"Yeah, he's been under for ages."

"Why do you think they kidnapped you? It seems a silly thing to do now, just before the conference."

"I think Torres was forced to act. There's a Mexican enforcer with him, a giant called Nacho. He's the one who did this." He gestured to his face. "My guess is he reports back to Lopez. When it became obvious I was following Torres, it forced his hand. If he'd done nothing, that would have looked suspicious."

That made sense.

"You've got to admire the guy," she murmured. "He's got balls."

Reid grunted in agreement.

They talked for a bit longer, then Kenzie stifled a yawn. She was exhausted, and her body, particularly her neck, was beginning to ache, but it was nothing compared to what Reid must be feeling. "I'd better get going."

"You're welcome to stay here." His gaze lingered on her.

She looked longingly at the space next to Reid, it would be so easy to lie down and fall asleep beside him. And more. But it would mean drifting back into a world of uncertainty, where she questioned everything, unsure of herself—of them.

They made such a great team. That was one of the things she loved about their friendship. The trust. Kenzie didn't trust easily. It was always easier to walk away.

She'd been to Colombia once, to the rainforest on an assignment for the paper. With her guide, she'd crossed a ropey suspension bridge, decaying and dilapidated. It barely looked strong enough to hold their weight. When she'd stepped on it, it had swung precariously. Step by step, she'd inched her way across, holding on for all she was worth.

This felt like that. Having taken the first few steps with Reid, the bridge had creaked and swayed. So now she could either keep going, risk falling into the abyss, or shuffle backwards to where it was more stable. Where she trusted it wouldn't break, and she wouldn't fall.

"Thanks, but I'm going to head home," she said quietly. "Keep me posted."

He dropped his gaze. "Will do."

25

REID STAGGERED into the police station the next morning to muted applause. By now, everyone had heard that the LT had been kidnapped, beaten up and managed to escape. This was a story that would be told over and over again at Sweetwater PD. Reid, however, wanted to get straight back to work. "Any news on the dawn raid?"

Ortega's team, along with a SWAT unit, had raided the warehouse where he'd been held first thing this morning. Reid hadn't bothered going, since he knew it would be deserted. It was more for show than anything else.

"Everyone was gone." Vargas filled him in. "There was nothing there."

He grunted. Just as expected.

"What about Torres's house?"

"Detective Ortega's team is keeping an eye on it. If he goes back there, they'll bring him in. You can count on it."

That's what Reid was afraid of. Torres had to remain in play until the conference.

"Torres will go to ground," Reid predicted. "Now that I'm free, he'll stay hidden. I wouldn't be surprised if he ships out again."

"There's a warrant out for his arrest," Vargas said.

Reid nodded. That, too, was expected. He might have to tell Pérez about Torres, but Ortega would question why they were backing off.

He called a meeting in the incident room. Spirits were high. The LT was back, and both cases were heating up. These were exciting times for the backwater police department.

"Thanks, everyone, for your concern and hard work in trying to locate me over the last few days. As you can see, I'm alive and kicking." He snorted. "Well, alive at any rate."

There were a few chuckles. The cut along the side of his face was healing, but it would leave a nasty scar, and his eye was still swollen, but he could see a sliver of light through it, which he took to be a good sign. The hospital had bandaged his torso to keep his ribs stable, but it meant he couldn't slouch, so was restricted to sitting upright or standing all the time.

Reid faced his team and tried not to think about his aches and pains. They would heal, and he had a job to do.

"I want us to concentrate on figuring out who ran Kenzie Gilmore off the road yesterday. Let's look at any CCTV footage we can find on the causeway, along with any LPR systems along the route she took. If we can get a plate, we can find out who it was."

In theory. The perpetrators may have been using a stolen car, or dummy plates, but it was a start.

"Where's Dempsey?" Reid asked Vargas once the others dispersed and got to work.

"He was in earlier, but said he had to go meet somebody. I figured it was one of his contacts."

Reid frowned.

"Er, boss," Vargas shuffled, clearly uncomfortable. "I want to apologize for the other day. You know...when Shannon came to see me at the department. I just want you to know that I don't talk about you, or work, to her."

He patted Vargas on the shoulder. "Don't worry about it. I know you're discreet. She seems nice."

"Yeah." He flushed. "She's great."

Reid shot him a parting smile and went to find Hamilton.

"He dashed out saying he had to do something urgent," one of his fellow uniformed officers said.

Good. The kid was still tailing Dempsey. He'd find out soon enough who he was meeting.

"I've picked up Kenzie's car on the license plate recognition system," said Diaz, pointing to her screen. "This was taken on the expressway before she reached the causeway. It doesn't look like anyone's following her, although it's hard to see in the storm."

The image was grainy, but there were no vehicles close enough to Kenzie to be suspicious.

"Keep looking." Reid blinked, his good eye compensating for the lack of vision in the other one. That Mexican bastard had a lot to answer for. "They must be there, somewhere."

Diaz nodded and went back to scrutinizing the camera footage.

Reid was making himself a cup of coffee to go with his handful of painkillers when Vargas bounced in. "I hope it's good news," Reid grumbled.

"It is, boss. The CSI team has a result from the paint scraping taken from the side of Kenzie's Honda. It's a high-performance automobile paint called—" He glanced down. "Something I can't pronounce. But the interesting thing is this particular color is only used in a few makes of car."

Reid perked up. "So, if we know what kind of car it's used on, we can cross-reference those with what we find on the roadside cameras."

Vargas grinned. "Exactly."

"Good work. Let me know when you have something." He picked up his coffee just as his phone rang. It was Hamilton. Moving into the incident room, he closed the door.

"Yeah?"

The officer's voice was hushed, urgent. "Dempsey is at the probation offices."

He went cold. "Shit, has he gone inside?" What the hell was he doing there? Was he in it with Hodge? Or was he so bitter that he was tipping him off to derail the investigation?

"Do you know who he's meeting?"

"No, he's waiting for the elevator."

"Stop him, Hamilton," he blurted out. "He could blow the entire op." He forgot that Hamilton didn't know which op he was talking about.

"Um... how, sir?"

"I don't care. Arrest him if you must, but under no circumstances can he talk to Hodge. Do you understand me?"

"Yes, but—"

"Go now. Bring him back here. I want to talk to him."

"He's in the elevator." Hamilton's voice was edged with panic. "It's going up."

"Stop him," barked Reid. "Stop him before he gets to Hodge's floor. That's an order, officer."

"Yes, boss!" Hamilton cut the call.

Reid stood there, breathing heavily, praying Hamilton would get to Dempsey in time. If the vengeful old geezer tipped Hodge off about their investigation, the entire organization would dissolve, and they'd never catch these guys.

He stormed back into the squad room. "Vargas, call the phone operator and get me Dempsey's call records, and get onto IT. I want to see all his emails for the last week." IT consisted of one tech geek who maintained all the computers, scanners, and printers at the Sweetwater Police Department.

To Vargas's credit, he didn't ask why, but simply picked up his desk phone and made the calls.

Reid paced up and down wishing he knew how Hamilton was

doing. It had been five minutes since the phone call. How long did it take to race up the stairs and arrest the old bastard?

Ten minutes later, his phone rang.

He snatched it up. "Did you get him?"

"Yes, boss."

Reid sank into the chair. "Thank God. Any fallout?"

"No, I have him in cuffs." He sounded distraught. "I didn't know how else to apprehend him."

"Good work, officer. Now bring him back here for questioning."

"On our way."

Thank goodness!

"He got him," he said to Vargas, who had no idea what he was talking about. "Dempsey. He got him."

A shocked murmur ran through the squad room when a nervous Hamilton brought in Dempsey in handcuffs. The old guy was fuming, muttering expletives, but the rookie cop held him firm.

"Put him in a holding cell," Reid snapped. "I'll deal with him later." He could stew for twenty-four hours until they'd been through his call records and emails. He'd also have to get internal affairs involved, and he sure as hell couldn't risk Dempsey getting out and going straight to the enemy.

He put Hamilton on the search as a reward for his quick thinking and decisive action. If he hadn't called Reid when he did, it would have been too late to do anything, and the operation would be in tatters. It was the rookie cop's first real taste of detective work.

"Look for any calls, texts or chats with a William or Bill, Hodge, or anything that looks suspicious," Reid explained. "Hodge was probably using an unregistered phone for his illicit activities. The same with the emails. Think you can handle that?"

"Absolutely, thanks, boss."

Reid nodded, and the young cop got to work.

"We've got a match," Diaz shouted a couple of hours later. "A gray Ford Mondeo was picked up a few vehicles behind Kenzie's on the causeway, and then again, but closer this time, on the bridge a hundred meters from where she crashed."

Reid gave a curt nod. "Sounds promising. Does the paint match?"

"It's the right make and model of car," she confirmed.

"Great work. Do we have a clear shot of the plate?" He didn't dare hope. The rain, the low visibility, the darkness would not act in their favor.

"We've got a partial," Diaz said, zooming in. "LR87..."

It was better than nothing.

"Okay, we can work with that. Let's dig up all the Ford Mondeos that start with LR87. With a bit of luck, that will give us our perp."

Diaz got to work.

Reid tried to go back to the report he was writing on his kidnapping, but he kept losing focus. He didn't want to remember how they'd beaten him up. Unable to defend himself, he'd taken blow after blow until he'd passed out.

His cheek throbbed at the thought of Nacho's fists pounding into him. He tried to get comfortable in the chair, but the stiff bandage around his midsection made it impossible. As it was, he had to be careful not to turn too fast, or cough or sneeze.

Another coffee helped, and he soldiered on. If he treated it like it had happened to someone else, it was easier. Almost like an out-of-body experience. He was looking down from above, wondering if this was it. If this was where his life would end. In an empty office in a deserted warehouse, at the hand of an ugly Mexican thug.

As he was nearing the end of his report, Vargas punched the air. "Yes!"

Reid looked over. Diaz was smiling, while Vargas patted her on the back.

"You got something?" They could do with some good news.

"I've got the full plate," she said triumphantly. "I'm running it through the DVLA database as we speak."

"Great work!"

They were getting closer. Soon they'd know who'd driven Kenzie into the barrier and caused her to crash. If that person was linked to the governor, all hell was going to break loose.

Reid wasn't going to back off, not even for a second. He was going to charge the son-of-a-bitch with attempted murder, in addition to the pedophile charges that would be brought when they blew the ring wide open.

It was just a matter of time.

26

"It's a rental," Diaz said, her shoulders slumping. "Registered to a company called Ready Motors."

"Do we know who hired it?" Reid asked.

"The records show it was leased to a Juan Rodriguez. Booked via telephone and the person who picked it up paid cash. It hasn't been returned yet."

Reid very much doubted it ever would.

"They're sending through his driver's license in the morning," Diaz continued. "They're shut for the day."

"Okay, let's pick this up tomorrow. We've done all we can today."

Driving home, Reid kept glancing in the rear-view mirror, half expecting to see the blue headlights appear again, even though it was unlikely. Torres would have convinced them it was safer not to mess with the police. Especially when there was a warrant out for his arrest, and that of Lopez's enforcer, Nacho Fierro.

Still, a sniper shot or a drive-by wasn't out of the question.

It was a relief to pull into the parking spot outside his house. Christ, he ached. Gingerly, he got out of the car and hobbled toward the cabin, clutching his side. His only thought was to lie down with a shot of something to take away the pain.

He was doing just that when he heard a crunch of tires on the gravel outside the window. A car door opened and closed, and light footsteps approached the house. A woman, probably Kenzie.

He groaned. The sliding door was unlocked so she could find her own way in.

True to form, she didn't bother knocking. Instead, walked around the house, jumped onto the deck, and pulled open the sliding doors with a low hiss.

"Reid?" she called, padding across the floorboards.

"In the bedroom." He'd taken his shirt off and undone the bandage to get some relief, and now there wasn't time to pull it back on.

Poking her head around the door, she said, "There you are." Then, her eyes fell on the bruises on his torso. "Oh, my God. Is that from—?" Words failed her as she stared at his side. It looked like someone had taken a baseball bat to him.

He nodded. "Compliments of Torres's enforcer. Fists of steel, that guy."

She took a closer look. "That's bad."

He grunted in agreement. "No kidding."

"Why didn't you tell me you were this badly injured." She sat down on the bed and he shuffled over.

"How did you get here?" changing the subject.

"Replacement car from my insurance company." Her gaze flickered back to his ribs. "Can I get you anything?"

"I got everything I need right here." He gestured to the glass of bourbon and painkillers on his bed stand.

"You've got to eat," she said.

"I ate on the way home." The packet of chips he'd found in the console counted, right?

"I've been researching the Morales cartel."

Reid noticed the dark circles beneath her eyes. They matched the bruise on her forehead. What a pair they made. "Did you know they're the biggest importers of cocaine into the Miami area? The DEA has been after them for years. If Torres is a plant, he's been undercover for at least five years."

"That's what I figured," he told her. "I've been looking for him for two years, and before that, we were part of a joint task force with the DEA tracking their key members. Torres has been around for a long time."

"And they never said anything to you then?" Kenzie wanted to know.

He shook his head. "No, but they wouldn't have wanted to risk his cover. If he was that embedded in the organization, even a secret meeting might be discovered. Any change in behavior could have given him away."

She puffed out her cheeks. "I don't know how he can live like that."

"It's his job."

"I know, but still..." She shrugged. "I'd be terrified someone would find out."

There was always that risk.

Leaning over, he opened the drawer in his bed stand.

Reid fumbled in the drawer and pulled out an old photograph. Gazing at it, he handed it to Kenzie.

She gasped. "That's Torres and Bianca. "They look so happy. How did you...?"

"You can't tell anyone this," he mumbled.

"I promise."

He knew he could trust her. "Earlier in the year, before your mother's case, I broke into his house and had a look around."

"You knew where he lived?" Those blue eyes were tinged with disappointment that he hadn't told her before.

"Yeah, you were right. I have been watching him. I discovered where he worked after the strangler case, and I've been watching him since then."

"That was the surveillance app Vargas found on your phone."

"Yeah, although I've had to remove it. It wasn't authorized surveillance. Luckily, Pérez turned a blind eye. I knew about his alias, his wife, everything."

She shook her head. "Yet you said nothing."

"I didn't want Ortega to go in guns blazing. I was waiting for something big to happen, something I could use against him."

She stared at him. "And did you find anything?"

"Not yet." He didn't mention the convoy of vehicles that had probably distributed the drugs throughout the state, because then he'd have to tell her he hadn't gone after them because of her, and he didn't want her to feel bad.

Kenzie ran a hand through her hair. It was loose today. Usually she wore it up in a ponytail. Efficiency over vanity. Her eyes were drawn back to the photograph. "What does this mean?"

He sighed. "I think I got it wrong. Bianca *was* in love with Torres, and he might have been in love with her. I think she knew he was an undercover agent."

Kenzie's gaze turned hard. "Yet he still shot her."

Reid exhaled. "Yeah, that's what I don't understand. I'm still trying to get my head around it."

They talked for a while longer, then Kenzie's phone rang. Taking it out of her bag, she gasped.

"It's him."

"Torres?"

"Yes." She bit her lip. "Should I answer it?"

"Yeah," he replied grimly. "We need some answers."

───────────

Kenzie answered the phone, her heart racing. "Hello?"

"Kenzie, do you know who this is?" No pretense this time, he'd used her real name.

"Yes, of course. Reid told me what happened."

"Is he with you?"

"Yes, do you want to speak to him?"

"No, I don't have time. Tell him to meet me at that bar in the Glades? Smiley's? Ten-thirty?"

"Tonight?"

"Yeah."

"Okay."

The line went dead.

Kenzie glanced up. "He wants to meet. Tonight, ten-thirty at Smiley's."

Reid glanced at his wristwatch. It was eight thirty. "Good, maybe we'll finally get some answers."

"I'm going to make us something to eat." Kenzie noted his pallor beneath the bruises. He didn't look well. "And don't try to talk me out of it. You need sustenance."

Reid gave a tired nod.

There wasn't much in the fridge, but she managed to rustle up a ham sandwich with some salad thrown in for good measure. Then she made them a pot of coffee. The bourbon would numb the pain, but if he wanted to talk sense, he needed to be in control of his senses. Torres was a slippery fish, and she wasn't about to underestimate him again.

At ten o'clock, Kenzie drove the few miles down the road to the swamp bar. The storm had cleared the air and although the evening was warm, it was much more bearable. Despite being midweek, the bar would be packed with the usual locals, and at this time of night, rowdy, but perhaps that was the point. A secret meeting would be far less noticeable.

Parking beside a row of motorcycles and pickup trucks, they walked towards the bar. Music spilled out into the still night, drowning out the sounds of the swamp. Kenzie shivered, nerves on edge. She glanced across at Reid, whose features were gritted with determination. He was in pain, she could tell.

Reaching out, she took his hand and gave it a squeeze. It was a compulsive gesture, but he looked like he needed it. She was rewarded with a small smile.

"Let's do this," she whispered.

He nodded, and they walked into the bar.

Torres wasn't there yet, so they took a seat in the far corner, away from the dart board and the pool table where most of the noise was.

Just before ten-thirty, the saloon-style door swung open and in walked Torres, baseball cap pulled low. Wearing a casual shirt, working man's jeans and worn boots, he fit right in.

A chameleon, just like her, he adapted to his environment and blended in, knowing how to live a lie. Nobody gave him more than a cursory glance as he walked over to where they sat. Reid stood up.

The two men glared at each other, the air bristled.

Reid said, "Take a seat."

Torres sat first, then Reid. There was a bruise on his cheek where Reid had punched him, although it was fading already, unlike Reid's, which were only deepening.

Kenzie didn't move.

"I think you'd better start explaining," Reid murmured. "Because we're not sure what to believe, and there's a warrant out for your arrest. I could take you in right now."

The DEA agent nodded, as if that was to be expected. "It wasn't my idea to abduct you." He chose his words carefully. "Nacho had picked up that you were following me, and if I didn't do something about it, it would have looked suspicious."

That made sense. It was Torres's job to handle situations like that.

"When did you find out about me?" Kenzie asked.

Torres shifted his gaze to her. "Right from the start. An attractive woman bumps into me at a club. I knew it was a set up. I saw Reid hovering at the back and thought he'd sent you. Bold move, considering..." He met Reid's gaze.

The silence drew out.

Then Reid said, "What happened the night Bianca died?" His voice was an icicle.

Torres breathed in sharply as if the memory hurt him, or maybe it was the question. "I was on my way to the bar to meet Bianca. The article had hit the papers, and she was scared." His eyes glazed over, lost in the memory. "I told her not to worry, that we'd get out, both of us." choking on his words, "But I was too late."

He looked back at Reid. "I got a call saying the police had surrounded the joint. Lopez was there, with Nacho. They knew it was her. It could only have been her." His eyes were haunted. Reid didn't say a word. Neither did Kenzie.

"I tried to call her to get the hell out. I swear, I tried, but she didn't pick up. Nacho confronted her, and she confessed." His face darkened. "They don't call him the Butcher for nothing."

Kenzie shivered.

Reid stared at him. "But it was your gun that shot her."

"No, it was Nacho's weapon. I used it to shoot a police snitch a few years back. He was going to get himself killed. They were on to him, so I shot him in the leg. Not fatal. The shot alerted the authorities." He paused. "I saved his life."

That put a different spin on it.

"Bianca never told them about you?" Kenzie whispered.

Torres's voice trembled. "No, she took that secret with her to the grave. She knew they were going to kill her. That was a given. Bianca died protecting me."

Reid balled his hands into fists.

He knows.

She'd meant Nacho, the Butcher. Not Torres.

All this time he'd been gunning for the wrong man.

"No one took her death harder than me." Torres stared at the dirty table. "After that, I left town for a while. I wanted out, but my handler convinced me to go back." He grimaced. "Lopez fled to Mexico, he took a bullet from one of your guys and needed surgery. We weren't sure he was going to make it."

"We suspected he'd gone back to Mexico," Reid grumbled.

"He had a friend with a private plane and pulled in a favor. He was out of the country in less than two hours and on an operating table in Mexico City in four."

"What did you do?"

"I came back to Miami, changed my name and started the off-dock loading business. I needed a way to bring in the product since the cops had taken down our old supply route."

"You've done so much damage," Kenzie remarked. "How do your superiors justify it?"

"It's part of what's referred to as Attorney General Exempted Operations, or AGEOs. The DEA is authorized to conduct under-cover illegal drug trafficking and money laundering activities to gather evidence." But his eyes burned. "My only goal now is to get to Lopez—and he's coming to town."

Reid straightened up. "Is that confirmed?"

"Yeah, he flies in on Monday. There is a series of meetings at the Ritz-Carlton Hotel in South Beach. It's our window of opportunity— the only time Lopez has been on American soil in the last two years. This is our chance to get him."

"Does your handler know about this?"

"No, that's what I need you to do. Tell him what's happened. He'll have seen the warrant for my arrest and be wondering what the hell is going on. I can't break cover for long enough to meet him. Tell him about the conference at the hotel. I'll send you the details when I have them. Once we have all the high-ranking cartel members together in one room, you can bust the lot of them. I can testify to everyone's involvement."

"What about you?" Kenzie frowned, concerned. "You're taking an awful risk."

"I know, but this is the culmination of five years of undercover work. This is why Bianca died. I *have* to take them down." His expression was grim. "Even if it's the last thing I do."

"Who's your handler?"

"Wilson, at the Miami field office. Say I sent you. Operation Long Haul, that's the codeword for the op."

That was very appropriate.

Reid gave a curt nod. "Did they suspect anything after you helped me escape?"

"I don't think so. You did a good job of making it look real." He gingerly touched his jaw.

"Sorry about that." Reid cleared his throat. "And thanks for what you did. You took a hell of a risk."

"I am an officer of the law." He shrugged. "I couldn't let you die, even if it meant forfeiting the mission. Anyway, after this, I'm out. Five years of pretending to be somebody else. I've had enough."

"One more week," Kenzie said, her heart going out to him. "Actually, four days, and then it'll be over."

Torres met her gaze. "I damn well hope so, because if this goes to shit, I've had it."

"I'll make sure they're there," Reid promised. "We'll take them down and get you out. I'll have to let the Miami PD know you're undercover, though, otherwise you're likely to get arrested on sight."

"Appreciate it."

They shook hands.

"Good luck," Kenzie said, as he left.

The end was in sight. She just hoped it would all go according to plan. Alberto Torres deserved a normal life. He'd given up enough of his own.

27

"You're shitting me!" Pérez yelled over his desk. Reid had gathered him and Ortega together and come clean about Torres. "He's fucking DEA?"

Ortega gaped at Reid. "*He* told you this?"

"Yeah, when he helped me escape. I couldn't tell you the other day because I wasn't sure what the best play would be, but after speaking to him last night, and his handler this morning, we agreed you had to know. It's imperative he isn't arrested until after the conference. If we want to take down Lopez and his top generals, this is the only way."

"Holy shit." Ortega shook his head in amazement. It took him a while to process what Reid had said, then he frowned. "What did he say about Bianca?"

"It wasn't him," Reid replied. "It was the Butcher, Nacho Fierro. He held a gun to her head after the article appeared and she confessed. He shot her before the police arrived. Torres wasn't even there. That's why there was no evidence of him at the scene. He was on his way there when he heard what happened."

"Crap!" growled Ortega. "All this time I thought he'd shot her."

Reid grunted. "That makes two of us."

It was the text message.

He knows.

Everyone had thought she'd meant Torres.

Pérez sunk into the chair. "What about the gun? We know it was Torres's gun."

Reid relayed what the DEA agent had said.

Pérez shook his head. "I had no idea. Carlos was my snitch, and he never said a word."

"Where's Carlos now?" asked Reid.

"No idea. Fled the state. Given what you've told me, it was probably for the best."

Reid agreed.

"This is a lot to take in," Pérez continued. "You said you spoke to his handler. What's the plan of action?"

"The DEA is going to raid the Ritz-Carlton when Lopez and his generals are convened. Torres is going to let us know when to move."

"What about us?" asked Ortega, eyes gleaming. This was the culmination of years of investigation for his team as well. "Do we get in on the action?"

"Yep, we're going to be at the hotel as reinforcements, but this is the DEA's operation. They're taking point."

Ortega nodded.

"Not a word to anyone," Reid warned, his gaze on Ortega. "We don't want to arrest Torres and risk blowing the op."

"Don't worry about me," Ortega assured him. "I learned my lesson the first time."

They all had.

"He was the second guy to infiltrate the cartel," Torres's handler, a seasoned agent called Wilson, had told Reid when they'd met earlier that day. "The first lasted a month before they made him. His mutilated body was found hanging from a signpost in Juárez, south of El

Paso. We didn't think Torres stood much of a chance, but he hung in there. The months went by and we heard nothing. It was like he'd dropped off the face of the earth." The DEA agent raised his bushy eyebrows. "We feared the worst, but then one day, out of the blue, he called from Mexico and said he was working for Lopez, readying the product for distribution. We weren't sure what that meant, but we left him in there. No contact. Completely on his own. Couldn't risk telling the Federales about him, since most of them are in the cartel's pocket."

It must be damn hard being out there all on your own, Reid reflected, after putting down the phone. In an odd twist, he was suddenly respecting the man he'd hated for so long. Deep in the enemy camp, trusting no one.

Then Bianca had come along. She'd picked the undercover agent up in a bar, and they'd hit it off. Really hit it off. At some point, she'd told him who she was, and he'd let on that he was a Drug Enforcement agent. Or vice versa.

Kindred spirits with a common goal. Both had so much to lose, but they were united in that they wanted to take down the cartel. The op had failed that time, and Bianca had lost her life.

Now it was up to them to make sure it didn't fail again.

The next order of business was to interrogate Dempsey, who'd been in a holding cell all night. Not surprisingly, he wasn't in the best of moods.

"I'll have your badge for this, Garret. You can't arrest me. I was a cop when you were running around in diapers. I haven't done anything wrong."

Reid pulled out a chair and sat down. The interrogation room was hot and stuffy and smelled of sweat and desperation.

"What were you doing at the probation offices?" he asked.

Dempsey glared at him from across the table. "Visiting a friend."

"What is your friend's name?"

"None of your business," he said sullenly.

"Was it Bill Hodge, by any chance?"

All he got was a noncommittal grunt in reply.

"We found his number on your computer."

The old guy's eyes widened, but he went on the defensive. "So what? Can't I visit a friend now?"

"Not when he's the target of an active investigation. A guy who's been a cop since I was running around in diapers ought to know that."

Dempsey sulked, his lower lip protruding like a naughty kid. "Still, it's not a crime."

"I doubt internal affairs will see it that way."

He threw up his hands. "Come on, man. You don't have to involve them. I didn't even speak to Hodge, I swear."

"It's Lieutenant, and I know you didn't speak to him because Officer Hamilton apprehended you before you got the chance."

He leaned forward. "Then why are you holding me?"

"How's obstructing an investigation, for starters? Then there's police corruption, collaborating with an organized crime group, pedophilia..."

"I'm not one of them," he shouted, his hands balling into fists.

"Then why are you protecting them? You'd better make that pretty damn clear because from where I'm sitting, it's not looking good for you, Dempsey."

Sweat patches appeared under his arms.

"I wasn't warning them. I don't give a shit about them."

"Then why were you there?"

"To get back at you," he hissed, his gaze accusatory. "I wanted you to fail, so you'd get transferred out or quit. Either way, it would have been a win."

Reid studied him. Was he so bitter that he'd derail an active investigation just to seek revenge? "Sorry you feel that way."

"Casillas and I go way back," Dempsey explained. "We used to be partners, back in the day. When you got him fired, I decided I'd do whatever I could to make you fail."

Ah, now it made sense.

"Casillas was a lazy, corrupt cop and had no business running a police department."

"We liked things the way they were," grumbled Dempsey.

"Only because it meant you did nothing," Reid retorted. "There are good detectives here, good police officers, and you had them sitting on their asses doing nothing all day except fiddling with paperwork. You ought to be ashamed of yourself. You and Casillas." He shook his head. "You're not worthy of that badge."

He got up to leave.

"Are you going to arrest me?"

"Yeah, damn right I am. I can't have you running back to Hodge and warning him we're on to them. Besides, IA is coming over, and they want to talk to you."

He hung his head. "I'm so screwed."

Reid didn't disagree.

"How are you feeling, boss?" Vargas asked, as he sat down gingerly at his desk.

"Better," he lied.

Vargas grinned. "Good. Uniforms have brought in Rodriguez, the guy who rented the hire car."

"Oh yeah, thanks."

"Shall I put him in the interrogation room?"

"Actually, Vargas, why don't you talk to him?" He couldn't face getting up again just yet and Vargas could use the practice. A good detective, but young, he needed experience.

"Me?" Pointing to himself.

"Yeah, why not? You can handle it. Find out why he hired the car and where he was the night Kenzie was driven off the road."

"Oh, um, okay."

Diaz gave him an encouraging smile. "You got this."

Reid pulled up the video feed on his computer and pulled on his earphones. The IT guy had set it up so that the interrogations could be watched by the detectives, should they choose to do so. Not even Miami PD had that function. They watched from a communal screen outside the interrogation room.

"Let's see how you do," he murmured, as Vargas walked into the room in which he'd just interviewed Dempsey. A few moments later, a police officer showed Rodriguez into the room. Looking scared and confused, his eyes fluttered from the mounted camera to the table to the detective sitting there.

"W—What am I doing here?" he stammered.

"Sit down, sir." Vargas gestured to the empty chair.

It was a good start. He didn't reassure the suspect or come across as disrespectful.

Rodriguez sat down. He was skinny, with greasy black hair and acne scars.

"Please state your name for the recording," Vargas asked.

"Juan Rodriguez."

"Thank you." Vargas glanced down at his notepad. "Mr. Rodriguez, is this your driver's license?" He slid a copy of the document across the table.

The suspect nodded.

"And did you use it to hire a Ford Mondeo on the twenty-fourth of June from a company called Ready Motors?"

Blank eyes stared at him. "Huh?"

Vargas repeated the question.

"I don't know what you mean," Rodriguez said. "I didn't hire no Ford Mondeo."

"Are you sure you didn't hire this car?" Sliding another photograph across.

"No, sir. I sure as hell didn't."

Vargas glanced up at the camera.

"You can do it," Reid murmured. "Think."

Vargas took a moment, then said, "Can you explain why someone with your driver's license hired this car two days ago?" Unfortunately, there was no CCTV camera at the rental company, so there was no image of the man who'd hired the car.

"That's impossible. My license is in my wallet." Reaching into his back pocket, he pulled out a tattered leather billfold. After fiddling through the card holder section, he looked up. "It's gone."

Reid leaned back in his chair.

What do you know?

"You mean your license was stolen?" Vargas asked.

"I—I don't... I mean yeah, it must have been." He was pulling all his cards out and laying them on the table.

Vargas scratched his head. "Where do you think you lost it?"

"I don't know." He looked panic stricken. "I never use it. We don't even have a car. The last one broke down, and I sold it for scrap."

"Did you leave your wallet unattended anywhere recently?" Vargas asked. "Like a bar or a restaurant?"

Reid nodded at the line of questioning. The detective was thinking on his feet.

"No, I would never leave my wallet..." He stopped, his eyes lit up.

"What?" asked Vargas.

"Nah, nothing."

"You thought of something. Where did you go?"

He sighed. "I met this chick in a bar. She was nice, and we got talking." He shrugged. "I suppose it could have been her. But what would she want with my driver's license?"

Good question. The "she" was a surprise, or not. Thinking about it, a woman would be an easy distraction for a guy like Rodriguez.

"Tell me what happened." Vargas said, his pen poised over the notepad. "Did she pick you up?"

"No, we were both at the bar, that's all. I offered to buy her a drink."

Make him think he was the one picking her up.

"And then what?"

"We talked. Her parents live in Nicaragua. That's where I was born."

A good hook, if ever there was one.

"Did you go home with her?"

"No, of course not. I'm married."

Vargas nodded. "So how did she get to your wallet?"

He thought for a moment, then snapped his fingers. I left my jacket on the back of the chair when I went to the restroom. Just for a minute, but...

Vargas scribbled on the pad.

That would be it. That was the opportunity she'd been waiting for, whoever she was.

"You didn't notice it was missing?"

"No, I told you, I don't use it for nothing."

Vargas asked him to describe the woman. Pretty, dark haired, good body.

Reid sighed. That described half the women in Miami.

A thought struck him, and he pulled off his earphones. Maybe, just maybe, they could identify her.

He called Kenzie. "Hey, do you know of a dark-haired woman who works for either Hodge or the governor? Pretty, good body."

Kenzie didn't hesitate. "It could be his personal assistant, Carol Porter. She met me at the Governor's Mansion."

"Carol Porter, right. Thanks."

"What's this about?" she asked.

"I'll tell you later. Gotta go, thanks, Kenz."

Hanging up, he searched for: "Carol Porter Governor Talbot". Several images popped up. Selecting the best one, he asked Diaz to take it to show Rodriguez.

The man nodded enthusiastically. "Yeah, that's her! How did you know?"

Vargas looked up at the camera and nodded.

"Gotcha," murmured Reid.

28

"Kenzie, a word, please?"

Kenzie got up from her desk and went into Keith's office, her editor. A sharp-eyed man with a nose for a story, he managed the content that appeared in the Miami Herald.

"How's the head?"

"Fine." The lump was almost gone now. Only a slightly raised area, rather than an actual plum like it had been.

She hadn't told him the full story, just she'd had a wreck and hit her head on the steering wheel. Nothing serious.

"I know you asked for a few days," he said. "But we need a follow up on the kid who was stabbed on his way home from school. Any news?"

"This has the potential to be huge," Kenzie told him. "I can't say much right now, but the coke that was found on the boy wasn't his. It was planted on him to make it look like a drug killing."

Keith studied her, his brows meeting in the middle, journalistic senses tingling. "You know this for sure?"

"Yep, and I know who. I also know why. I just can't prove it."

Yet.

"Huge, you say?" Keith knew she didn't hyperbolize lightly.

"Politically," she hinted. "Heads will roll."

"Can you be more specific?" He was leaning across the desk now.

"Unfortunately, no. We've got to be careful with this. I need more evidence." She rubbed her forehead.

Keith clicked. "That's what the accident was about, wasn't it? You didn't get rear-ended."

She studied him, unsure how much to say. Keith wasn't known for his discretion. He was a newsman. Anything newsworthy went in the paper. Still, he was the one who'd taught her to double source her material.

"I was forced off the road, Keith. It wasn't an accident."

"Do you know who it was?"

"The police have traced it back to a political figure who I think is involved in a pedophile ring."

"What?" he stood up. "And you're only telling me this now?"

"It's unconfirmed." She looked up at him. "But I'm getting close. Why else would he try to have me silenced?"

Killed.

An image of Matteo Davis flashed through her head. A drug-related incident.

Kenzie Gilmore. A car accident.

It was raining, she lost control of the vehicle and hit a pole. She could see the headline: REPORTER DIES IN CAUSEWAY CRASH.

"You're not in danger, are you, Kenzie? I don't want a repeat of the Ingleman debacle."

Would they try again? Not if they thought she'd backed off.

"I don't know," she admitted. "But I'm being careful."

He sighed. "At least you've got that detective boyfriend to look after you."

She frowned. "He's not my boyfriend."

"Isn't he?" Keith looked down at the documents on his desk. "I thought he was. You need someone like that with the scrapes you get into. Not to mention he's a great contact."

That was true.

"He's a friend," Kenzie insisted, consolidating the thought in her head as she said it. "That's all."

Keith didn't look up. He'd moved on to another story, another headline. "Get me copy as soon as you can, Kenzie. In the meantime, the follow up on the girl in the canal needs filing. Get one of the staff reporters to chase it up with a more general feature on the rise in drug deaths in Miami."

She hesitated. "Actually, I am working on that story as well. There might be a big break in the police investigation soon."

Glancing up, he fixed his gaze on her. "Something else you can't talk about?"

"Sorry," she said. "It might even be related to the other case."

Keith put down his pen. "Now I am intrigued."

"I promise, as soon as I have something definite, I'll let you know."

He arched his eyebrow. "I'm giving you a lot of leeway on this one, Kenzie. Don't let me down."

"I won't." Shooting him a parting smile, she went back to her desk. Both cases were too sensitive to talk about right now. She'd learned her lesson—it was better to wait and get the scoop just before it broke.

Carol Porter, Talbot's secretary, had stolen the license that was used to hire the car that tried to kill her. Reid had called her back and filled her in. She hadn't been the driver. That was a man. Two men, side by side, their outlines blurry in the rain, but she could tell by their stocky build that neither was a woman.

Kenzie tapped her nail on the keyboard. Maybe it's time to have a little chat with Carol Porter. Off the record.

. . .

Carol Porter lived in a quiet neighborhood close to the governor's Miami mansion, where her boss lived. Kenzie had been watching her apartment since eight o'clock. It was a Saturday, so it was unlikely she would be going in to work.

At eight-thirty, Carol appeared in leggings and a loose-fitting T-shirt, along with a pair of running shoes.

Kenzie sighed. She wasn't dressed to follow on foot, and the rental car would look obvious tailing a jogger, so she settled down to wait. Hopefully, Carol wasn't one of those fitness fanatics who ran for hours.

Pulling out her laptop, she did some work on the other articles she had to deliver for the paper. Now that she was the senior investigative reporter, she worked on features, while her team of four staff writers covered the basics, and her research assistant, Raoul, fluttered around digging up information for everybody because she had yet to put him to good use.

Confiding in people was not her strong suit. Keith told her she had trust issues, and maybe he was right. Her ex-colleague, Clayton, had been more of an adversary than a teammate. So much so that he'd blown her cover on their last investigation, which almost had deadly consequences.

It didn't pay to trust anyone. Not in this business.

Except Reid. He was the only person in the world she did trust.

A pang of guilt hit her. She ought to tell him what she was doing, but he'd just warn her off. It was foolish and dangerous; she was putting herself in the line of fire again.

Yes, she knew all that, but this time she had leverage. Carol Porter would not want her boss to know she'd messed up.

Kenzie waited until she saw Carol returning. The governor's assistant had a determined gait and ran with a long-legged stride up the street to her apartment complex.

A shower, a coffee, and then what? Kenzie wanted to catch her off guard, and somewhere where they wouldn't be overheard or spotted on camera.

Half an hour later, Carol emerged wearing shorts and a long, white cotton shirt. Her dark hair was up in a casual chignon, and she wore gold hooped earrings that glinted in the sun.

Kenzie watched as she got into her car.

Here we go.

She followed Carol to a nearby shopping mall. The personal assistant found a parking spot and then took five minutes to get into it. Her efficiency clearly did not run to parking.

Kenzie pulled in nearby and got out of the car. Waiting for her moment.

Carol got out and flung her purse over her shoulder. Kenzie moved in.

"Hi," she said.

"Oh, you startled me!" Carol exclaimed, then her eyes widened as she recognized Kenzie.

"Yes, it's me." Kenzie smiled. "I think we need to have a chat."

"I'm sorry, I really don't have the time."

"Yes," Kenzie said, her voice like steel. "You do."

She'd blocked Carol in, so there was no escape. "Why did you try to run me off the road?"

"I–I have no idea what you're talking about."

"Juan Rodriguez remembered you. You chatted him up in a bar, stole his driver's license – which is an offense, by the way–and hired the car that side-swiped me."

"What? No!" But the fear in her eyes gave her away.

"Was it on the governor's orders?"

"I'm sorry, I have to go." She tried to push past.

Kenzie blocked her. "You're not going anywhere until I get some answers." Kenzie's voice hardened. "I don't take kindly to attempts being made on my life."

"I don't know what you mean."

"Yes, you do." She held her ground. "Carol, do you know who I am? I work for the Miami Herald. I'm an investigative reporter.

Unless you want to see your name in the paper tomorrow morning, tell me what happened."

The personal assistant hesitated, tense and wide-eyed reminding Kenzie of a horse about to bolt.

"I know it was you. I have proof."

Her shoulders sagged. "I didn't know you were going to get hurt. I was told to hire a car and make sure it didn't trace back to the governor."

Yes! Hallelujah.

Kenzie didn't tell Carol she was recording every second of this conversation. Although not admissible in court, it would verify her source, if it came down to it.

"So you picked Rodriguez up in a bar?"

"I thought that was the easiest way to do it. That guy didn't even have a car. I didn't think he'd miss his license."

"He didn't. It was only when we asked him why he'd hired a vehicle that he realized he'd lost it. That was a clever ploy on your part."

"How did you know it was him?" she asked.

"We had a partial plate."

Carol bit her lip.

"Who was driving?" Kenzie asked.

"I honestly don't know." She spread her hands. "I just booked the car, I didn't pick it up. I swear."

"Whoever picked it up had the license."

"I left it at reception in an unaddressed envelope as instructed."

"Your boss give you those instructions?"

Carol sniffed and gave a tearful nod.

Kenzie needed to be clear about this. "Governor Talbot?"

"Yes." It was a whisper, but it was enough.

Kenzie stepped back, easing the tension. "Okay, Carol. You can go. Thanks for talking to me." Not that she'd given her much of a chance.

"Will you tell the police?" whispered Carol. "I don't want to be arrested."

Kenzie pretended to think about it. "Not if you don't tell the governor you spoke to me."

She shook her head. "I won't."

"Okay." Kenzie smiled. "Then we have a deal. I protect my sources. You don't need to worry."

Carol sighed in relief. All her urgency gone, she was defeated.

Kenzie went back to her car.

As she drove away, she saw Carol standing in the same position, still staring after her.

29

THE RITZ-CARLTON WAS a plush hotel in South Beach. The reception area was modern, with a funky back-lit wall and a gleaming black terrazzo floor. A classic cocktail lounge led off from the lobby, which made it difficult to keep tabs on the guests checking in as people kept wandering in and out.

Reid would have thought a congregation of cartel members might have chosen somewhere a little more inconspicuous, however, it seemed they enjoyed luxury as much as the next person.

One of the advantages of the hotel was that it offered a choice of two and three-room suites large enough for a small conference. They'd been reserved under a false name, of course, and paid for in advance, in cash.

The hotel was only too happy to accommodate—they'd had such requests before, this was Miami, after all—until they were informed the DEA would be holed up in a nearby suite and would possibly be raiding the rooms at some point in the next forty-eight hours.

"We suggest you keep the guests away from the seventh and eighth floors," Agent Wilson told the hotel security, who were both bewildered and intimidated in equal measure.

The hotel was cooperating fully, despite the inconvenience. The last thing they needed was collateral damage, especially since the hotel had spent a fortune promoting its shiny new image after the renovations due to Hurricane Irma.

Reid and Kenzie were allowed to tag along, mostly because they were the only people to have had any contact with Torres in the last few months, and it was possible the undercover agent would call one of them with the intel. Ortega, Vargas, and Diaz hovered at the back.

Kenzie was working on her laptop, both her phones visible on the table. "That one's my everyday phone," she explained to the agents, "and the other is my burner, the one I use for my alias and the number I gave Torres."

Reid raised an eyebrow. He should have guessed she'd use a separate phone for her sources. Untraceable and completely off the record.

"They'll be arriving soon," Reid told her. "One of the agents at the reception desk will let us know when they check in."

"I hope this goes according to plan," she murmured for the umpteenth time that day.

"I'm sure it will." He wished he felt as confident as he sounded. After the last cock-up, they couldn't afford to let Lopez get away again.

The sun rose higher in the Miami-blue sky, the air conditioner droned quietly, and the agents in the room discussed contingency plans in low voices. Eventually, after what seemed like an eternity, Agent Wilson's walkie-talkie crackled, making everyone jump.

"The party has checked in. I repeat: The party has checked in."

"Roger that," barked Wilson, nodding to his team. The waiting uniformed agents began checking their equipment and readying their weapons. There was a lot of clicking and murmuring as rifles were loaded and communications tested. Reid felt the familiar buzz of adrenaline.

This was it.

Until this point, he hadn't been sure if the cartel boss was going to show up. It wasn't unusual for them to have a last-minute change of venue. A criminal's paranoia.

Thankfully, nothing like that had happened, and Lopez was in the building. According to the agent at reception, Torres had checked everybody in.

"They won't arrive together," Reid told Kenzie. "It's too noticeable. They'll walk in alone and at different times so as not to draw attention to themselves. Lopez may not even enter through the main reception. He'll be secreted in through a side entrance or something."

Wilson nodded in agreement. "We have men covering all possible entrances, but Lopez will be in disguise. We'll have to wait for the final confirmation from Torres that he's here."

It came an hour later. A text message sent to Kenzie's burner phone.

The wolf is in his lair. Room 712.

As soon as she'd shown him, Reid passed it on to Agent Wilson, who briefed his team. Another buzz of activity as they went over their action plan for the raid.

"What about us?" Diaz asked, fidgeting with her pen. "What do we do?"

"We're here as a courtesy," Reid told them. "We'll only be needed if it all goes to shit."

Ortega ground his jaw. "Let's hope that doesn't happen."

"When do you think they'll meet?" Vargas asked, his eyes wide.

"No idea. Could be tonight, could be tomorrow. We'll have to wait for word from Torres."

The sooner the better in Reid's opinion. Tensions were high. A lot was riding on getting this right, not to mention the years of undercover work and investigation by the DEA as well as the Miami Police Department. It was what Bianca had given her life for.

Wilson was admirably calm. He paced a little, talked to his team in a hushed tone, but mostly stood with his back to the window, a composed but determined expression on his face.

Time wore on.

Nobody left the suite, and nobody came in. Other than the hotel manager and his head security officer, nobody knew they were there.

Reid glanced at his watch. Eight o'clock. "Any sign of activity from suite 712?" he asked Wilson.

"Nothing yet," came the gruff reply.

Nine o'clock.

Kenzie's burner beeped. Everyone turned to her.

With shaking hands, she picked it up.

It was from Torres.

"They're meeting in room 710," she whispered, her cheeks flushed. "Ten o'clock."

Wilson grabbed her phone and double checked the details himself.

"We're on," he barked.

His team sprang into action. They'd spent hours going over their plan of attack. Everybody knew where they needed to be and in what order.

Agents would be dispatched to the front and back entrance of the building in case anyone made a run for it. There were operatives in the underground parking lot and outside in the hotel grounds.

The assault team lined up inside the door, purposeful and professional.

Kenzie typed furiously on her laptop, capturing the moment for her article. She had an exclusive, on condition that the op was a success. Nobody wanted to consider the consequences if it wasn't.

At quarter to ten, Wilson's walkie-talkie crackled. The agent in the security room told them that seven men had entered room 710. The men were wearing hats or baseball caps, so it was hard to identify them on the security cameras, but they assumed Lopez was with them since the meeting was taking place on schedule and all the guests were accounted for.

At five to ten, Agent Wilson gave the command.

Reid exhaled.

Time for action.

30

Kenzie's phone buzzed just as the assault team was leaving the room. She gulped. "It's another message from Torres."

Annoyed, Wilson held up a hand. The assault team halted in their tracks.

"What is it?" he asked her.

Silently, she handed the phone to Reid.

"Damn it," he muttered under his breath.

"What does it say, detective?" snapped Wilson. The team was in the corridor, exposed.

"Lopez isn't there. It's a false alarm. The meeting has been postponed till tomorrow morning at eleven hundred hours."

Wilson scowled. "What the hell is going on?"

"According to Torres, this is a preliminary meeting. Everyone is there except Lopez."

"You mean they're having a meeting about tomorrow's meeting?"

Reid shrugged.

"For fuck's sake," growled Wilson.

"We could still go in," Ortega suggested. "We'd get the cartel's top management."

"But not Lopez," pointed out Kenzie.

Wilson made a snap decision. "We haven't come this far to rush it and lose Lopez again." He turned to his men. "Stand down."

The assault team filed back into the suite, their expressions neutral. They were used to this. Delays, false starts, aborting the op. All part of the job. Kenzie watched as they safed their weapons and relaxed. For now.

Suddenly, her other phone rang. The caller ID was blank. "It's diverting from my work phone," she whispered.

Everyone stared at it like it was a ticking bomb.

Kenzie glanced at Wilson, who nodded. "Answer it."

"Hello?"

"Kenzie, it's me."

It's Torres, she mouthed to the room. His voice was strangely normal, upbeat even. The suave charmer she'd met in the club, not the secretive undercover agent. "I have a proposition for you, if you're interested." The call was on speaker so everyone in the room could hear.

"I'm listening."

"Lopez... Well, he's expressed a desire to have a reporter write an article about him, about his background, his humble beginnings, his rise to the head of the cartel. He wants to do it while he's in Miami and asked if I knew anyone. I thought of you."

"No way in hell," growled Reid.

Wilson held up a hand.

Kenzie didn't know what to say. She was mouthing like a guppy.

"If you're up for it, you're to come to room 710 as soon as possible. You'll be granted one interview. The article must be written by tomorrow morning, at which point you'll be asked to leave. That's it."

"Um..." Kenzie glanced at Reid, who was glaring at her like this was her fault. Wilson was thinking hard.

"C—Can you give me a minute?"

"Sure. Call me back on this number."

The line went dead.

Kenzie exhaled shakily. An article on Federico Lopez, the biggest drug dealer since El Chapo, and just as notorious. Her heart was racing. This would be the scoop of the year, if not the decade—and just before the DEA arrested him and brought down the Morales cartel.

This was huge.

"Don't even think about it," Reid warned.

She jumped up. "How can you say that? This is the opportunity of a lifetime."

"I'm not letting you anywhere near Lopez and his goons," Reid replied, towering over her. If he was trying to intimidate her, he wasn't going to succeed.

"I think that's my decision, don't you?"

"Actually, it's my decision," cut in Agent Wilson. "This is my op, and I'll decide what happens."

Both turned to face him.

"There's no way I'm not doing this," Kenzie argued, at the same time as Reid blurted out, "She can't do it. It's too dangerous."

Wilson held up a hand. "Enough, both of you."

They fell silent.

He studied Kenzie. "Would you be prepared to wear a wire?"

"Jesus Christ." Reid raked a hand through his hair. "We are not sending her into the lion's den. She's a civilian with no training. This guy is a cold-blooded killer."

Kenzie nodded. "Yes, as long as it's well hidden."

"It's too risky," Reid snapped.

"We'll make sure it's concealed," Wilson promised her.

"She's not doing it," reiterated Reid.

"I'm in," said Kenzie.

Reid threw his hands up and stalked over to the other side of the room. Kenzie gazed at Wilson, her pulse racing. "What do I have to do?"

"They won't be expecting you to be wired up," he said, "which makes you the perfect candidate to go in there. You're a run-of-the-mill reporter, and he'll check you for a tape recorder, probably confiscate your mobile phone for the duration, but he won't suspect you to be wired up."

Kenzie swallowed nervously. "Won't they pat me down?"

"Technology's changed a lot since those days." He pursed his lips. "I'll give you a tiny mic to wear. Nobody will know it's there."

She took a deep breath. "I'd better call Torres back."

Wilson nodded.

It rang four times before he answered. "Kenzie?"

"I'll do it."

There was a pause. "Okay, we're at the Ritz-Carlton in South Beach. Let me know when you've arrived, and someone will meet you at reception."

There was someone listening. He had to make it look like he was delivering this information for the first time.

"I understand."

Kenzie hung up, her heart hammering. Holy crap, she was actually going to interview The Wolf. Keith would be beside himself when he found out.

"Can I call my editor?" she asked.

"No!" came several voices at the same time.

She held up her hands. "Okay, sorry."

Agent Wilson took her aside and went through the preliminaries. Don't be over eager. Let him lead the conversation. Do exactly what he says. Don't put yourself in danger.

Got it.

They attached the wire, which was in the form of a hair clip. "It's got a tiny transmitter in it," Wilson said. "It'll relay the conversation to our tech guy who'll pick up every word, so you don't have to do a thing."

A hair clip was inconspicuous enough. Reid was watching from the other side of the room as if too furious to come near her. Probably just as well. She didn't want him yelling at her again.

She knew this was dangerous. There was a risk, but it was her career. It was what she did—and they were offering her the biggest story of her life on a plate. How could she refuse? Besides, the hotel was literally surrounded by DEA agents. At the end of this, Lopez and his crime syndicate would be in custody, or dead. Shivering, she didn't want to think about that.

The story.

That's what she'd concentrate on.

"Ready?" asked Wilson. The assault team had left the premises but were on standby in case of an emergency. They'd return early tomorrow morning in plenty of time to prep for the eleven o'clock meeting.

She took a deep breath. "Yeah."

"Right. Sammy will take you downstairs in the service elevator. You'll go outside through the kitchen entrance and walk around to the front. Go into the lobby and call Torres."

It all went as planned. They managed to get outside without being seen, and a moment later, she was walking into the hotel lobby as if she'd just arrived.

Standing in the middle, she texted Torres.

I'm here.

Instead of a reply, an enormous Mexican with a tattoo running up his neck and a bulge under his jacket appeared. "Kenzie Gilmore?"

She gulped. This guy looked like he could snap her neck with one twist of his massive hands. Was he Lopez's bodyguard?

He glanced at the laptop bag in her hand. "Is that yours?"

"Yes."

"You won't be needing it." He took it from her.

"But... the article?"

"You will be provided with a laptop. Give me your phone, too."

She handed it over.

The Mexican gave a satisfied grunt and said, "Follow me."

She didn't question him, just followed him into the elevator. Inside, he turned to her, making her heart skip a beat. She backed into the corner.

"You understand I've got to search you."

Kenzie exhaled and lifted her arms. He patted her down without being offensive. He might look like a thug, but he was completely professional.

Satisfied, he gave a curt nod. "Okay."

Kenzie breathed a sigh of relief. The elevator doors opened, and they stepped out into a plush corridor.

"Come with me."

She followed him down the hallway to room 710.

Kenzie took a few steadying breaths. She was about to meet the infamous Federico Lopez. In the flesh. Her heart was hammering so hard she felt like it would leap out of her chest.

The bodyguard glanced at her. "Ready?"

She bit her lip. "Is he in there?"

A strange pause, then he said, "Yes."

He opened the door, and Kenzie walked in.

In the middle of the room stood a woman. Petite, with glossy black hair, a haughty expression, and a glint in her eye.

Kenzie halted. "Oh, sorry. I was expecting Lopez?"

The woman's red lips parted in a smile.

"I am Lopez."

31

"WHAT?" spluttered Reid in the DEA suite.

Wilson frowned. "What's he think he's doing?"

They listened hard, crowding around the receiver. "My husband died two years ago," the woman said in a smooth, accented voice. "I've been running the Morales cartel ever since."

"Holy shit," breathed Reid.

"Fucking hell." Ortega jumped out of his seat. "All this time we've been searching for Lopez, and we nailed him at the raid."

Both Vargas and Diaz were rendered speechless. The color drained from Wilson's face, and he sank into a chair.

"You have?" Kenzie's voice. Hesitant, uncertain. Reid could picture her expression as she tried to keep it together. To adapt to the new information.

"Of course. Who else was going to do it? My son, Dominique, was too young. My husband had no brothers, nobody he trusted. Only me." She spread her arms. "So here I am."

"But everyone thinks you're him."

Laughter filled the room.

"That was the idea. Until now. If my competitors knew I was a woman, they might have decided I was weak, and attempted a takeover." She shook her head. "Well, I am here to prove them wrong. I want you to write an article 'outing' me as the head of the biggest cartel in Mexico. The world must know that Federico Lopez is dead, and Maria Lopez is in charge now."

There was a pause.

Kenzie's voice. "Yes, of course. If that's what you want."

"It is what I want."

There was a rustle as Maria Lopez walked around the room. "Torres speaks highly of you."

Kenzie's voice was steady. She'd recovered from the surprise, confident now in her role. "He's too kind. I work at the Miami Herald, that's all. Just a reporter on the crime beat." She was playing herself, the intrepid reporter eager for a story.

"Yes, I know. I had you checked out."

Reid gulped. Would she discover their connection?

"But..." continued Lopez. "More importantly, you are a successful woman. You know how hard it is to excel in a man's world."

Reid sensed Kenzie's smile. "Yes, I do."

"Please." Lopez's tone changed. More congenial now, like a friend who'd invited you to dinner. "Take a seat, and we will begin. I will tell you my story, and you will write the article. When you are finished, I want to read it. That is the deal. It doesn't get published until I'm happy with it. Did Torres explain that to you?"

"He did," Kenzie acknowledged.

It was how these things worked. A scoop, but only once it had been approved by the source. Still, it would be gold dust in the publishing industry. Reid understood why Kenzie didn't want to pass on it. He couldn't blame her, not really. It was just... He swallowed over the lump in his throat. What would he do if he lost her?

Shit.

No, that wasn't going to happen. Kenzie might be in the enemy camp—but he would make damn sure he got her out. Failure, this time, was not an option.

Reid, Vargas, Diaz, Ortega and the DEA agents listened with rapt attention as Maria Lopez told her story.

Growing up in a mountain village in Sinaloa, Mexico, she'd seen her brothers do back-breaking work in the marijuana and poppy fields, and knew if she wanted to get rich, she'd have to be involved in the drug trade.

She met Federico in her twenties. He was tough, charismatic, and smart. At that stage, he was working for the Sinaloa cartel, rising through the ranks. She was young, beautiful, and motivated. They made a formidable couple.

After a falling out, Federico left to start his own cartel. He gained a somewhat mythical status by providing essential services to the remote communities in the Sinaloa mountains, funding everything from basic necessities like food and medical supplies to infrastructure like roads and dams. A cold pragmatist, she'd seen her husband shoot a man in the head for messing up a shipment.

Maria stood by his side the whole time. She understood that this was how you made money in their country, and how you gave back.

Unlike many of his compatriots who turned to kidnapping and murder, Federico was a businessman, first and foremost.

"He only resorted to violence when it benefited his business interests or posed a threat to his family," Maria explained.

A natural strategist, he built the Morales cartel up to be dominant in the region. At last count, they were responsible for shipping more than a quarter of all cocaine, heroin, methamphetamine, and marijuana into the United States.

There was pride in Maria's voice. She'd helped her husband build an empire, then taken it over when he'd died.

"I continued his legacy," she said. "Then I expanded it. We now distribute to Central and South America as well as the United States. Places like Colombia and Brazil are usually thought of as producers, but that's all changing. It is a huge emerging market." She was on a roll now, her voice strong and confident. With a firm grasp on her late husband's business, she was taking it further than Federico would ever have considered.

"We're branching into synthetic drugs—ecstasy, MDMA, acid—controlling the manufacturing and the distribution. We've taken over local distribution networks, incorporated them into the family, so to speak. Now they work for us."

Reid was sure the smaller distributors hadn't been given much of a choice.

"That's impressive." Kenzie again. There was a note of admiration there, maybe even awe. The thing with Kenzie was that she was so good at playing a part, he never knew if it was an act or not. Probably a bit of both. What Maria had done was clever, ambitious, and calculated.

Even more so because nobody knew it was her.

"Why have you decided to come clean now?" Kenzie asked.

Agent Wilson's jaw tightened. "I told her to let Lopez lead the conversation," he muttered.

"She knows what she's doing." Reid found himself defending her.

Kenzie was a seasoned reporter who knew how to extract information from sources, information people wanted to read about. The human interest.

"It's time." Maria didn't seem to mind the interjection. "I'm proud of what I've done. I've proved I can lead the cartel. Two years of meteoric growth and business has never been better. The world should know who's in charge."

"What about your competitors?" Kenzie asked. "Are you afraid of challenges to your leadership because you are a woman?"

A pause. Reid held his breath. Vargas shot him a worried look.

"No," she said stiffly. "That is why I need this article written. Everyone must know that we will not be threatened. That we are here to stay."

He heard scribbling. Kenzie was making notes on a piece of paper.

"We lead by example," Maria continued. "We do a lot of good things for the community and it ensures we have support in our local region. Can other cartels say the same?"

"Sort of like Robin Hood," Kenzie murmured.

Maria clapped her hands. "Exactly...No, I am not afraid."

"She's worse than her husband." Agent Wilson turned away from the receiver in disgust. "We have to take her down."

Reid pursed his lips. "She's smart, so we have to do this right. We can't afford another screw-up."

"You think I don't know that?" Wilson snarled. "Two years ago was not our fault. The leak came from your side."

Ortega walked over to the window, saying nothing. Reid wasn't about to shame him in front of the DEA agents. They'd put that behind them.

"I'm not disputing that," he acknowledged. The joint op had been a disaster. "But I've got a civilian in there, and we have to make sure she comes out of this alive."

"We'll do our best," Wilson grunted.

"That's all I ask." Reid sank into an armchair. Kenzie had moved on to Federico and was inquiring how he'd died. The room quietened down.

"He knew something was up. He told me that morning he suspected he was being watched. When the police raided the bar in Little Havana, my husband escaped out the back, but not before he was shot by a DEA agent." She hissed the words, still bitter. "His bodyguard got him to the car, and they drove straight to a private airport where a friend had a plane waiting. The goal was to get him to a hospital in Mexico, but he died during the flight."

"He never made it back to Mexico," muttered Reid.

"That's why they could keep it quiet," Wilson added. "There weren't many people who knew he'd died."

Only the pilot and whoever was on board with him. Reid bet they were no longer alive to tell the story.

"I was informed as soon as they landed," Maria confessed. "I was devastated. But I decided that his legacy must continue, and I would be the one to do it."

"That was courageous of you," Kenzie remarked.

"My husband included me in his decision making. He often bounced ideas off me. I knew the business, although there was an adjustment period. With Nacho's help, I learned all I could. Nobody but the three of us knew my husband had died."

"I knew that big fucker was calling the shots," Reid murmured.

"How did you issue orders?" Kenzie inquired.

"Through my deputies. Obviously, we had to tell them what had happened. They are intensely loyal."

The secret was incredibly well kept. Nobody had an inkling that Lopez wasn't still alive and ruling the cartel with an iron fist.

"When I spoke to anybody else, I used voice altering software to make myself sound like my husband. It wasn't hard." She smirked. "People believe what they want to believe."

Reid knew that to be true. They'd all been fooled, including Torres.

Kenzie and Maria Lopez talked for two hours. Reid had to admire Kenzie's tenacity. Asking pertinent questions, she gave them all a glimpse behind the woman in charge of the Morales cartel. Even Wilson was impressed.

"You have until eleven o'clock tomorrow morning," Maria told Kenzie, as the interview ended. "Nacho will show you to your room. A meal will be brought to you, and you won't be allowed to leave until the article is complete. Do you understand?"

"Yes, ma'am."

"Good. I will see you tomorrow, Miss Gilmore."

There was the sound of a door opening and closing. Kenzie had left the room.

Footsteps, muffled in the corridor. The ping of an elevator. Wilson spoke into his walkie-talkie. "Do you have eyes on them?"

The security team was watching all the floors on CCTV from the control room.

"Eighth floor, sir. I can't see which room."

Reid exhaled. She'd be safe for a while. An armed guard was at her door so there was no way he could get to her, but her microphone was still transmitting, and would do so for at least forty-eight hours.

Another door closing... A rustling sound as Kenzie moved around the room... Running water... Then Kenzie's voice whispering through the microphone.

"Reid? Are you there? Did you get all that?"

32

THERE WAS NO RESPONSE. Of course not. The transmitter was one way only. Reid and the DEA agents could hear her, but she couldn't hear them.

Kenzie turned off the water and left the bathroom. She was pretty sure they'd bugged her hotel room. A journalist, writing a story on a major cartel boss. They couldn't trust her even if they wanted to. Hence the running water. It would drown out her voice.

She thought about searching the room, however, if they'd installed a camera, they'd know she was looking. That would be suspicious.

Act normally. Be the professional she was and write the article as Maria had specified.

Alone in the hotel room, Kenzie sank down on the bed. Her legs were shaking. That interview had been intense. Maria Lopez was a formidable woman, despite her diminutive size. She was striking rather than beautiful, in her mid-fifties, with hard eyes that gleamed with purpose.

CEO of one of the largest crime syndicates in Mexico. And all in secret. Until now.

She shivered.

This was going to be bigger than she'd originally anticipated. With Federico Lopez out of the picture and his wife holding the reins, it would be a human-interest story like none other.

Time to get started.

Kenzie studied the suite they had put her in. On the desk was an open laptop, just like Nacho had promised. She walked over and turned it on. The battery was fully charged, the cable plugged into the socket.

There was tea and coffee, as well as a mini fridge stocked with tiny bottles of alcohol should she need some liquid stimulation. Unlikely.

She had plenty to work with. Maria's story was inspirational enough.

Kenzie made herself a coffee and sat down to work. It was going to be a long night.

The final line of her article was written at four a.m. She'd barely paused, only to eat the sandwich they'd provided and to use the bathroom. Her eyes felt grainy, and her mouth was dry.

She glugged down some bottled water, then lay down on the bed to get a few hours of sleep before tomorrow. The big day.

Maria Lopez's reign would be short-lived. It was almost a shame after she'd worked so hard to build up the cartel. If it was any other business, Kenzie would admire her, but she couldn't dredge up much sympathy for a ruthless cartel boss.

She thought of the teenagers Reid had pulled out of the canal. Bianca. There was a lot of blood on her hands.

You have until eleven tomorrow morning.

Eleven.

That was when it would all kick off. The assault team, lethal in their body armor and automatic weapons. Would they arrest her too? They'd have to, to keep up appearances. Would Reid be there?

The op was fraught with danger. Was she a fool agreeing to do this?

Then she thought about what she'd written and smiled. No way. Maria wanted the world to know who was in charge, and they would. The woman. The wife. The cartel boss.

At ten-thirty, there was a knock on her door. It seemed to hang in the air.

Kenzie sucked in a breath.

It was time.

Nacho stood there, same clothes as the day before, same dark eyes watching her. "Finished?"

"Yes."

A nod. That's all. Then he turned and walked down the corridor.

Kenzie followed, resisting the temptation to look up at the camera. She knew the DEA agents would be watching, recording, monitoring her every move. She'd worn the clip all night, too afraid to touch it. It helped knowing they were there. Her invisible army.

They took the stairs. Down one level. Along the corridor to room 710. The Wolf's lair.

Nacho opened the door and stood back so she could enter. At first glance it was empty, except for the security guy with the big ass rifle in the corner. He was hard to miss.

"This way," Nacho said.

Through a connecting door, into another room. Bigger this time. The sun slotted in through half-open blinds like lasers on a boardroom table with twelve chairs around it.

Maria Lopez sat at the head, resplendent in a white power suit, her glossy black hair up in a bun, long red nails tapping on a mobile device.

Kenzie waited, clutching the flash drive.

Maria put the phone on the table and looked up. "Ah, Kenzie. You're finished?"

"Yes, ma'am."

Kenzie placed the flash drive on the table.

"Sit down." She patted the seat next to her. Kenzie did as she was told.

A laptop appeared and Maria connected the flash drive. The document opened and the cartel boss began to read. Her eyes flitted across the page, pausing over certain words.

Kenzie held her breath. Would she like it? Or hate it?

It was good, she knew that much. But did it do what Maria wanted? Did it tell the world she was now in charge, that she was here to stay?

For at least another thirty minutes.

Maria came to the end of the article, and her red lips turned up in a smile.

Kenzie felt her legs go weak.

Thank God.

"You're very good." Maria looked up.

"Thank you."

A firm nod. "I approve. You can go now."

Great!

She got up to leave just as the door burst open and a man ran in. Alarm bells went off in Kenzie's head.

"What?" Maria got to her feet.

He glanced at Kenzie, then whispered something to his boss.

Maria's face tightened. Her lips thinned into a straight red line. The dark eyes turned stormy.

Uh-oh.

Kenzie began backing away. She'd been made.

Was Reid listening?

"Is something wrong?" She heard the tremor in her own voice.

"A disappointment, that's all. Why don't you take a seat? I'd like you to stay for the meeting. It will make an interesting follow-up."

She smiled, and Kenzie got the feeling she was being sized up as prey. She sat down in a vacant armchair by the window. Nacho positioned himself beside her. He didn't meet her eye.

"Tell them to come in," Maria demanded.

She stood up as a group of men filed in. The team in Miami. Her distribution network. Kenzie saw their eyes widen as they saw Maria. A few nodded in greeting.

"Take a seat," Maria said.

One by one, the men sat. Torres, who came in last, was the only person not surprised to see a woman standing at the head.

A door behind them opened and two other men emerged and stood on either side of her. Her deputies. The only men who had known Federico Lopez had died on that plane. Grim-faced and loyal, each with a handgun tucked into the back of their pants. Kenzie could tell by the way their jackets fell.

Her mouth went dry. There was no shortage of hardware in this conference room. When the assault team arrived, bullets would fly.

The meeting commenced.

"I know you must be surprised to see me standing before you," Maria began. "I am here to tell you my husband is dead."

Shocked murmurs rippled around the table.

Maria didn't flinch.

"He died two years ago. For the last twenty-four months, you have been working for me."

Their eyes grew wide, mouths dropped open.

Maria seemed to be enjoying the moment.

"The cartel has gone from strength to strength under my leadership, and I see no reason why this should change. Do you?"

Her eyes roamed over their faces, challenging them to contradict her.

No one did.

Kenzie had to admit, she had a way with words. A natural ability to be both friendly and intimidating at the same time.

"If you have a problem with this, you may come and speak to me afterwards."

That was a veiled threat if Kenzie had ever heard one.

"Now onto cartel business. It has been a long time since we've all been together. Thank you for your hard work and dedication to our business. You are all valued employees." She paused, and her bosom rose as she inhaled. "It has come to my attention, however, that there is a traitor among us."

No!

Kenzie's gaze flew to Torres, who sat straight-backed and expressionless in his chair. She had to give him credit, he had balls of steel.

The men were casting furtive glances around the table. Torres kept his eyes on Maria.

"A DEA agent, in our midst. Can you imagine?"

Kenzie's heart sank. They knew it was him.

Reid, where are you?

Maria reached under the table and withdrew a pistol. It must have been taped there, out of sight. Before anyone had time to react, she'd aimed it at Torres and pulled the trigger.

Kenzie screamed.

Torres flew backwards, his chair crashing to the floor. The gun hadn't made more than a loud pop, and she realized it had a silencer on it.

Kenzie tried to move towards him, but Nacho held her back. "Let go of me!" she yelled.

"Ah, so you knew about this too, did you?" Maria turned her gaze —and the gun—on Kenzie.

"He's my friend," she hissed, staring at the blood drenching the front of his shirt.

"Did you know he was an agent?"

"No!"

Why wasn't the assault team here? What had happened?

"I don't believe you." She turned to her men. "This venue is now compromised. Leave quickly, disperse, and stay alert. We will reconvene in a day or two. Go now."

They scrambled to their feet, making for the door.

Kenzie grabbed the clip out of her hair and yelled into it. "Now, come now!"

Nacho snatched it from her and crushed it underfoot, just as the door burst open.

Finally.

"Torres, he's been shot!" she yelled as gunfire erupted.

Nacho dragged her into the next room and out onto the balcony. For a moment, she thought he was going to throw her off.

"No, please!" she begged. Then she saw the rope ladder. She stared in amazement as Maria kicked off her shoes, climbed over, and disappeared beneath the edge.

They were seven floors up!

"Your turn," ordered Nacho, lifting her over. If she hadn't gripped the rope, she would have fallen to her death.

"Oh, God," she whispered, as she climbed over, praying she wouldn't slip. Wind whistled around the building, lifting her hair off her neck.

Strong hands grabbed her waist and hauled her onto the balcony below. She nearly collapsed with relief.

Shots echoed from above. Deafeningly loud. No silencers now. No half measures.

The image of Torres lying on the floor bleeding out flashed through her mind, and she stifled a sob. He'd given so much to catch Lopez. Now it seemed it might be in vain.

She was ushered into the hotel suite, through an adjoining room, and out into an empty hallway. They took the stairs down another couple of floors, then the service elevator. It came out in an underground parking lot. Waiting at the door was a white van. It had Milo's Catering stenciled on the side.

Nacho pushed her inside, then a barefoot Maria climbed in after her, the white suit barely rumpled. He handed her a gun, which she immediately trained on Kenzie.

Like she was going to go anywhere?

Maria looked remarkably calm, considering what had happened. The van door slid shut.

Kenzie could still hear the gunfire in her head.

She closed her eyes and saw blood soaking Torres's shirt.

The engine started, tires screeched, and they were off. Lopez had gotten away. Again.

33

REID CHARGED into the hotel suite behind the assault team. "Where is she?"

He couldn't see Kenzie or Maria Lopez.

Shit!

Bodies littered the floor. He scanned them, his heart in his throat. Three men he didn't recognize, two members of the assault team, one holding his leg, the other his arm, then...

Torres!

He rushed over. Shit, there was blood everywhere. Ripping open his shirt, he saw the hole in his chest. It was still leaking blood, lots of it.

Reid pressed down on the wound.

The undercover agent let out a garbled moan. He was alive.

"We need an ambulance!" Reid yelled without thinking.

Wilson stared at him. "You think?" Then he spoke into his walkie-talkie. "All clear. Send 'em in."

Paramedics burst through the door.

"Over here," yelled Reid.

"Get that door open!" yelled Agent Wilson.

His men used a battering ram to send it flying off its hinges. More gunfire erupted. Reid ducked down beside Torres. The paramedics backed out of the room.

Torres didn't have long.

"Where's Kenzie?" Reid asked.

Torres just shook his head.

Wilson and the remaining agents managed to subdue the shooters, and a moment later, came out holding two men in cuffs. One was limping.

Torres groaned.

"Sorry, buddy." Reid kept his hand on the wound. If he didn't, Torres was going to bleed out.

He yelled at Wilson. "Anything?"

"Lopez is gone," Wilson replied.

Reid hadn't been talking about the cartel boss. Suddenly he didn't give a shit what happened to Lopez, he was only concerned with finding Kenzie.

"Is Kenzie there? Is she okay?"

"She's not here." Wilson came back, his face grim. "They got away."

Reid frowned. "How? The corridor was covered."

"Over the balcony."

"What?"

"Down a ladder to the floor below. We've sent men down there, but it's too late. They've gone."

"Jesus." His heart sank.

Maria Lopez had Kenzie and knew she was working with the DEA. Things couldn't get any worse.

"Hang in there," he said to Torres, who's eyes were flickering closed. "You can't die yet. You hear me? This isn't over."

The paramedics returned, more cautiously this time. Reid beckoned them over.

Torres was given oxygen and his wound bound. They treated

him, silent behind their masks. Once he was stable, they took him out on a stretcher.

Reid looked up, feeling like he was on the scene of a Tarantino movie. Glass shards covered the carpet, the armchair had hemorrhaged fluff, the light fixture had shattered on the boardroom table. Three body bags lay on the floor, zipped shut. The carpet was stained red.

It was a bloodbath.

Hazily, he got to his feet, wiping his hands on his shirt. Torres's blood.

"We'll get forensics in here," Wilson sighed.

"Don't bother."

Reid walked into the adjoining room and out onto the balcony. He peered over, it was quite a drop. The ladder was still there, flapping in the wind. Kenzie would have been terrified. He was proud of her for climbing over, for not losing her nerve.

If only they'd gotten there sooner. If only the stupid transmitter hadn't glitched out.

One moment Maria was telling Kenzie she could go, the next Kenzie was screaming.

He did a count of the bodies. Nacho, the tattooed ogre, was missing. Lopez's right-hand man, her enforcer. The one who did the dirty work for her, who'd pulled the trigger and killed Bianca.

He gripped the railing.

Please, not Kenzie too.

Wilson stood in the center of the room, his hands on his hips, but his stance told Reid how devastated he was. "We need to see the CCTV out in the corridor," Reid told him. He had to do something.

Wilson gave a terse nod. "Follow me."

They raced down the stairs to the security room. Inside, the two DEA agents posted there were yelling at hotel security to bring up the right footage. "Floor six, not eight. Jesus Christ."

"Here it is," said Wilson.

They watched as the door to room 609 burst open and the big

Mexican emerged. Glancing left and right, he gestured behind him. Maria Lopez stepped out into the corridor. She was barefoot. Kenzie followed in her running shoes, pale and terrified. Racing to the stairwell, they disappeared inside.

"Are there cameras in the stairwell?" Reid barked.

"Only on the first floor," the operator said.

"For fuck's sake." Wilson raked a hand through his hair.

"What about the basement?" Reid asked.

"There's the underground parking lot," the operator said, hesitantly, scared he'd get shouted at again.

"Bring it up," snapped Wilson.

Nothing.

"Where'd they go?" said Reid. They sure as hell didn't go out the main lobby, the agents would have seen them. They didn't go out the kitchen either, or the side entrance into the garden.

"What else is down there?" Wilson asked.

"There's the delivery entrance," the operator muttered, not looking up.

Shit.

"Any cameras there?"

He knew the answer before the poor guy said it.

"I'm going down." Reid took off out of the security room, across the lobby, to the stairwell. Wilson followed. Racing down a flight, they stopped on the lower landing. On the left was the door to the underground parking lot. Reid went right.

Flinging open the door, he emerged in another, smaller parking lot, wide enough for two vehicles. Straight ahead was a roller door, standing open.

Reid threw his hands up. "This is how they got away."

Wilson stared, dumbfounded.

Ortega burst in behind them, looked at the delivery entrance and winced.

Reid turned on the DEA agent. "Why didn't you know about this?"

His shoulders sagged. "It wasn't in the plans."

Ortega stared at the open garage door. "They must have added it when they did the alterations after the hurricane."

Vargas squeezed in beside them. "What do you want to do, boss?"

He shook his head.

"What about her other phone?"

Reid's pulse spiked. "Did they take it off her?"

"I don't know. He asked for her phone, but who's to say she gave them both to him?"

Vargas had a point. Wilson looked up hopefully. "Worth a try."

Reid couldn't stop his hands shaking as he pulled out his cell. He dialed her burner. It went straight to voicemail.

Gritting his teeth, he tried the other one.

It rang.

His heart surged. "It's on." He cut the call, not wanting to give her away. "We can use it to find out where they've taken her."

Yes! She was so smart. Somehow, she'd managed to hold on to her normal phone. They hadn't considered she might have two.

Reid dialed Pérez at Miami PD and briefed him on the situation. Then he gave him Kenzie's number and told him to ping her phone. ASAP. "Call me back when you have her location."

Please, he prayed as they made their way back upstairs. *Please let them not be too late.*

34

Kenzie tried not to retch. The frantic motion of the van and the inability to see outside was making her carsick.

Maria Lopez glanced away from her. On the outside, she appeared calm, but Kenzie could tell by the tension in her neck and shoulders that she was seething.

The van turned a corner, and Kenzie put her hand out to steady herself. The corrugated slats on the side of the van dug into her back, but she had to push back to not go sliding off the hard seat.

The drive seemed to take forever, but eventually the van came to a stop. A metallic whine told her electric gates were opening. Were they at a private residence?

The tires crunched up a gravel drive and then the van stopped, the engine cut off. Kenzie let go of the side. They were at their destination.

The sliding door opened, and daylight intruded. She blinked, her eyes adjusting.

Nacho grabbed her arm. "Come with me."

His fingers pressed into her skin, pulling her up a gravel drive. She had no choice but to go with him.

"Where are we?" she asked.

Nacho didn't reply, he just kept dragging her towards the house.

Kenzie gazed up at the Spanish-style villa. They went under a wide arch and into a shady courtyard. Exotic plants poured out of terracotta urns while bougainvillea clambered up the white-washed walls as if it too was trying to escape.

An open patio door led into a tiled living room. Maria had already gone inside; Kenzie could hear her heels clicking on the tiles.

Then her voice. Urgent, in rapid Spanish. Issuing instructions.

Damage control. Would she run for it, or stay and wait it out?

Kenzie wondered what had happened to the flash drive. It had been in that laptop before all hell had broken loose. Had Maria had time to take it?

It didn't really matter, Kenzie could remember what she'd written. She just didn't know whether she'd get a chance to write it again.

Nacho led her up a flight of curving stairs to a wide landing. A balcony overlooked the inner courtyard. Downstairs, Kenzie could see a group of men congregating, weapons slung over their shoulders.

She had an army.

"This way," barked the Mexican, squeezing her arm. They went down a hallway to an open door. Kenzie hesitated. Once she was inside, there was no escape. Except for a bullet.

"Why am I here?" she asked. Was this to do with the article? Why was Maria Lopez keeping her alive? Surely it was easier just to kill her.

In response, Nacho nudged her inside. The door shut with a definitive click, and a moment later, a key turned in the lock.

Great.

A prisoner again, but at least she was still alive.

She looked around the room. It was bright and airy with a futon-style bed, a bamboo dresser, and an adjoining bathroom. A guest room, of sorts. There was a large window, but it was shut. The thick glass and no handles made her doubt she'd be able to open it. The air-conditioning was on, so the room was temperature controlled, but there was no fresh air.

A beautiful jail cell.

A purpose-built prison. With listening devices?

This time she didn't care. Who was she kidding? She searched the room from top to bottom, which wasn't hard since there wasn't much furniture in it. Surprisingly, she didn't find any bugs or hidden cameras. Maybe they didn't need them, with no way out.

Reaching into her sports bra, she pulled out her second cell phone.

Reid answered his phone on the first ring. "You got it?"

"Yeah," came Pérez's voice. "Sending her location through now."

Reid exhaled.

Thank God. Kenzie was alive.

Ortega blue-lighted it across town to a district on the outskirts of Miami. Reid sat beside him in the passenger seat, issuing directions. Vargas and Diaz hung on in the back. Wilson, along with four DEA agents, had taken their own vehicle.

Kenzie's phone had triangulated to a large villa in an upmarket residential area. They flew down a leafy avenue, sirens silent now, not wanting to announce their arrival.

"It must be a safe house of some sort," Ortega said as they parked down the street out of sight.

"Cameras." Reid pointed to a mounted eye staring down at them from above the electric gate. An inhospitable fence surrounded the property, blocking out the world.

Wilson joined them. "We're going to surround the house," he said. "We'll go in fast and hard. I've got another team coming."

It was the only way. Once they got in view of the cameras, they'd encounter armed resistance. One thing the Mexicans did not lack was firepower.

While they were waiting, Reid's phone buzzed. Glancing down, his heart soared.

Kenzie.

I'm okay. Locked in a room in some house. Out of town. Roughly thirty minutes.

He replied:

I'm outside. Waiting for backup.

He got a thumbs up and a smiley face in return.

She was playing it down, trying not to show how scared she was. His heart swelled.

ETA?

He texted back.

Not sure. Will let you know. Soon!

As he put the phone in his pocket, he heard vehicles coming down the avenue behind him. Turning, he saw a black tactical vehicle approach. The assault team. They pulled over and Wilson spoke to the driver.

"We're going in," he said when Reid joined them.

"Kenzie's inside. I've received confirmation."

"How is she contacting you?" Wilson asked.

"She had a second phone. Somehow, she managed to hide it when they searched her."

Wilson raised an eyebrow. "Clever girl."

Yes, she was.

"Let's go get her," Reid said. He'd already put on his armored vest, as had the rest of his team.

Wilson issued the command and the tactical team lined up on the road outside the house. Vargas and Diaz spread out around the property along with the remaining DEA agents. Anyone who came out of their house was told to go back inside and keep the doors and windows shut.

A lone dog barked at the intrusion, but no one paid any attention.

The tactical vehicle revved its engine and took off down the road. Reid watched as it sped through the wrought iron gates, sending them flying off their hinges. There was a shout, followed by rapid gunfire.

The assault team entered the property, guns blazing. They snaked up the driveway to the villa. Reid followed, his weapon drawn, Ortega right behind him.

Armed men stood on the balcony shooting down at the team below, but there were only a handful of them, and Wilson's men took them out within minutes. Reid dashed under the arches and into a courtyard.

"Kenzie!" he yelled.

"Up here," cried Ortega, taking the steps two at a time.

Reid followed. A dead guy lay on the landing, blood making the marble slippery. He jumped over and went down a hallway. "I'll go this way."

Ortega went the other.

Reid kicked open a door, only to hear a woman's voice behind him say, "Drop the gun."

He froze.

Maria Lopez.

Slowly, he put the gun on the ground. "The house is surrounded, Maria. There's nowhere to run."

"I'm not running," she said.

He turned around. Her hand was steady, the gun pointed right at his chest.

"Then why are you doing this?"

"You're coming with me."

"Where's Kenzie?"

"Don't worry about her."

How could he not?

Icicles clawed at his chest. "She's not..." He couldn't even say the words.

Maria laughed. "Of course not. I'm not a monster."

He felt weak with relief.

Walking up to him, she kicked his gun further down the hallway, out of reach. He thought about attempting to take her weapon off her, but she might just pull the trigger. He didn't like the maniacal glint in her eye.

"Put your hands where I can see them."

He did as he was told, and she got behind him. "Now, you and I are going to walk out of here, nice and easy."

He nodded.

She pushed the gun into his back. "Move."

He walked forward, back down the hallway to the landing. Wilson, who was standing in the courtyard, looked up and saw him and gave a yell.

"Easy, detectives," Maria called. "Unless you want your man to die."

"Stand down," Wilson shouted.

Reid watched as the agents with him lowered their weapons.

Shoot her, he wanted to yell, but they wouldn't take the chance. Not when he was acting as a human shield.

Down the stairs they went, him with his hands in the air, Maria with the gun pointed at his back. They were halfway down when he heard a thump, and Maria fell forward into him.

He spun around to see Ortega taking the weapon out of Maria's hand. She lay in a crumpled heap on the stairs, groaning.

He'd knocked her on the head with the butt of his handgun.

"Thanks," he said.

Ortega grinned. "You're welcome."

Wilson ran forward, along with his agents. They picked Maria up and cuffed her. She stumbled, groggy and disoriented.

Reid felt his pocket vibrate.

He pulled out his phone. Another message from Kenzie.

Are you ever going to come and get me?

Kenzie enjoyed the feel of Reid's arm around her shoulders as he led her from the room.

"It's about time," she complained, but her eyes were smiling.

"Sorry, got delayed."

They walked downstairs and out into the driveway where a stony-faced Maria was being ushered into a waiting police car.

"Kenzie!"

She stopped.

"You will print the article, won't you?"

Kenzie didn't reply.

Maria's voice was tinged with desperation. "Promise me you will. The world needs to know."

Kenzie started walking again. She would print the article, but perhaps not the one Maria wanted.

"I'll make a deal," she cried.

Reid stopped.

"No," Kenzie whispered. "No deal."

But Reid had turned around. "Give us your Miami and LA networks and the article is in tomorrow's paper. Front page news."

"Reid," hissed Kenzie, "you can't do that." Keith would have a shit-fit.

"I already have," he said. "You know how important this is. We can take down her entire organization."

Kenzie hesitated. She did know.

They could always do a follow up on the arrest. The story would feed off itself for weeks.

Maria stared at them. "I can't do that."

"Then no article."

Kenzie broke away from Reid's hold and approached her. "I'll publish the article exactly how it is. I promise."

Maria's eyes glistened. "No one must know it was me," she whispered.

"No one," Kenzie agreed.

"Then we have a deal."

35

"She'll only talk to you," Reid said as Kenzie got out of the car. He'd driven them to the Miami-Dade County Detention Center, where Maria Lopez was being held until her trial.

The *Herald* had printed the article as promised, and there weren't many people who didn't know who Maria Lopez was. Admire her or despise her, she was achieving the sort of infamy attributed to El Chapo and Pablo Escobar.

"This isn't right," Reid muttered, as they entered the prison. "She doesn't deserve fame."

"You know how fascinated the public is with drug kingpins and mob bosses," Kenzie pointed out. "It was bound to happen, especially since the arrest."

Follow-up articles had included Maria Lopez's arrest, the sting operation led by the DEA at the Ritz-Carlton, the story of the nameless undercover agent who risked his life to infiltrate the Morales cartel. It was publishing gold.

Kenzie, of course, was the star of the show. The journalist who'd broken the story, who was there at the final take-down, kidnapped by Maria Lopez herself and asked to record her story. Her editor, Keith, couldn't praise her enough. Forgotten was the fact a few short months ago he'd nearly fired her, forcing her to put herself in danger for the sake of the story that would save her job.

They passed through security and waited until Maria had been put into an interrogation room.

"She's ready for you," said a female prison guard.

Like they were visiting for tea.

Reid went in first and saw Maria frown. "Don't worry, Kenzie's here," he said dryly.

"Hello, Maria." Kenzie smiled and sat down opposite the cartel boss at the cold, metal table. It was nailed to the floor, as were the chairs. Reid didn't know how she could be so polite, given what had happened. He wasn't feeling especially charitable towards Maria after she'd held a gun to his head.

But Kenzie was the consummate professional, and she knew a good thing when she saw one. Everyone was waiting to hear what would happen to Maria once her trial began, and Reid suspected Kenzie would be there every step of the way.

Reid was surprised at how good Maria looked, her hair freshly washed, her skin smooth and clear despite the lack of makeup. Not even the prison uniform detracted from her appearance. It paid knowing people on the inside, people whose palms she could grease to make her stay easier. Although, in a place like this, she would be prison royalty.

"I want to talk to Kenzie alone." Maria stared at Reid.

"That wasn't part of the deal, Maria."

"It's okay," Kenzie said.

Reid gritted his teeth. He hated giving Maria the upper hand. He hated any criminal, thinking they had control over the situation, over him.

Still, he needed that information. With Maria's help, the DEA could bring down her entire network in both Miami and Los Angeles. Destroy the distribution networks that shipped drugs into the United States. It would be an important battle won in the war against drugs.

"Fine. I'll wait outside." He left the room.

Outside, under the deep blue Miami sky, he called Agent Wilson at the DEA field office. "How's Agent Palmer doing?" he asked.

Alberto Torres aka Alex Guerra aka David Palmer.

He had his real identity back now. Reid wondered if he'd even recognize his own name after five years living as someone else.

His wife had been taken to a safe house by DEA agents. She professed to having no idea her husband was anyone other than a hard-working off-dock warehouse owner from Miami.

In fact, David Palmer was from Pittsburg, Pennsylvania, and had grown up with a Mexican mother and Irish immigrant father. Fluent in both Spanish and English, he'd moved to Miami after he became a DEA agent to get used to the world he would soon be infiltrating.

Reid wondered if he'd realized how close this assignment would push him to the edge.

"He's awake," Wilson said. "But he's not out of the woods yet. They're keeping him in critical care until he's stable."

The undercover agent had made it to the hospital, thanks to the heroic efforts of the ambulance team, and undergone emergency surgery to remove the bullet in his lung.

"That's good news," Reid said. Yesterday, they didn't know whether he was going to make it. "Is he allowed visitors?"

"Yeah, during visiting hours. They're pretty strict about that."

"Great, thanks." Reid smiled. Palmer had played an instrumental role in bringing down the Morales cartel and deserved to be recognized for it. There was talk of a medal.

"Have you got my list yet?" the agent asked.

"We're working on it. Kenzie's with Lopez as we speak."

"Right. Keep me posted."

"Will do."

Reid paced up and down, waiting for Kenzie. What was taking her so long? All Maria had to do was give her the freaking names.

An hour later, she still hadn't come out. Reid had spent the better part of it sipping bad prison canteen coffee and reading the paper.

Eventually Kenzie emerged, her cheeks flushed.

"About time," Reid remarked, putting down the newspaper. "What took so long?"

"I got the names you wanted." She handed him a sheet of paper and sat down. "That's her entire network," Kenzie confirmed. "She assured me she hadn't left anyone off."

"Forgive me if I don't take her at her word," Reid said with a smirk. However, Wilson would be happy to get his hands on this. "Good work."

She leaned back in the chair. "I'd kill for a coffee."

A prison guard glanced over. "Figure of speech," she clarified, chuckling.

Reid got her one, but couldn't shake the feeling he was missing something. She seemed too chipper, too excited for the occasion.

He put it down in front of her. "What else did you talk about?"

Her eyes were wide. Innocent. "What do you mean?"

"Kenzie, I know something else happened in there. What's got you so excited?"

She scowled. "Damn it. I can't hide anything from you, can I?"

That wasn't exactly true. When she was acting a part, she was impossible to read, but when she was excited about a story, she was an open book.

Kenzie took a deep breath. "Maria Lopez has asked me to write her memoirs."

That took a while to sink in. "Memoirs? What's that? Like an autobiography?"

"Yeah, she wants to document the rise and fall of the Morales cartel, and of course, her role in it."

Reid shook his head. "Even now, after she's been captured, she's still using this to her advantage. Doesn't that woman ever give up?"

Kenzie shrugged. "She's a businesswoman taking advantage of the situation."

He frowned. "You approve of this?"

Kenzie thought for a moment. "I believe in freedom of speech, so if she wants to write a book in prison, I don't see why she shouldn't be able to."

"Because she's a murdering drug baron and shouldn't be allowed to profit from her crimes."

Kenzie spread her hands. "If I don't do it, someone else will. I'd rather I got the job."

Reid grimaced. "I suppose you're right. At least you know the context of her arrest. Another writer might glorify her story way out of proportion."

"I'll keep it real," Kenzie promised.

And that was the best he could hope for.

Kenzie was still on a high when they went to visit Agent Palmer in the hospital. Propped up in bed, the left side of his chest was covered with dressings and a loose-fitting hospital gown hanging off his lean frame.

"You look better than the last time I saw you." Kenzie smiled as they walked in. That image of him bleeding on the floor would never leave her.

"I still can't believe she shot me."

"It was sudden," Kenzie said. "I got the shock of my life when she pulled out that gun."

It seemed Maria Lopez's justice was as swift as her late husband's.

He grunted. "I didn't see it coming."

Reid walked up to the bed and shook his hand. "All that matters is that you made it. That was a close one."

"I believe I've got you to thank for saving my life."

Kenzie thought she saw Reid flush.

"No, I just did what any other law enforcement officer would have done. I shoved my hand over the hole."

"The doctor told me if I'd lost any more blood, I wouldn't have made it."

Kenzie didn't want to think about that.

"Not this time," muttered Reid.

Palmer grinned. "No, not this time."

"Maria Lopez gave up her network," Kenzie told him. "Wilson and the DEA are rounding them up as we speak. This will be the biggest drug bust in Miami's history."

A light shone in Palmer's eyes. Everything he'd worked for had led to this moment. His sacrifice hadn't been in vain. Bianca's sacrifice hadn't been in vain.

Justice was being served.

"That's great," he mumbled, clearly emotional. "How'd you get her to make a deal?"

"Kenzie," Reid acknowledged.

She flushed. "I agreed to write her memoirs."

Palmer's eyes widened. "I guess this isn't the last we've heard of Maria Lopez, then."

Kenzie grimaced. "Guess not."

It wasn't good news for the DEA agent. As long as Lopez was alive, he'd always be at risk. Which was why Wilson had come up with the genius plan to let him die.

"Nobody knows you made it," Reid explained. "As I'm sure you've been told, you're here under a false name, and if anyone calls the station, you died on the way to hospital. Alberto Torres and Alex Guerra no longer exist."

"But David Palmer does," said Kenzie softly.

Palmer let out a shaky breath. "Not for long. They want to put me in WITSEC. Give me a new life."

Again.

"At least you won't have to look over your shoulder anymore."

"What about my job?" His expression was strained. "I'm a DEA agent. I don't know how to be anything else."

Kenzie's heart went out to him. After everything he'd gone through, he now had to start all over again. A new city, new friends, new career. Still, he was alive. Surely that was the main thing?

"I'm sure they'll work something out," Reid said, but Kenzie knew he was only trying to make Palmer feel better. There was no way he could continue to operate as a DEA agent, not while Maria Lopez was still around. A whiff that he was alive, and a hit squad would be after him. Next time, he might not see who pulled the trigger.

"Focus on getting better," Kenzie said. "You can sort the rest out later."

He gave a tired nod. "Yeah, you're right."

"We'll leave you to rest." They walked outside into the late afternoon sunshine.

"He's a good guy," Reid said. "And a great cop. It's strange how everything's flipped on its head." Kenzie knew what he meant. He'd hated him for so long, and now he'd saved his life.

"I hope he's okay. He deserves to be happy."

They walked back to Reid's pickup. On the way home, Kenzie turned to him. "Reid, I have to tell you something about Governor Talbot. Promise you won't be angry."

He pulled over and stopped the car. "Kenzie, when you say those words to me, I know I'm going to get mad."

She bit her lip. "With everything that's happened, I haven't had a chance to tell you, but now seems like the appropriate time."

"What?" His eyes narrowed.

"I spoke to his secretary, Carol Porter, the other day. She admitted to stealing that man's driver's license and hiring the car that ran me off the road."

Reid's brows shot up. "You spoke to her? Are you crazy? Now he's going to come after you even harder."

"No, he won't."

"He *will*, Kenz." He stared out the front windshield, both his hands still on the wheel. "This is bad. I wish you'd said something sooner. We're going to have to get you some protection. After last time, there's no telling what he'll resort to."

It wasn't everyday Reid got so uptight. She knew he was just concerned about her. "Reid, listen to me."

He turned to her, exasperated.

"She won't say anything because I threatened to go to the police if she did. Don't forget she committed a crime. She doesn't want that coming out."

"Do you believe her?"

"Yes, she wouldn't risk it. Carol Porter is ambitious, not stupid. An arrest would destroy her career. She'd never work in politics again."

Reid drummed his fingers on the steering wheel. "Do you have proof? Something other than the circumstantial evidence we've got."

She grinned. "I caught the whole conversation on tape."

Reluctantly, he nodded. "Okay, that's good, even if it's not admissible in court. It won't help us arrest the governor. It's his word against hers."

He was right. No one would believe a personal assistant over an upstanding member of society like Governor Talbot.

"He'd say it was a smear campaign," Reid said. "A plot to discredit him. Happens all the time."

"I know," Kenzie agreed. "We need something concrete if we're going to bring down this pedophile ring."

"I can always bring in Hodge," Reid said. "If we come down hard on him, he might buckle and agree to a sting op. Although it's risky."

"We wouldn't know whether he'd warned them or not," Kenzie pointed out.

"Yeah, I'll discuss it with my team."

She kept forgetting she wasn't part of his "team." Sometimes, he forgot too, they worked so well together.

Turning onto her road on Bay Harbor Island, he pulled up

outside her house. "Let me know at the first sign of anything suspicious, okay?"

She smiled at the worry in his eyes. "I promise."

Kenzie was walking up the short path to her house when her phone beeped. Glancing at the screen, she gasped. Turning around, she charged back down the path. "Reid, don't go!"

He'd turned the car around but had heard her shout and pulled over, the window down. "What's up?"

"I just got a text message from the juvenile offender I spoke to the other day. There's another party. Tonight. He's given me the address."

Reid arched his eyebrow. "One of *those* parties?"

"Yes. This is the perfect opportunity for a way to take them down. This is it! No one will suspect a thing." Her heart was racing.

Reid thought for a moment. "We need to put an officer undercover. I'm not going to make a move until we know all the players are there, particularly Talbot."

Her eyes lit up.

"Not you, you're a woman. It needs to be a man, right?"

Damn, he was right.

"Vargas is too young," she pointed out. "He's early twenties, barely older than some of the offenders."

"So are most of the team," he said ruefully. "No one has the experience to pull this off."

"You'll have to do it," Kenzie said.

He hesitated. "It's been a long time since I've done any undercover work."

"You're perfect," she insisted, warming to her idea. "You're old enough, you can take on the role, and you look good in a suit."

He grinned. "How would you know?"

"I have an active imagination." They shared a smile. "Anyway, I can help you get ready."

Reid held up his hand. "Hang on, let's not get ahead of ourselves.

This needs to be planned out. Send me the address, and I'll brief the team."

"You'll keep me posted?" she asked, apprehensively.

"Yes, of course." He gave her a knowing look. "You don't think I'd leave you out, do you?"

She laughed. "I'd like to see you try."

36

REID TOOK A STEADYING breath as he approached the sprawling two-story property where the party was being held. It was set back from the road, on an innocuous palm-lined avenue, with a landscaped garden and a lazy, curving driveway.

Jazz music emanated from the open windows along with the soft hum of voices. It was nine o'clock, a respectable time to arrive, or so he'd been told.

The boy's text had given the address, and little else, so he was going in blind. That would have made him nervous, except Kenzie had called Pat and asked him what Matteo had told him about these parties.

"It was weird at first," the young student had told Kenzie. "There weren't many people there and Matt thought it was going to be lame, but then as it got later, men began to arrive. They came in alone, dressed up, you know, like for a work thing, reeking of cologne and headed for the bar."

To take the edge off what they were about to do. To assuage the guilt.

"By nine p.m. the place was packed. A man approached Matt

and took his hand. He led him upstairs, and that's when Matt clicked to what was going on. He locked himself in a bedroom, opened the window, and scrambled down a drainpipe. He was lucky to get away."

A brief respite, considering he was murdered the following day.

Reid paused, wondering if he was making a mistake being here. What if they didn't grant him access? What if they saw through his flimsy act? Unlike Kenzie or Agent Palmer, he wasn't a chameleon who could morph into other roles, play another character at the drop of a hat.

Too late for second thoughts now. Gritting his teeth, he rang the buzzer. The door opened, and a man stood there. "Can I help you?"

"I'm here for the party," he said, as they'd discussed. "Governor Talbot invited me."

"Oh." The man's face broke into a smile. "In that case, come in."

It was as easy as that.

Reid followed him in, scoping out the crowd. He knew the governor hadn't arrived yet, as they'd been watching the house. Until he did, his lie was safe.

Reid didn't recognize anybody, but he wasn't into politics. He did, however, spot several gold Rolexes, custom-made suits, and signet rings. This was an elitist group, a privately organized pedophile ring. He felt sick being around them.

But he had a job to do.

There were several youths, presumably the young offenders. Nervous, defiant, jaded. He read their expressions as he walked around, making it look like he was inspecting the merchandise. He had learned from Kenzie that some of them knew what was in store and had agreed to go along with it because it meant a shorter probation period, while others were new and had no idea what awaited them upstairs. They walked around with bewildered expressions, drinking beer, and wondering why they'd been invited.

A man approached a boy who couldn't be more than sixteen years old. After speaking, the man nodded towards the stairs.

Reid swallowed over the bile in his throat. He wanted to stop it, to rip the boy away and arrest the scumbag, but he couldn't. Not yet.

Not until the governor was here.

Where the hell was he?

Kenzie had contacted Carol Porter again, much to the woman's horror, and asked her if the governor was in town tonight. He was. And he'd penciled a personal evening in his calendar. Reid bet he wasn't going to spend it with his wife.

Any time now.

More boys were led upstairs. Reid was beginning to feel nauseous. He *had* to put a stop to this.

"Where the hell is he?" he murmured into his microphone. The tiny earpiece was embedded firmly in his ear. It was unnoticeable to anyone talking to him, and on loan from the Miami PD surveillance team.

"Still hasn't arrived," Vargas replied. He and Diaz, and the rest of the team were in a rental house across the road, watching the property through darkened windows with state-of-the-art surveillance cameras. Also on loan.

This house belonged to an Edward O'Hara. Reid had never heard of him. Apparently, he was some big shot investment banker or fund manager, something like that. He ran a multi-million-dollar company, and his clients included heads of state, billionaires and celebrities.

Reid wondered which of the self-important peacocks he was. That must be him, holding court in the drawing room, a tumbler of whiskey in one hand and a cigar in the other. The picture of wealth and power. He laughed at something the man he was talking to said, tilting his head backwards in a loud guffaw, oblivious to the pain and suffering going on upstairs.

Sick bastards.

Reid prowled around. He purposely didn't make eye contact with anyone, preferring to observe, to survey, to remember. The tiny camera pinned to his jacket pocket was recording everything, storing details away for backup in court, should they be allowed to use it.

A sting operation was always risky. To ensure a successful prosecution, they had to catch the perpetrators in the act. To go in now, would allow them to round up the bastards upstairs, and prosecute them to the full extent of the law, but they wanted more. They wanted the big fish.

Outside the tall bay windows, the sky had turned a deep indigo and a twinkling of stars dotted the darkening canopy. Inside, the men continued to drink and to select their targets for the evening.

The bitter taste in his mouth intensified. "Any sign of him?" he growled, low enough not to be heard.

Diaz's voice. "No, not yet. Hang on, a Merc's just pulled up."

Reid held his breath, his heart thumping in an agonizing rhythm. He couldn't stop thinking about what was going on above his head.

"Yes," hissed Diaz in his ear. "It's him."

Reid positioned himself at the bar, waiting for the moment the governor walked in. He heard the discreet knock, the sound of a greeting, a warm voice, deep and authoritative. Governor Talbot had arrived.

He sauntered into the living room and a drink was handed to him. A fine single malt. His tipple of choice. Two other men greeted him, while several nodded and jostled for his attention. Sex wasn't the only thing on the agenda.

Away from prying eyes, this was the perfect place to make new acquaintances, to do a little discreet business, facilitate a few backhand deals.

The group of men talked in low voices, enjoying their drinks.

Diaz's voice: "Is it time?"

His team was running the op, but Pérez had provided a tactical support team for the raid.

"Negative," he murmured.

To catch the governor in the act, they had to wait until he'd gone upstairs. Right now, he seemed in no hurry. He was relaxing, getting in the mood.

"Come on," Reid muttered, as yet another young boy was led upstairs. "Let's get this over with." The boy hesitated and looked like he might back down, but the businessman held firmly to his hand.

"Two security guards inside," Reid murmured, noticing the burly bouncers for the first time. One had just walked in from outside the patio doors at the back, while the other must have been in another room. "Both are armed." Their jackets were bulging in the obvious places.

"Roger that," came Diaz's voice. "When we enter, can you subdue them?"

"One, yeah, but not both." By the time he took down the first, the second would have had time to get off a shot, if not a few. There was the potential for collateral damage.

"The back door is open," Reid murmured. "If someone can get over the wall and enter through the garden, they can join the party."

"Who?" came Diaz's voice.

"Send Vargas," said Reid, without hesitation. "He's wearing jeans and a T-shirt. Get rid of the police insignia. He'll be mistaken for a juvenile offender."

A pause. "Okay, boss."

"Hurry, Talbot is on the move."

The governor's eyes were roaming, cat-like, around the room, and his gaze settled on a gangly youngster with longish hair and acne. His next victim.

"Not today, pal," murmured Reid.

He turned to the patio door to see his deputy stroll in, a suitably surprised expression on his face. Reid glanced at him, then at one of the security guards. Vargas gave an indiscernible nod.

The governor approached the pimply faced boy and exchanged a few words. The boy nodded, and while he followed Talbot upstairs, everything about his body language screamed no.

Reid waited for them to disappear, then followed. He got to the landing and looked around. Five bedrooms, five closed doors. He heard a grunt, the creak of floorboards, and some shuffling. Which door had the governor gone into?

It didn't matter. He was here. He was going to be caught in flagrante.

"Get ready," he murmured into his microphone, swiveling on his heel and going back downstairs. Nodding to Vargas, he followed security guard number two into the living room. Guard number one was in the drawing room closest to Vargas.

"Now!"

Not five seconds later, the front door to the house burst open and a dozen police officers swarmed in. There were shouts of consternation, some of fear, and a scramble as both businessmen and young offenders bolted for the patio door.

Except it was shut. Vargas had made sure of that.

Guard number one knelt on the floor in front of him, his hands on his head.

Guard number two reached for his weapon, but Reid knocked it out of his hand and pressed his own gun into the man's back. "I wouldn't."

The man put his hands up.

Reid cuffed him and confiscated his firearm, handing it to one of the police officers.

Vargas marched the first security guard out of the house, hands cuffed behind his back.

"Good work," Reid complimented, as he handed his prisoner to a waiting officer.

Six members of the tactical force had charged upstairs and, judging by the shouts of complaint, had successfully arrested the abusers. Not a shot had been fired.

Everybody watched as the governor was led downstairs in handcuffs, protesting vehemently. Nobody listened.

"You've been caught with your pants down," Reid remarked as

the politician walked past. "It's over for you." He couldn't keep the disgust out of his voice.

The governor stared at him, eyes wide with shock. The gravity of the situation was sinking in. His reputation was ruined. His career was over. So was his marriage, and all the trappings of power he so enjoyed.

The young men were also rounded up and shepherded outside. They'd be taken to the police department where they would give their statements, be offered counselling and then be released.

Reid holstered his weapon and joined the rest of his team celebrating outside.

"We got him." He high-fived Vargas.

Out of the corner of his eye, he saw Kenzie get out of the surveillance van and walk up to Governor Talbot.

"You should be ashamed of yourself," she hissed. "And I *will* press charges, so you can add attempted murder, as well as first-degree murder, to your list of despicable crimes."

"Murder," he spluttered, his eyes unfocused. "I haven't killed anyone."

"Matteo Davis," she retorted. "The young boy who ran away from your last party. The one you got your goons to kill on his way home from school. The one you planted drugs on to make it look like a gang killing."

He turned a ghostly white under his fake tan.

"We know everything," Kenzie hissed. "You'll be lucky if you don't get the death penalty."

"You okay?" Reid asked, as Talbot was led away.

Kenzie stood there, seething.

"Yeah. I am now."

37

THE FALLOUT from the arrest was immense. In a way, the governor was lucky, because he wasn't the only public figure to be annihilated in the press when the story of the pedophile ring broke. There were bankers and lawyers and heads of industry. It was carnage.

Keith was in raptures. "You've really done it this time, Kenzie. You're a household name."

The story had eclipsed every other news item, even the articles on Maria Lopez that were still running. The online version of the paper went viral, and the internet was aflame with bloggers and influencers, expressing their shock at what had taken place. Those involved were named and shamed. Memes circulated. The public interest grew like a tidal wave and neither the *Herald* nor the police could contain the flow of information.

Governor Talbot was filmed being led from the Sweetwater Police Department to a waiting transport vehicle to be taken to prison. Kenzie, of course, had special access, so her cameraman, Clyde, captured the shots of the governor that rocked the political world.

The broken man. The guilty secret. The scandal of the century.

And beneath every headline was Kenzie's byline.

"I wouldn't be surprised if you won a Pulitzer for this," Keith told her.

She shook her head. Prizes were great, but it wasn't why she did this. "The truth had to come out."

Hannah came to see her at the office. "Thank you!" She gripped Kenzie's hand. "I knew you were the right person to ask."

"Glad I could help," she replied. "Matteo deserved justice."

Then she gave Hannah a tour of the newspaper offices and introduced her to the Editor-in-chief, Keith.

"Send over your resume when you've graduated," he told her. "We might be able to give you an apprenticeship here at the *Herald*."

Hannah was so overwhelmed, she could barely answer.

"Sweet kid," he told Kenzie, once she'd left.

"With a keen intuition," Kenzie told him. "She's the one who came to me, knowing those drugs had been planted on him, despite what the police told her. She'll make a good reporter one day."

Later, when she finished work, Kenzie drove over to Reid's house, still in her loaner car since the insurance company had written off her little Honda. At some point, she'd have to think about buying a new one.

The sky stretched impossibly blue above her, and it felt good to be alive. It was moments like this when she was glad she'd become a reporter. It hadn't been her dream, but it was a close second. In this latest investigation, she'd been the reporter, a victim, and part of the team who'd brought down the pedophile ring. Kenzie was used to playing roles, but this was a record, even for her.

"Governor Talbot is trying to cut a deal," Reid told her. They were standing on his deck, gazing out over the water. She hadn't seen him for a couple of weeks. Things had been that busy at work, and he'd had to put in overtime readying both the cases for prosecution.

An eagle squawked above them, then swooped down to the surface. They watched as it almost touched down, its talons extended, then rose again, soaring on the current.

"He confessed to everything. Apparently, the principal of the school, Hogarth, was in on it too, not only Hodge."

"That's why Matteo was killed," Kenzie whispered, shocked. "He told the headmaster what had happened. Little did he know he was talking to the enemy."

Reid's gaze softened. "You did good, Kenzie."

"*We* did good," she corrected, smiling at him. She was glad to see him looking so well. The black eye had healed, and the angry slash on his cheek had knitted together. He'd always have a scar there, but in her opinion, it only made him more dashing.

"How are things at the station?" she asked.

"Sweetwater is firmly on the map." He grinned. "Thanks to the shots of Talbot leaving the station in chains."

A shocking image. A man used to being splayed over the tabloids for his political policies and goodwill was now being led, head down, in irons to a waiting police car. The desolate look on his face had said it all.

"That's great. You've only been there a couple of months and you've already made your mark."

"I'm not done yet. The department needs cleaning up. Dempsey, the detective who was going to warn Hodge, the probation officer, that we were onto him, has just been arrested. Internal Affairs don't take that sort of thing lightly."

She raised an eyebrow. "I'm sure he deserved it. If he'd warned Hodge, you'd never have got Talbot."

Reid nodded. "Vargas has been great, I'm thinking of promoting him."

Kenzie smiled. "I hear he's got a new girlfriend?"

He chortled. "Yeah, they're hot and heavy. She's quite something, too. I would never have put them together."

"Oh? Why's that?"

"They're so different. She came to celebratory drinks at the Blue Water Tavern last week, and..." He shook his head. "She's a little wild."

"She might be good for Vargas."

He shrugged. "Maybe."

"The Police Chief must be pleased," she said.

"Yep, I've been asked to speak at a police symposium next month." He pulled a face. "You know how I hate that shit."

She laughed. "It's good for your career, Lieutenant Garret."

"Oh, and one of the bouncers at the party confessed to killing Matteo Davis and planting the coke on him. He got it from a Cuban street dealer by the name of Carlito the Rat."

"Catchy."

"Yeah, Ortega thinks it might be the start of a new network, filling the space the Kings left behind last year." Kenzie remembered the gang violence of the year before. Not many in Miami didn't. It had caused countless deaths and affected hundreds of people.

Ortega and the Miami PD had brought them down eventually, but it was always going to be only a matter of time before some other gang filled the void. It was the way things went. The endless battle against drugs.

"Do you want a drink?" he asked.

"Sure, why not?"

He got them each a beer and they sat on the swing seat he'd put out on the deck. "I'm glad to see you've got some outdoor furniture," she commented, leaning back and feeling it sway softly beneath her.

There was a creak as Reid sat down beside her. "Yeah, I figured I spend so much time out here, I may as well make it homey."

They sat in companionable silence, drinking their beers. The eagle swooped again, and this time it got lucky. When it rose, it had a wriggling fish in its talons. The sky changed color, turning a dusky pink, then purple.

"This is nice," Kenzie said quietly.

"Yes, it is."

She looked up at him. "Can we keep things this way, you know, between us?"

His eyes glittered. "What way?"

"Friends."

"Friends?" He arched an eyebrow.

"Okay, a little more than friends, but you know what I mean."

"Yes, I do." Smiling, he put his arm around her. "And yes, of course we can."

The End

The story continues in *Burnout*, the next Kenzie Gilmore thriller. Head to the next page for a sneak peak!

Stay up to date with Biba Pearce's new releases:
https://liquidmind.media/biba-pearce-sign-up-1/
You'll receive a **free** copy of *Hard Line: A Kenzie Gilmore Prequel.*

BURNOUT: CHAPTER 1

Reid stared down at the twenty-foot python. Its body was so swollen and distended, you could just about make out the figure of a human form inside.

"It's double the size." The gator hunter, a beefy man who'd introduced himself as Selwyn Price, waved his single shot bolt-action rifle in the air. "As soon as I saw him, I knew there was a body inside. Could be a hog or a boar, but my money's on a human being." He pronounced it like bean.

The snake lay on the dry ground beside the waterway, its skin glistening in the harsh midday sun, stretched to breaking point around whatever it had eaten. It had died of natural causes, most likely an acute case of indigestion.

"We thought we'd better get you down here before we cut it open," Officer Dwayne Griffith said, sweating in his new Sweetwater PD uniform. "Just in case."

Beatrice, his wife, had helped him out of a sticky spot a few months back, so when her husband had approached him for a transfer, he couldn't say no. As soon as he met the tough old beat cop, however, he'd known it was a good decision. Sweetwater was on the up, thanks to their successes over the last year, and they were recruiting. Reid was slowly building a team he could rely on and getting rid of the old legacy of laziness and corruption that had turned them into a backwater laughingstock.

Dwayne Griffiths was in his mid-fifties, experienced and tough as old nails. There wasn't much he hadn't seen in his time, and he knew the streets of Miami like the back of his hand. A valuable asset to any department.

"Okay, let's do it." Reid nodded to the gator man who put down his rifle and picked up a lethal, foot-long hunting knife. "If it's human, I'm calling forensics and we'll need to get this reptile to the morgue."

Selwyn inserted the knife, a foot below the head, where the bulge started and sliced downwards along the snake's belly, careful not to knick whatever or whoever was inside.

"Easy." Reid stood on the other side, his eyes fixed on the reptile.

"I knew it!" The gator hunter straightened up. "That's human legs in there."

A putrid stench oozed out of the snake carcass, and they all took a step backward. "Yeah, that's a body alright," Reid agreed grimly. Two feet with narrow ankles covered in a slimy substance and partially decomposed were clearly visible.

"Holy Mary," murmured Dwayne.

"Get on the phone," ordered Reid. "Call the local CSI unit and get them out here."

He gave a shocked nod and turned away to make the call. Reid bet that in all his years as a beat cop, he'd never seen anything like this. The Glades were as dangerous as the streets of Miami, but the predators weren't always human.

"ETA forty minutes," he told Reid, pocketing his phone. In reality, it could be longer. The dirt road into the Glades was narrow and dusty, and they were pretty far in. The swamp stretched for miles around them in all directions, the surface of the water hidden by an endless sea of sawgrass and cattails.

Above them, the careless blue sky seemed inordinately far away, while the white-hot sun beat down, relentless in its intensity. It was Miami's dry season, and they hadn't had rain in weeks. After the notorious heatwave last summer, which had resulted in monstrous thunderstorms and a mini deluge, come October it had dried up and now, they were entering a brand-new year under drought conditions. The vegetation was dry and brittle, and the environmental services were talking about organizing a controlled burn ahead of schedule to prevent wildfires.

"Okay." Reid swiped at his brow. "Officer Griffith, I'm putting you in charge. Make sure whoever is in there gets to the morgue safely."

"You don't want me to slice her open all the way?" the gator hunter asked hopefully.

"No." Reid turned to him. "I want to preserve him or her as much as possible."

No doubt he'd be telling his buddies at the swamp bar how he'd cut open a twenty-foot reptile to reveal a human body. It was a once in a lifetime story.

"You don't expect foul play, do you boss?" Griffith loosened his collar, his dark skin glistening with perspiration.

"I don't know," Reid replied. "But until I do, I'd rather be cautious. At the very least we need to know how he or she died."

"Squeezed to death," the hunter supplied with a shrug, as if that was obvious. "That beast's a constrictor. Strangles the life out of its prey before it eats it."

"Most likely," agreed Reid, "but we'll let the medical examiner determine that."

He jiggled his car keys in his pocket. "Right. I've got to get back. I'll see you at the station, Griffiths."

The beat cop gave a firm nod. "Sure thing, boss. I got this."

"It's female," the medical examiner declared. Reid wasn't sure if she meant the snake or the person inside. The snake lay dissected on the steel table, spliced open like a science project.

It was a Burmese python, according to the gator hunter. An invasive species and a threat to local wildlife. So much so, state initiatives had been introduced to eliminate them. According to Selwyn, you could earn $8.46 an hour and $50 per snake measuring up to four feet and an extra £25 for every foot over that. Not bad, if like the gator hunter, you were out working in the Glades anyway.

"About five foot two, Hispanic origin, roughly forty-five years of age."

Reid grunted in acknowledgement. That cleared that up.

"She is partially digested, so it's hard to make out her features," the ME continued, bending over the body.

He grimaced. "Any indication of how long she's been dead?"

"I'd say minimum forty-eight hours, judging by the state of her. Stomach acids are incredibly powerful," she added, as if to back up her statement. "Especially in these types of creatures."

Predators. Hunters. Animals that ate anything and everything.

Two days. "What about fingerprints?"

"Gone, I'm afraid. Completely corroded. I'll take a DNA swab."

Her DNA might be in the system. Fingerprints would have been useful, though. "What about the cause of death?" he asked.

"Give me a minute."

The ME, assisted by a lab helper, lifted the woman's body out of its slimy cocoon, while a second lab assistant pulled the carcass out from under her. It landed with a thud on the floor, before it was dragged to the side of the room, out of the way. Reid was glad he was watching from a viewing gallery through a pain of thick glass, rather than standing next to the body. The stench must be overpowering. He marveled at the ME's fortitude – even her assistants were wrinkling their noses – but then, she would be used to such things.

She inspected the victim's body in its entirety, starting at the head and working her way down the torso and finally the legs. Reid watched as the fluorescent light in the autopsy lab illuminated the partially digested body. He could make out dark hair, a slender frame to which fragments of clothing were still attached, and running shoes, fully intact. They might be able to get some forensic evidence from those.

"Her ribs are broken." The ME pushed in the middle of her torso. "And there is bruising around her midsection consistent with constriction. I'd say she died from cardiac arrest."

Reid raised his eyebrows. "A heart attack?"

"Yes, it happens when the body is deprived of oxygen." She glanced up. "If it's any consolation, she would have been unconscious in minutes."

That did help. A little.

It was as the gator hunter had said. No foul play.

"Okay, thanks." He turned to go.

"One moment." The ME frowned and reached behind the woman's leg. She glanced at her assistants. "Help me turn her over."

They rolled the woman onto her stomach. Her limbs were as stiff and unyielding as a plastic doll's. Reid sucked in a breath. It always shook him up, seeing a once-healthy person so rigid and inflexible. Perhaps because it drove home the indignity of death, or maybe the movements were so unnatural that his brain struggled to process them.

She pulled the spotlight closer. Reid waited, unable to see what she was looking at. One of her assistants was blocking his view.

"Anything?" he asked, after a long pause.

She grunted, then straightened up. "There's a small circular wound in her upper right thigh. It's raw and inflamed."

"Like a snake bite?" he asked, even though he knew reticulated pythons lacked venom.

"More like a knife or bullet wound," she corrected, pulling in a giant magnifying glass on a stand beside the table. "Scrap that. *Definitely* a bullet wound."

"She was shot?" Reid leaned his forehead against the glass. Now that was a surprise. "Before she was eaten?"

The ME probed the wound with a pair of surgical tweezers. "Looks that way." She removed a small, silver chunk of lead. "There's your bullet," she said, triumphantly, dropping it into a petri dish.

Reid stared at it, frowning. "Is that what killed her?" Maybe it had hit an artery or something.

"I doubt it." She touched the skin around the wound with her gloved finger. "She didn't bleed out. A shot like that wouldn't have killed her, not right away, but it would have slowed her down."

"Slowed her down enough for the snake to grab her?"

"It is possible. Predators like snakes and alligators rarely go for prey that is already dead. A live victim would be far more appetizing. The most likely scenario is the victim was dragging herself though the swamp, trying to get to safety when it attacked. She'd have been too weak to fend it off. It would have squeezed out whatever life was left in her."

Before eating her.

Jesus.

Reid raked a hand through his hair. "Okay, thanks." It amounted to the same thing, though. The bullet would have killed her if she hadn't found help, and out there, remote as it was, help would have been a long time coming. Chances were, she'd have been out there all night by herself with no shelter, no protection, wounded and bleeding.

He left the morgue deep in thought. This was no accident. Whoever fired that gun was responsible for that woman's death. Snake or no snake, they were looking for a killer.

BURNOUT: CHAPTER 2

Kenzie showed the austere prison officer her press ID card and driver's license and waited to be escorted through to the meeting area. Maria Lopez, the notorious head of the Morales cartel was being held in the Miami-Dade County Women's Correctional Center, whilst serving out her 30-year sentence. Last year she'd been found guilty of four counts of engaging in a criminal enterprise, drug trafficking, money laundering and conspiracy to commit murder.

Her saving grace had been that she'd only taken over from her husband two years prior, and so hadn't had time to amass any more counts, otherwise Kenzie was sure she'd have gotten life.

There was no private interview room, no soundproof chamber, no recording devices. Kenzie had to join the other desperate relatives during visiting hours to conduct her interview. Maria got no special privileges, not to the general observer, anyway. She appeared just like everyone else.

Inside the prison, however, was another matter. The cartel queen was revered. So much so, she had her own cell, a television, and a cushy job in the prison kitchen.

The guards tiptoed around her, reluctant to make an enemy of one of Mexico's biggest cartel bosses. She still had a lot of influence, even though the Miami branch of the cartel had imploded. Last year's sting operation had seen several of her inner circle gunned down in a DEA-orchestrated bust.

Maria still had an ace up her sleeve. The Californian leg of the cartel was flourishing, and part of the deal the DEA had made with her was that she would hand over the names of those involved, in exchange for Kenzie writing her memoirs.

"When you publish the book," she'd told Kenzie, "I will give you the list."

Maria was using her incarceration to document her rise to power, and how she'd gone from a poor kid living on the streets of Mexico City to running one of the biggest drug cartels in America's history. It was an inspirational story by anyone's standards, and if she'd been running a legit business instead of a criminal enterprise, she may have graced the cover of Fortune Magazine. Such was life.

A buzzer sounded and Kenzie walked through an interlocking door into a wide, drafty meeting area filled with two-seater tables and metal chairs bolted to the floor. The message was clear. Nobody could be trusted. Not here.

Fluorescent lights served as a stark reminder that they were in an artificial environment where smiles were forced, tensions ran high, and many meetings ended in tears or arguments. Even the windows, too high to see out of, had thick wrought-iron bars across them canceling out the sunlight.

She took a seat at a table, her notepad and pencil in front of her. They wouldn't let her bring in a cell phone or recorder, so she was old-schooling it. Not that she minded. There was something comforting and familiar about holding a pencil in her hand and scribbling notes on lined paper. In this place of desolation, it gave her a sense of control. It might just be over words on a page, but it was something.

A steel door on the opposite side of the room clicked open and a line of prisoners shuffled in bound by ankle restraints, but their hands were free. Kenzie supposed the logic was that even if they got out of the meeting room, they couldn't move fast enough to escape.

Maria was first out of the gate. Slim and upright, she drew the eye. In her forties, she was an attractive woman with long dark hair, an elegant neck, and a haughty tilt to her head. Kenzie thought she appeared taller than her five-foot four frame, but that had everything to do with her commanding presence, rather than her stature.

Orange looked surprisingly good on her. It made her black hair appear more lustrous and her skin bronzer. Was that mascara she was wearing?

Maria sank into the chair opposite with a broad grin showing her neat, white teeth. "Kenzie Gilmore. How lovely to see you again."

Kenzie plastered a smile on her face. "Likewise, Maria." Last time they'd talked, Maria was holding a gun to her head.

This assignment had her tied in knots. Sure, it would do wonders for her career – a book on the notorious female crime boss – but one wrong step and the DEA wouldn't get the names they needed to bring down the Californian branch of the network, and she'd make an enemy of a woman who had more clout inside prison than most politicians had outside it.

A shiver passed over her. "How have you been?"

Maria shrugged. "You know..."

Kenzie didn't, but she could imagine. Life inside the penitentiary couldn't be fun.

The unusually retro digital clock above the door flipped over to the next minute, making the passing of time audible to everyone in the room. They had just under one hour. "Shall we get started?"

Maria gave a little nod.

Kenzie had thought long and hard about how she was going to structure Maria Lopez's memoirs. "Let's begin with some background material, your upbringing, your life before you met Federico." It would frame the early chapters of the book.

Maria's eyes became hazy as she looked through Kenzie into the past. "It's not a pretty story, but I want to tell it," she began, her shoulders hunching as she caved in on herself. A protective gesture, perhaps. A subconscious defense mechanism to prevent the past from breaking through the wall she'd built around herself.

"Let's start with your parents," Kenzie probed.

"I don't remember my father. He left when I was a baby." She spoke like it didn't matter, like he was a man who'd come round to visit once and never returned. A forgotten guest. "My mother raised me while working at a factory as a seamstress." Her eyes hardened. "We were very poor. Sometimes we didn't have enough money to put food on the table."

Kenzie bit her lip, but kept writing. She didn't look up. Maria wouldn't want her sympathy. "That's when she would go whoring."

That got her attention. "Excuse me?"

Another enigmatic smile, dark eyes flashing defensively. "I used to hide in my room while she entertained men downstairs. They didn't stay long, and it paid well." She scoffed. "Better than factory work anyway."

Kenzie stared at her. "I'm sorry, I didn't know."

"Why would you?" She inhaled and Kenzie got the impression she wished she were dragging on a cigarette. She could almost imagine the smoke curling up towards the ceiling with the exhale.

Kenzie glanced back down at her pad.

"I was eight when José moved in." She shuddered. A small, involuntary movement, but noticeable to one trained to look for clues in body language.

"Who was José?" Kenzie asked.

"Her pimp." She shook her head as if trying to shake off the memory, but of course, that was impossible. Kenzie knew that better than most. After her mother's disappearance, she'd tried to put on a brave face, to pretend she wasn't hurting, but it was all a facade. Inside she'd been screaming for answers. Answers that never came.

"At first, he occupied most of her time. I didn't like it, but at least she was happy, or pretended to be. He didn't like her seeing clients, so the parade of nameless men stopped. I was glad about that."

Kenzie sensed there was a 'but' coming.

"I was twelve when he first noticed me."

Kenzie went cold.

Maria didn't flinch. "He used to come into my room at night and make me do things. Horrible things." The words tumbled out of her, raw and edgy, even though her expression was blank.

Kenzie felt the bile rising in her throat. Twelve years old. What kind of sick man abused a twelve-year-old girl?

"Did you tell anyone?" she breathed.

Maria snorted. "I tried. Mother called me a tattletale and a liar. *He* backed her up. I just wanted attention. I was jealous of their relationship. The usual shit."

Kenzie's skin crawled. Unfortunately, this story was far too common.

"What did you do?"

"I endured it for two years, then I threw acid in his face and ran away."

Kenzie's eyes widened.

Holy crap.

Maria squared her shoulders. The worst was over. She was back in control. "It was the day before my fourteenth birthday. I stole a bottle of bleach from beneath the kitchen sink and hid it under my bed. When he came to me, I threw it at him and ran out of the house. I never went back."

Kenzie stopped writing. "You left at fourteen?"

Maria gave a firm nod.

"Where did you go?"

"The park. I slept on a bench that night. The next day I turned fourteen."

Kenzie's heart went out to her. "I'm so sorry, Maria." Losing her own mother had been hard, but not like this. Maria had been in an impossible situation and had resorted to drastic measures to escape the abuse.

"Don't be. Shit happens. It's how you deal with it that's important."

She wasn't wrong there.

"How long did you sleep rough?" Kenzie asked.

"Not long. I found a squat and stayed there. I stole from shops and pickpocketed to stay alive. Those druggies and wastrels became my friends." Her eyes lifted to meet Kenzie's. "That's where I met Federico."

The retro wall clock thumped, and a male voice called, "Finish up, folks."

Shit. This was just getting interesting. "He was homeless too?"

"No, he was supplying the kids staying there with cheap drugs. He was a runner for a low-level drug dealer connected to the Morales cartel. I got his attention." She smiled, the first genuine smile in the last hour. "I was mature for a fifteen-year-old, I looked a lot older than I was."

"Is that how you got together?"

"Time's up, people." The guard's voice grated through the cool air.

Maria stood up in a smooth, effortless motion, as if their weighty discussion had never taken place.

Sighing, Kenzie put down her pencil. "I'll come back next week."

Maria dropped her voice. "You know the deal. None of what I tell you in here gets out before the book. No leaks. If anything appears in the press before the publication, your policeman friend won't get the names."

Kenzie stood up so she could meet her eye. "I know the terms of our agreement."

Maria nodded, then turned away and walked with as much dignity as a person in chains could muster, through the door, and back to the cells.

Loving *Burnout*? Follow the link below to order now!

https://links.withoutwarrant.ink/8y2b

ALSO BY BIBA PEARCE

The Kenzie Gilmore Series

Afterburn

Dead Heat

Heatwave

Burnout

Deep Heat

Fever Pitch (Coming Soon)

Detective Rob Miller Mysteries

The Thames Path Killer

The West London Murders

The Bisley Wood Murders

The Box Hill Killer

Follow the link for your free **copy of** *Hard Line: A Kenzie Gilmore Prequel.*

https://liquidmind.media/biba-pearce-sign-up-1/

ALSO BY WITHOUT WARRANT

More Thriller Series from Without Warrant Authors

Dana Gray Mysteries by C.J. Cross

Girl left Behind

Girl on the Hill

Girl in the Grave

ABOUT THE AUTHOR

Biba Pearce is a British crime writer and author of the Kenzie Gilmore series and the DCI Rob Miller series.

Biba grew up in post-apartheid Southern Africa. As a child, she lived on the wild eastern coast and explored the sub-tropical forests and surfed in shark-infested waters.

Now a full-time writer, Biba lives in leafy Surrey and when she isn't writing, can be found walking through the countryside or kayaking on the river Thames.

Visit her at bibapearce.com and join her mailing list at https://liquidmind.media/biba-pearce-sign-up-1/ to be notified about new releases, updates and special subscriber-only deals.

67846142R00164